Dedica

*To friends who love one another, t[...]
incase it ruins your friendship
Be brave, be courageous and take the chance on love. You never
know it might just surprise you xoxo
To all the girls out there who love to be loved, who want that
someone special, he is there just gotta keep on looking
Follow your heart, follow your dreams*

You Hang The Moon

Willowbrook, Volume 2

Kerry Kennedy

Published by Kerry Kennedy, 2024.

This is a work of fiction. Similarities to real people, places, or events are entirely coincidental.

YOU HANG THE MOON

First edition. September 30, 2024.

Copyright © 2024 Kerry Kennedy.

ISBN: 979-8227497802

Written by Kerry Kennedy.

For all the girls out there who never think they'll find their one. He's out there and he is waiting just for you xxx

Other titles by the author
Dakota
Who's Watching Who
Santa Fe Billionaire
Hidden Desires
The Sound
Meet Me In Casablanca
The Willowbrook Series
Healing Hearts book1
You Hang The Moon book2
Love At Lazy Dukes coming 2025
Children's books
Boris Flies To The Moon
Boris Meets Father Christmas
Little Miss Daisy The Strawberry
Boris Flies To The Moon bilingual version Spanish & English

Web Novels
Ice Bound Hearts
Mafia's Arranged Princess Bride
Crushing On My Bad Boy Billionaire, Best Friend
Ice Hockey Study and His Best Friend's Sister (Book 1 of On The Ice)
Puck Love Reunited (Book2 of On The Ice)
The Betrayed wife Becomes A Secret Billionaire
The Ex's Daddy
Audiobooks
Boris Meets Father Christmas
Boris Flies To The Moon
Who's Watching Who

Chapter 1

Daisy
"Well would you look at that mighty fine ass on the Marshal." My best friend, Lottie says as I nearly choke on my cappuccino as we sit in Bluebell's diner.

"*Lottie.*" I hiss. "He can hear you, and you shouldn't be saying things like that about the damn marshal."

"Listen girl, you think it and I say it. Simple facts. Don't tell me you haven't been checking his ass out like ninety times a day." She chuckles. Oh. My. God. Lottie is a scream.

"No, I haven't actually."

"Well, girl let me tell you, you're more dumb than a rabbit in the headlights. That fine ass is meant to be looked at. If I weren't so married up, I'd have that under me in a heartbeat."

"Lottie, stop. He's only at the counter, he can hear every word you say."

"Well it's about time you and he got it together." She says and winks at me and drinks from her cup of green tea. I personally need caffeine, I'm a bit addicted to the stuff and since I get up so early, five a.m to do my morning yoga on the deck then go meet Logan and pick up Hector his gorgeous Airedale Terrier, to take him to my seamstress shop, it's a pretty full on morning and I do like a coffee to zing me through my morning. Okay, so I like it in the afternoon and early evening too. Oh yeah, and also after a meal in the evening when I'm at a restaurant. Sleep, well that comes way too easy for me because I also don't go to bed too early. I like to stay up until gone ten at night reading. So when my head hits that pillow, I am out like a light.

"We are never going to get it together, you know Deacon and I are just good friends. Always have been and always will be. Ever since we were kiddies in the sand pit."

"Oh *please*, Daisy. The way that man looks at you, seriously? It's written all over his face how much he'd like it to be more than friends."

"Yeah, well that as it may be unless he asks me I ain't gonna do nothing about it." I retort and fold my arms in front of my small chest. Unlike, Lottie I was not blessed with a great set of boobs, sure they're fine but there's just not an awful lot of them. I toss my long, blonde hair over my shoulder to give her that look that means, *we are not discussing this right now*.

"Just saying." She says getting the last word in, which makes me chuckle because my bestie always has to get the last word in. Lottie and I have known each other since we were around seven when her family moved to Willowbrook.

At first she was so shy so I kind of took her under my wing and offered her to sit with me during lunch. I shared my strawberry milk with her, offered her some of my pineapple chunks and a bond was formed from then. We were literally inseparable growing up.

Her bouncy waves hand around her shoulders and sometimes I am so envious of her ebony hair with its high sheen and gloss, although Lottie does tell me that it takes a lot of effort and products to get it to look the way it does. Her caramel skin is soft and glowing and she's inherited her coloring from her Mexican mother and her part Irish father. With high cheekbones, I'd die for and some models no doubt, it's fair to say that Lottie is a stunner.

"Well, stop just saying and tone it down a bit." And with that she finishes her coffee.

"How's the stall going for the fundraiser?" She asks. I'm setting up a crafting stall for the event which is taking place in a couple of weeks time. It's in aid of raising funds for the local baseball team and Logan, my elder brother who runs the doctor's practice here in Willowbrook started the fundraiser several years ago. He's invested in the future of our kids and liked the idea of giving them a place to play ball, be safe and meet other kids. It really took off in our community.

"It's going. I've got some new ideas I want to plan a little more and make some cute things up like bunting, pillows, stuffed toys, you know that kind of thing."

"Sounds perfect. I'm around if you want me to keep you company at the stall on the day. I hear Logan's playing with the band, that'll be awesome. He sure can play a mean guitar that brother of yours."

"Yeah, they're playing. I can't wait. Sage may get up and do a song with them." That's Logan's fiancée, they were together before she left him for Michigan State and some fancy medical career but ended up returning not too long ago and well, they're back together again after ten years apart. It's romantic and makes me swoon when I think about how they got their second chance. In fact, I've never seen my older brother so happy. It's the best.

"Wow, that girl has an amazing voice. It's been a while since we heard her sing, right?"

"Sure has, since we were kids ourselves. I think we were seventeen or something." I say and Lottie nods her head. God, where has the time gone, I'm now twenty-seven. I try not to think how badly I want a man in my life to be my forever man, some kids and to be settled. It'll happen for sure one day but to be honest, I do have a thing for Marshal Deacon and no man has come close to him, so I'm kind of stuck to be honest.

Sure, I fantasize that Deacon will one day just come on right out with it that he wants to take me on a date but maybe like me, he's too worried to ruin an amazing friendship and like with Lottie, I've known Deacon since I was a small kid. He's Logan's best friend and I bet he still sees me as Logan's kid sister.

"Afternoon, ladies." He says. I blush. Oh for goodness sake, I hate it when I act like a hormonal teenager around him. I feel embarrassed.

"Hey there, Deac." I say and smile. He smiles back. I love the way his eyes crease and his blue eyes shine. A girl could well and truly get lost in those eyes, I'm telling you know. Girls hang on to your hats because this man has the potential to sweep you right off your feet given half the chance. I just wish he was sweeping me off mine.

Chapter 2

D*eacon*
　　Every time I see that girl, she makes my heart skip a beat and race. My mouth goes dry and I just get tongue tied and twisted. She does strange but wonderful things to my body and I have to resist the urge to touch her. She's my friend. She's my best friend's kid sister and there isn't anything I would want to do that'd upset our relationship.

Hell, we've known each other since we were knee high. She was my prom date too but I chickened out of kissing her at the very last minute, even though that beautiful face of hers was uplifted and her lips were ever so slightly parted. Just the thought of it makes me feel it in my groin. Jeez, I am standing in Bluebell's diner I've got to think of something other than Daisy and real quick.

"How are you ladies this fine day?" I ask Daisy and her bestfriend Lottie, they've known each other for a long time too and if you see one, you're bound to see the other. The mischief those girls would get up to still makes me shake my head. And the way they got the boys all twirled around their fingers in school, well that was something else. Those girls never had to carry their books to school, there was always some kid in tow willing to do that for them.

They needed help with anything and the pair of them had it. Logan and I used to shake our heads a lot at how these girls played on their looks, but not only do Daisy and Lottie have superior looks, they have the nicest and sweetest personalities too. Unless you cross them. Well then, Daisy sure is a little firecracker, another reason I like her so much. That girl is nobody's fool.

"We're all good, thanks Deac. Talking about the fundraiser in a couple of weeks time." Daisy says. Lottie is looking me up and down. She makes me feel like an object at the best of times. I smile at her, she doesn't stop taking in my body. Yeah, I feel a bit uncomfortable. But you know I work out, I'm the law here in Willowbrook and as such it's my job to stay fit and be active so I can protect the folk here as and when I need to. Although to be fair, here in Willowbrook there isn't much that goes on. We're a tightknit community and we don't get much trouble.

The odd drunken brawl at Lazy Dukes, some petty shoplifting with a couple of teenagers, mostly those from Copper Town. We don't have bad kids here in Willowbrook, thank goodness.

"So," Lottie begins, "what are you doing for the fundraiser? Are you doing the dunk again?" I shake my head. I'm never doing that again. Last year, Logan threw the balls for Daisy and Lottie and I spent most of my time in the cold water, he hit the disc every damn time.

"Not this year. I think last year was my last year on that, I think it ought to be Logan this year so I can get my own back." The girls chuckle.

"He's playing band this year again but having a longer stint. And he and Sage are going to help his ma out on the cake stall."

"Ah, well then I'll have to get him some other way." I smile at the ladies. Being so close to Daisy with her long blonde hair, that hangs over her shoulders in waves and those baby blue eyes of hers, makes me all hot under the collar.

A man could lose himself in those eyes for eternity and then some. "You heading off anywhere nice after your coffee?" I ask, tongue tied.

"I'm heading back to work." Daisy says. Man, I don't know why I don't just ask her out on a date. But I am not risking our friendship and I don't want to have a no by way of response, I'd feel like a complete idiot.

Instead, I shuffle some. "Deacon your table is free." I hear Babs, who owns the diner say from behind the counter. "Get yourself seated and I'll bring your coffee and pancakes right over."

I turn to her and thank her. "Ladies, have a good day." I say and tip my hat, then leave for the table. Mr Jefferson one of the older residents of Willowbrook is seated next to mine.

"See you later." Shouts out Lottie and then I hear the two of them giggle. I've got used to that, they've been giggling over me for as long as I can remember. But I did notice how Daisy got a cute, blush to her cheeks when I spoke to her. It's adorable.

I try not to think what it would be like to touch her and make her blush some more. "Morning, Marshal Deacon." Old man Jefferson says.

"Good morning Mr Jefferson." I say as I sit down and place my hat on the table in front of me. Debs arrives with my strong black coffee and a stack of pancakes.

"Fill your boots. If you want a refill just holler." She says and beams with her wide smile. I like Barbara she's been running Bluebell's diner for a long time, it was always our go to place when we were kids and I'm pleased she has no intention of retiring just yet. Besides, I'm sure one of her kids will take it over and keep it running.

That's what folk tend to do here in Willowbrook, they take the businesses over from their parents and everything seems to stay the same. Sure, some of the premises get a new lick of paint to freshen them up, maybe new signage but for the most part this small town hasn't changed ever since I was a kid. It's homely, the folk are welcoming and yeah, it can be a bit much when everyone knows your business but it's home and I wouldn't want to be anyplace else.

"See you chatting up that Miss Daisy again." Jefferson says. I raise my eyebrows.

"No, Sir. Not chatting her up. We're friends is all." He humpfs.

"She likes you, young man." He says with all the wisdom of an older man. I almost choke on my coffee.

"I don't think so, not anymore than she does any of the other guys around town, Sir. She's my good friend." I tell him and begin to cut into the stack of pancakes which I've now drizzled Maple syrup all over. There's a small pot of blueberries to the side and I throw those over for good measure.

"Trust me, young man I know when a young lady likes a man."

"As you say, Sir." I say and tuck into my pancakes. Sure, Daisy does like me but only as her friend. I can wish though.

Logan teases me about her all the time, he keeps telling me I ought to do something about these darn feelings of mine and ask her out on a date. Maybe one of these days I might but for now, I'm way too scared of being rejected and ruining what we've got. What if she said yes and everything is perfect then goes horribly wrong.

Trust me, I've seen the best of lovers end up as enemies and it sure ain't pretty.

I finish my pancakes and watch as Lottie and Daisy finish their drinks and stand to pay. Daisy is wearing a cute summer dress with cherries on it, she looks like the perfect wholesome American girl that she is. Fire burns in the pit of my stomach for her. What I wouldn't do to have my arms around that tiny waist of her and her chest pressed up against mine.

A man can dream, right?

Chapter 3

D^{*aisy*} I don't have my brother, Logan's dog Hector today. Usually, I go pick him up in the morning and he comes to my shop with me for the day. Out the back of the shop I have a nice deck area and a good space that leads to some woodland secured with fencing. Courtesy of Logan, putting up the fencing that is. Since he can't very well take Hector his Airedale into the doctor's practice with him, although I'm pretty sure none of the patients would mind, in fact isn't having an animal around supposed to be good for stress and soothing? And, Logan does own the practice.

Anyway, after my breakfast coffee with Lottie and seeing Deacon which left me blushing when he came to say, hi. Honestly, you'd think after knowing him most of my life, I'd have grown out of this only I haven't.

In all honesty, I have crushed on Deacon since I was a kid wearing braces and long pigtails and braids. Any excuse I could, I'd be hanging around Logan who has always been Deacon's best friend. Actually, Logan has two very close friends, Deacon being one and Abe who runs and own the Lazy Duke's bar is his other best friend.

Those three were like the musketeers growing up, where one was the other two would be close by. Usually with knee scrapes or mud on their faces. They couldn't stop getting into trouble with trees, tarmac from skateboard falls or just generally being boys. My mom used to despair of Logan when he'd come home with yet another bloody knee. It makes me smile.

Then, when I hit around fourteen I had a serious crush on Deacon. With his dark hair that he now wears close cropped due to being the Marshal, but back then it was longer, down to the nape of his neck and the way it used to curl, that definitely was sexy as hell. He still looks sexy, sexier than any one man should be allowed. Honestly, if he were on the front of a GQ magazine, he'd not look out of place. I've seen what he packs under that uniform of his and it's HOT. HOT. HOT.

I shouldn't really be thinking of his six pack or the way he has that whole V thing going on leading down to what I can imagine is definitely a girl's orgasmic night but I can't help myself as I slide the key into the lock of my shop's front door. Needless to say, when Logan merely hints at a pool party out back of his cabin or a night in the hot tub and BBQ, I am there like a bee to a honey pot because I just know that Deacon, if he's not on duty will be swanning around with his muscular chest and biceps on display and trust me ladies, they sure make me swoon not to mention making me all hot down there.

The door to my shop opens easily. Good job since it was jarring not that long ago and Logan had to come over and take the damn thing off its hinges and give it a good greasing. I step inside onto the rustic oak flooring and close the door behind me.

Inside I am greeted by the two walls on either side of me to my left and my right of shelves and racks of fabric from every color under the sun. I have them in color coordination starting with blacks through to greys, whites, reds, pinks, purples, blues, oranges and yellows. It's so pretty and magical, I could spend all day and night in here. I even have fairy lights set up for the winter months to add a bit of sparkle and charm.

In front of me is an archway that leads to my small kitchen area with all the appliances I need, coffee machine being the most important, microwave because I'm a lazy person and prefer to just heat my food up, even though Sage keeps on telling me I need to be more invested in my health and choose healthier food options. To be honest, I'm rubbish at cooking, whoever steals my heart for real one day, that is if I never get to be with Deacon, okay so I'm guessing that means nobody is ever going to steal my heart because he already has it and how could I ever be with anyone else when I'm in love with Marshal Deacon? I sigh. Microwave food for me then for the rest of my life.

To the left inside the arch is a door that leads to the bathroom area, it has a shower, not that I use that but it came with the property and I saw no point in ripping it out, a sink and the toilet, naturally. It's painted a petrol blue with daisies stenciled on the walls. They're my favorite kind of flower and my mother's hence why she called me Daisy. I do love roses but only the blush kind, I find the others way too dark for my liking.

Placing my battered leather bag down on the counter, I flip on the lights and the whole place lights up. I went for the industrial stainless steel lighting that you'd see in a factory unit, in my opinion they work well with the old wooden, oak beams. Apparently they come from a ship's hull. They're striking and when it's a bright sunny day, they have an almost honey like glow to them. My shop makes me feel peaceful and content, it's like stepping into your most comfy slippers.

My pale blue, Singer sewing machine takes pride of place on the right of the shop on my metal and wood sewing table. It was a present from my folks when I decided I wanted to go it alone and open my own sewing shop. We sometimes hold workshops here for the locals and guys turn up too. On a Tuesday night, I have just the retired folk in who love to come and chin wag with each other, I lay on some bottles of wine, Whisky for the hardcore ladies and of course coffee and tea. No men allowed on a Tuesday night. Us ladies like to gossip about the town's men.

Mom usually bakes the cakes and scones and it's just a lovely evening to be had by all. Lottie joins us and she is an absolute scream and keeps us abreast of all the new happenings with any fresh young men coming into town. There is a reconstruction of the old mill going on and there is no shortage of young guys coming in to fix it up. Apparently the owner is making it into a lodge since Willowbrook is very close to Snowshoe Mountain and it's a hot tourist spot for skiers in the season.

The first thing I do is go through to the back and make sure my machine has water in it and start to busy myself prepping my nice strong coffee. I take out my mobile and place it on the side then grab some skimmed milk from my fridge.

Whilst I wait for it to do it's thing, I go back to my sewing machine and make sure it's set up for the prom dress I'm making for Janice, who is Barbara's granddaughter. She's a pretty little thing and so damn cute and polite. I know for sure that this emerald fabric she has chosen is going to look like a dream on her with her red flaming hair.

The machine makes a beep noise to let me know my caffeine fix is ready. Once I'm all set up and ready to go, I lay the fabric out and check the measurements I have for Janice.

I love nothing more than to create and together with her ideas and my vision, we've come up with something stunning. It'll be in the fashion of a 1950's full skirted prom dress with a sweetheart neckline. It's always exciting to start something fresh. I'm so excited for Janice's first fitting.

As I glance up from my sewing machine, I catch Deacon passing by. He stops at one of the windows, I catch my breath willing him to pop in and just you know, chat. But he doesn't and I feel a little deflated.

I'm going to have to take Lottie's advice and give him some strong old hints.

Chapter 4

D*eacon*
I glance through the shop window and see her head bowed down over some green fabric. She moves her hands delicately over it as if she's smoothing it out. Damn am I a stalker now or a voyager? Shit. I feel like one.

"What you up to there, Son?" The rusty voice of one of the town's elders, Mr Hicklebottom takes me away from the window. Shit. Now I've been caught red handed looking in on Daisy. All I wanted was a last little glance before I go on about my day.

"Good morning, Mr Hicklebottom. How's your morning?" I don't give him an answer. He gives me a wink, his pale blue eyes have that little glint in them.

"I know what you're up to young man. 'Bout time you asked the young lady in there for a date." I keep my jaw from dropping to the ground. Everyone says this, well not quite everyone. Jasper Hilton doesn't that's because the slimeball has got his eye on Daisy. I swear I'd have to cuff him and throw away the keys if he ever laid a hand on Daisy's head. There's nothing per se wrong with the guy, but he's not for Daisy. Am I jealous? Okay, so maybe I am.

"We're just good friends. What is it with the folk in this town?" I say and start to walk towards my truck that's parked up at the end of Main street. I have to head into the station and catch up on some reports that need filing.

"Well then you ought to stop spying on her like some creepy pervert." He says, huffs and tips his beaten, brown cowboy hat to me. Great, now the oldies are calling me a creepy pervert. Fantastic.

"You mind your step today, Mr Hicklebottom."

"Right you are, Son." He raises his gnarled cane. I grin, he's a good old man that one. Heart of a dinosaur but shrewd as they come. He owns a large chunk of land at the edge of the town, and about five years ago he sold me some off so I could keep a couple of horses and build myself a cabin with a view over the lake and to the West Virginian mountains. It's a sight I'm telling you. One day I'm going to find my happy ever after woman and our lives will be a dream.

Mitzi is my Appaloosa girl, she's now four and rides like a dream. I got her from the rescue auction in Copper Town when she was two and we've been tight ever since. That girl loves her daddy and her apples. My other horse, Lady Night is a magic black, Arabian and she is something else. Her brain must be the size of an elephant, she's smart as hell and doesn't let anyone close except me. They're my girls and I love them to pieces.

As I walk towards my truck I pass the hardware store and can see Bob busy with a customer showing him something or other, I tip my hat as he looks up and greets me with the wave of his hand. Next to him is the new florist that opened back up a few months ago, after a complete revamp. Shyann took it over from her mother who sadly passed away eight months ago, before that it belonged to her granny. It's good to see that some of the younger generation are keeping the old business going. What she needs now is a good young man to sweep her off her feet. She sure is a hardworking lass. Never went to college or nothing but I understand from Daisy that she's completed her diplomas in business via an online course. Fair play to her.

"And what are you two up to?" One of the Baxter's boys is ambling towards me with a deck of cards in his hand, he's with another kid I don't recall seeing around here. I stop so they can't pass me on the sidewalk.

"Nothing, Marshal Deacon." They say together.

"Haven't you got school today?"

"Yes, Sir. It's a free period is all. We're on our way to Bluebell's for a shake. We've got an hour to kill." Baxter's boy, Johnny says. Free period, wow these kids sure are growing up fast around here. Was only like yesterday when his mother, Tate was pushing him around in a damn pushchair and I was his age at school. Time has flown.

"Okay, off you go then but straight back to school in time. You hear me."

"Yes, Sir," both kids say as I let them pass. At my truck I press the fob and get inside the large cab and switch on the radio. I have my laptop installed and radio in.

"Curtis, anything to report? I'm heading back to the station now." I tell my right hand guy.

"Nothing new, Marshal. Come on in and get these reports done so we can get them cleared."

"You got it." I turn the ignition on and hear as the engine ticks over. It's a beast of a truck, a Ford Ranger. I glide her easily off the small dust parking area and reverse onto Main street then swing the wheel and head into the other side of town where our station is.

Outside of the two floor, brick building with black metal window frames I step out. There's a couple of other officers having a cigarette. "That shit is going to kill you." I shout over at them.

"We know, Marshal." They continue to smoke in any case. I shake my head. Never did understand why folk want to pollute their lungs like that and increase their chances of all sorts of nasty conditions and diseases.

"Hey. What took you so long this morning?" Curtis asks as he looks up from his desk.

"Coffee at Bluebell's. Stopped to say hi to Daisy then caught up briefly with Mr Hucklebottom. He's looking good for an old 'un."

"Didn't you bring me a coffee, Deacon you're such an ass."

"Yeah, I know. What can I say? You can run out and grab us some coffee and doughnuts in an hour or so. Let's get cracking on the paperwork."

Curtis nods and bends his head back down to his laptop and starts clicking away. My other two offices come back in, acknowledge me and get to their desks.

"Y'all up for pool tonight?" Lacey asks. He's broad and brooding, dark as jet black hair and eyes like emeralds. He's a ladies man, I don't ever see him settling down but you never know, some young girl may just walk into town and he'll be a gonner.

"Not for me. I've got a date with my girls tonight." I reply.

"You know, Deacon you sure ought to find something else you can ride aside from those girls of yours." We are of course referring to Mitzi and Lady Night. I throw a paperclip at him.

I do have a woman I see from time to time, we're not serious. She wants nothing from me and I want nothing from her. I enjoy my company with Molly Jenkins and that is as far as it goes. We don't date as such, you know it's more kind of to hook up. Like me, she is twenty-nine and doesn't want any relationship right now. A few years back she left her over-bearing ex who was from the sound of it a total dick, moved herself from Idaho and hasn't looked back.

Molly works as vet assistant in Copper Town, and it's safe to say that nobody round here knows about Molly and my goings on. I'm a man with a healthy libido so don't judge me. Although I'm not going to lie, I do have some dirty thoughts about Daisy from time to time, then guilt washes over me since she's my friend and I kind of feel ashamed.

It's a pickle, right?

Chapter 5

D*aisy*
My phone rings and I reach for it off the table that is to my right, it forms an L shape with my main sewing table. I've been so engrossed in the prom dress that I realize, as I look at my mobile that it's already lunch time. Where has the time gone? No wonder my stomach is making all sorts of strange noises.

It's a message from Sage, Logan's wife-to-be. It's so exciting that he and Sage will be finally going down the aisle. Funny, if she had never left Willowbrook for Michigan where she started her medical career, they'd probably have been married a long time ago and maybe I'd be an aunty to his kids already. I sure am looking forward to that. Sage and Logan will have beautiful babies.

Are we still on for girl's night out later. Thought we could chat wedding stuff too? I smile at her message. It's been so great to reconnect with Sage. Even though I am a lot younger than Sage and Logan, when I was a kid she'd always have time for me. There's about an eight year age gap and when Sage started dating Logan back in school, she'd always take me out on the swings, on her shopping trips and basically treated me like her kid sister. It was adorable, we'd have girls movie nights and it never seemed to fuss her that I was so much younger. Now of course it doesn't seem like there are any years between us, but you know what it's like when you're say eight and your bro's girlfriend is sixteen. You wouldn't expect them to take much interest, but Sage, she's always loved me.

Sure am up for it. Lazy Duke's still? I can be there for eight.

Fantastic, Holly is going to meet us there. That's Sage's best friend she stayed here in Willowbrook, got married after school and had the kids. Her husband works in insurance the last I heard.

What about Eliza and Sadie? I ask. Eliza pretty much runs the practice for Logan and acts as his assistant and Sadie is their nurse. I adore Sadie, she takes no crap from anyone, says it how it is and the best thing is that you never quite know what color hair she's going to have from one week until the next. Currently, she is sporting hot pink, it must be her favorite shade because she hasn't changed it for a while. She also wears a pretty cool nose ring, I'd love to get one but I'm way too chicken for that.

Absolutely, they are both going to be there too and will Lottie be able to come? The more the merrier.

I'll shoot her a message and let her know to join us. I doubt she's got anything going on.

Great, I have to fly, I have a patient in a few minutes just wanted to tie up this evening's girls night out.

You got it. See you tonight. Oh, wait. Isn't Logan playing tonight?

Nope, he and the guys including Deacon are off to his folks for a poker and beer night.

Ah, that means we can have a few drinks and get a bit silly. Maybe they'll hook up the karaoke for us. That'll be huge fun.

Absolutely, can you drop Abe a message and ask him to set it up for us please? Right, I really do have to go. See you tonight. Love you, D xx

Love you too, Sage. See you tonight at 8:00 P.M.

I smile, I can't wait to see the girls tonight and let your hair down. It's not something we do often, what I mean is we usually meet up on a Friday but some of us have to work on a Saturday and it isn't funny with a hangover, as much as I love Tequila and Apple Cider, it doesn't like me too much the next morning.

Tomorrow, I have a clear deck so I can afford a couple of drinks this evening and Karaoke is my favorite. I can't sing, not at all but who cares, I love it. Sage on the other hand, when she sings a ballad it can send shivers up and down your spine.

Before I put the fabric away I reach out to Lottie to check she can come tonight.

Absolutely I will be there. Count me in, lover girl.

Lover Girl???

Yeah, you and Deacon.

Oh, not that again. Honestly, Lottie give it a rest. All these years and people are still talking about me and the damn Marshal, when will they learn I'm just his friend. Besides, what would a man in his early thirties want with a woman like me in her twenties? That man is experienced and then some, and I, well I've had one partner and it was a disaster. I think I'll stick with my romance books.

Girl, you have got to let that man in.

Nope, he needs to be with someone more his own age, he thinks I'm just a kid still. He's all mature and grown up, he's the Marshal for effing hell's sake. I'm telling you now bestie, Deacon does not see me like a sexy, red blooded woman. He sees me as the kid with braces, thick glasses and braids to my ass.

Lottie sends me several laughing emojis.

See you tonight and let's get all dressed up. I tell her. She sends me some love hearts and thumbs up.

Not long after, I close up the shop, turn the sign on the door to say I'm out for lunch and lock the door. First stop will be Bluebell's to get myself a nice blueberry muffin, she makes the best muffins for miles then I think I'll head to Carmichael's and have myself a nice Mexican chili taco or two.

As I walk down Main street, I have a spring in my step. The air is typical cool, fall weather but the sun is shining and there isn't a cloud in the sky. I marvel at the shade of blue and how perfect life seems to be right now. I don't need a man in my life, not right now. I have everything I need and more with my shop and business, my friends, my folks, and living in the best place possible, Willowbrook.

You keep telling yourself that, Daisy. You know you want that Marshal in your bed keeping you warm at night and those lips kissing yours. Yes you do. Stop denying it. I feel myself blushing, good Lord.

I step inside Bluebells, the bell above the door goes off. "Hey, Honey. What can I get you?" She shouts from the counter where she is just taking a customer's money.

"Blueberry muffin to go please, Babs."

"Coming right up." She says goodbye to the customer and opens the casing holding the blueberries, they look soft and moist. My stomach grumbles. *In a minute.*

Since it's lunchtime, the diner is busy, there's the usual townsfolk who swing by every day for their coffees, cakes and a bit to eat, but I see some fresh faces too. We have a lot of visitors come in from the surrounding towns, Willowbrook is a tourist destination with it's beautiful mountains, Main street is a picture and nothing beats it right through from Halloween to Thanksgiving and Christmas. We get inundated with tourists.

"Thanks, Babs. I'll see you tomorrow morning." She nods and smiles. I am always in here for my morning coffee, there is something about her brew that makes my morning a brighter one.

Minding my own business I continue to walk down Main Street heading for Carmichael's Mexican restaurant, as I walk I look in the store windows. There's a cute little vintage dress shop just opened, passing it I spot a gorgeous 1950s type dress, it's red with white polka dots and oh my, it is so pretty. I'm not watching at all where I'm going as I keep looking at the dress. I think I'm going to have to make time to go in and try it on.

The next thing I know I've walked into something hard. "Ouch." I say and look up only to see Marshal Deacon and those swoony eyes of his looking down at me with his mouth upturned.

"Hey, Daisy. You need to watch where you're walking." He says with a grin.

"I was." Lame. I'm flustered, I am up against his chest with his muscular arms around me, his large hands on my hips to steady me. I can smell his cinnamon fragrance, mm it's so good. I lick my lips. Oh shoot.

"That's how come you manage to walk right into me then is it?" He chuckles, it's deep and throaty but what I'm feeling more is the intense heat rising from between my legs up through my stomach. Oh. Wow.

I gaze into his eyes for a few seconds, wondering just how fine his lips would be on mine, and the feel of his tongue in my mouth. I cough and step back. Too much, right? I know, but if you were standing in front of Deacon with all that manliness I'm telling you, you wouldn't want to break away.

His eyes are glinting mischievously. "I'd say you did it on purpose, sweetheart."

"Don't you sweetheart me nothing. It was an accident. I was looking at that pretty little dress right there and not paying attention."

"Is that right? It'd look damn fine on you, Daisy." His words make me blush. He's just being nice, right?

"Thanks." I mumble. "I've got to go, I'm on my break. I'll catch you later." I practically run away from him. He tips his hat at me and nods, and I hear him chuckling as a scurry like a church mouse.

Damn it.

Chapter 6

D*eacon*
She sure does get me all hot under the collar especially in that cute summer dress of hers and her blonde locks falling over her face. It's all I could do not to reach out and touch her. She's going to think I am over stepping the friendship boundary, besides, what would a younger woman want with me? I'm in my thirties already and she's still in her twenties. I'm way too old for her. Aren't I?

Although, now I'm thinking about Catherine Zeta Jones and Michael Douglas only because I cannot think of any other older woman, younger men relationships that have worked.

I love how she's blushing right now. It's so damn cute. Everything about Daisy is cute and yet so womanly and sexy. Her long colt like legs would be the perfect fit around my waist as I hoist her up into my arms. Is it me or is it hot outside? This woman is killing me and my dick is starting to ache.

"I'll catch you around." I say smirking at her as she rustles off and gives me a small wave.

"Oh, are you girls going out tonight?" I shout after her, because you know, I just don't want her to be gone yet.

"We sure are, Deacon. We're going to paint Lazy Duke's tonight, kick up our heels and do some singing and dancing."

"Oh my, that's going to be a sight. You best behave yourself, Daisy. I know what you can get like when you get some of those tequila shots in you." I smirk and give her a wink. That girl can roar up a bar in seconds. I'm telling you. The last time she had far too much to drink, she was dancing on the table tops and kicking her legs up high. It took Logan to fireman lift her off and hurl her in that truck of his and take her home.

Needless to say the following morning, Daisy looked a little green. Still gorgeous but you know, that hangover was a mean ass one.

"Of course I'm going to behave myself, I'll not dance on any tables tonight. I'll keep my skirt down to my knees and behave like a proper lady." She laughs, the sound hits my hears like a symphony. Delightful, her laughter and gaiety has a certain tinkle to it. I love it. If there was one sound I'd have to choose to listen to for eternity, it'd definitely be Daisy's laughter.

"Make sure you do, or you'll have me to deal with and I do not want to be called away from my poker game to arrest any unwanton men harassing you."

"Oh, Deacon, relax. It's just Sage, Holly, Eliza, Sadie, Lottie and I."

"Exactly, when you and Lottie get together, chaos ensues." I remark. It's true those two seem to get into all sorts of trouble. Because they're both stunning men fawn after them and with their playful ways, they can sometimes be misread.

Only a couple of weeks ago, Logan and I had to set some guy straight because he was hitting on Daisy and pawing her at the bar. All she'd said was "hi," and "nice to meet you," then chatted about Willowbrook and the folk. You know some guys just misread a situation and he certainly did. Not being a local, Logan had his eye on the guy from up on stage and when he went t0o far with his hand on the base of Daisy's back, Logan was off the stage like a shot and pushing the guy.

Yep, that meant I had to step in from my small corner of the bar at Lazy Duke's and pull the whole nine yards, Marshal shit. That's how it goes. That girl is a damn magnet.

Daisy blows me kisses, "have a good game of poker. No taking all their money you card shark you." It's been known for me to clean up since I am pretty good at the game, I've been playing cards ever since my grand pop sat me on his knee. We'd spend hours on a Sunday after lunch my grand mama would make, playing cards. Okay, so poker came a bit later when I was around thirteen. I'm a pretty mean player and I like to win.

I tip my hat at her and head for Bluebells to collect my ham and cheese bagel, coffee to-go and a nice warm muffin. I happen to know that Debs always makes an afternoon batch and if you get the timing just right, you'll get a nice warm one.

"Hey Deacon, how you doing? Long time no see." She smiles as she makes fun of me a little. So, I come here twice a day, once for breakfast coffee and a pastry and again during the afternoon. Debs is the best baker in Willowbrook, she has this secret ingredient thing going on with her cakes and muffins, I swear she puts some kind of drug in them that keeps you coming back time and time again.

"Afternoon, Debs. How was the morning?" I ask as I set my hat down whilst she gets to my regular order.

"It was good, busy you know, the usual regulars a few new faces from Coppertown. Good for business." Her pale blue eyes are soft and gentle, the skin around them creases. Her auburn hair is tied up away from her face.

"Glad to hear it. Heard there were some new folk over in Coppertown, do them good to show their faces around here too. We like to keep things friendly between the two towns. Talking of which, are you speaking to Linda from the diner out that way for the fundraiser for the baseball kids?"

Linda runs the equivalent to Bluebell's diner over in Coppertown, she's a slightly more mature lady, at a guess mid-sixties with the most dynamic violet eyes you ever laid eyes on. She's funny and witty, takes no prisoners and makes a mean lemon meringue pie.

For the last few years, Linda has helped out with the fundraiser by baking the pies and setting up a stall. She makes a killing for our fundraiser for the little leaguers here in Willowbrook that Logan started off funding until he realized he needed to make it bigger and more profitable to support the kids around here. And since a lot of the kids from the neighboring towns come to play at our ground and use it for practice, we thought it a good idea to extend the fundraising activities to the business owners there too.

Now we have around fifty owners who all take part. Each year it grows a bit more and the entire day is filled with festivities, ranging from dunk the boss, the scavenger hunt that we sell tickets for, we have a themed luncheon where everyone buys a ticket and we take the difference from the cost of the luncheon and put it into the little leaguers pot. Not sure what the theme is this year, Eliza from the practice, Logan and Sage are on that. Last year it was Disney which was huge fun with over sized characters and I got the part of Goofy. The kids were nuts for it. I know this year they want to organize a film festival for the early evening something for the family to all enjoy.

"She said she's more than happy to participate again this year. She's already started baking the pies and will do the fillings closer in. I can't believe it's only a few weeks away now. Logan, Sage and Eliza still have a fair bit of planning to do."

"They do indeed, but they will pull it off, especially now Eliza and Logan have Sage on board." I take my bagel from Babs. "Thank you for the lunch order. I always look forward to this and a warm muffin."

"Straight out the oven, Marshal."

"I'll be heading off to enjoy this over in the park and then back to the grindstone." I nod and pick my hat up off the counter. As I turn I bump into Logan.

"Hey, Deacon. Skiving off again are we?" His brown eyes are smiling.

"Could say the same about you, Logan."

"Just picking something up for us at the practice, we're having a working lunch to discuss the fundraiser." He says as he turns to Babs. "Four coffees, one with vanilla please for Sage. Four slices of today's special cake and some brownies all to go please, Babs."

"We were just talking about that too. Babs and I were saying you've got a fair bit to do, right?"

"Boy, do we and with the wedding plans on top too and the extension on the cabin so Sage can have an art studio."

I raise my eyebrows. "Art studio? I didn't know Sage painted." And I've known her just as long as Logan has since we all went to school together.

"She took it up whilst she was in Michigan, her stuff is pretty good. I told her she should open a small shop and get someone to man it for her whilst she's at the practice all day with me. Honestly, I reckon she'd make good money. Her stuff is amazing."

"Why doesn't she set up an online shop, cut out the costs of an actual store to start with?"

"Good idea, I'll mention it to Sage. Her work needs to be seen, it deserves it, she deserves it."

"See you at poker tonight, Logan."

"Yeah, you ready to lose all your money tonight, Deacon?" He chuckles.

"You have got to be kidding me, your whole game has been sour over the last few sessions. Get ready to bring your wallet," I say. He gives me the sly finger so Babs can't see the good small-town doctor doing so. I grin and slap him on the back and head back outside.

My mind is back on Daisy and how pretty she looked today, that and who the hell is going to try chatting her up tonight on her girls night out at Lazy Duke's. Maybe I can wrap the game up early tonight and convince the guys to go get some drinks at Lazy Duke's. Someone's gotta keep an eye on that girl.

Am I being a bit over protective? Yeah, hell. Maybe.

Chapter 7

D^{*aisy*} I'm so excited to be going out with the girls tonight and for our chats and karaoke. The rest of the day whizzed by. I had a couple of walk ins. One was Mr Henderson who is such a sweet elderly gentleman and visits Logan in the practice on numerous occasions mainly for his arthritis. He needed some trousers taking in which I will drop off to him on the way home this evening. I may even pop into Debs on the way back and pick him up a nice homemade cherry pie. I happen to know it is his favorite.

Mrs. Winters, one of the teachers from the school, who teaches the little ones has also popped in to place an order for a vintage tea dress to wear to the fundraising event. We've picked out a beautiful navy fabric with bluebells on it. It'll suit her auburn hair and blue eyes. Mrs. Winters has taught at the school since I was in middle grade, she has always lived in Willowbrook and is one of the nicest ladies you will ever meet.

Now time to close up and I am ready for a night out with the girls. I do drop by Debs and pick up the cherry pie and go knock on Mr Henderson's door. "Good evening, Daisy." He says as he has one hand on his cane. His grey eyes twinkle at the sight of me, it's endearing.

"Mr Henderson your trousers are ready. Any adjustments be sure to let me know and I bought you a nice cherry pie." I hand the bag to him. He places it down on the small pine table he has in his hallway, then I offer him the pie.

"That is so kind of you, Daisy. I do love cherry pie. From Bluebell's?" He asks.

"Absolutely, no other place to get it. Enjoy, Mr Henderson. Let me know if you need anything. I'll be going grocery shopping tomorrow, would you like me to pick anything up for you?" I like to help the elders in Willowbrook out where I can, one day I will be their age and I like to think that we will have people like me around on hand to help us out too. Even though we have a good community service here for the elderly.

"I don't think so. Eliza came by the other day and made sure my cupboards were stocked and the fridge."

"Okay. I will see you around in that case." I lean in and give him a little peck on the cheek which makes him smile. Bless him, he is the cutest.

My cat Bonnie is meowing when I get in, she's an adorable tux, black and white with a black smudge on her pink nose. "Hey girlie. How was your day?" I pick her up and cuddle her into my chest. She purs and leans her head in so it's under my chin. I fuss her for a few minutes then put her back down. She trots after me as I go into the kitchen and reach in one of the knotted pine cabinets on ground level to reach for her kibbles.

Happy with her treats she munches away. I kick off my shoes and pour myself a nice glass of cold wine. It's already six and I am home later than usual, since ordinarily I will close shop at around four. But having stopped at Mr Henderson's and spending the extra time with Mrs. Winters pushed my times back a bit. I don't mind.

The wine is nice and cold as it glides down my throat. Now are we all eating out? I have forgotten. I message Sage.

Did we say we're eating at Lazy's?

Yes, we'll get something there.

Perfect, I'm starving. Just got in but will be with you ladies for seven.

Great, looking forward to us all catching up. I've only just got in too. We had a few extra patients walk in from Copper Town. The expansion programme over there is making us busier, not a bad thing. At this rate, Logan may need to consider hiring in another doctor.

Sounds good, sis-to-be.

We end the chat so we can both get ready. I love calling her my sis-to-be, in all honesty Sage has always been like a sister to me and when she left Willowbrook to follow her medical career in Michigan, it felt like a gaping hole had been left in my heart. I don't even want to think how it felt for Logan but he was a hot mess. That's all water under the bridge now that they've found each other again and are getting married in a few months time. It'll be a Spring wedding and I am making the gown for Sage. We're still discussing it and looking at different designs and of course Pinterest. I swear I'm addicted to that platform.

Bonnie brushes against my leg. "Come here, little one." I pick her up and walk through my open plan lounge-dining space, down the short corridor and into my bedroom. My small cottage has three bedrooms, one I use as a workout room as it has sliding doors that look out to the beautiful West Virginia mountains and forestland. It's a sight to be seen with the abundance of trees and foliage. I find it relaxing to do my yoga and Pilates in here of a morning when the sun is rising and peeking above the tops of the trees. It makes me feel so grateful for the life that I live.

Another room is my guest room and then there is my main bedroom with full bathroom en-suite.

I place Bonnie down on my large bed, covered with a beautiful white and blue patchwork quilt that my mom made for me. On each side of the bed are two side tables that my father carved for me. He's amazing with woodwork and seriously he could sell the stuff he makes, but he prefers to just treat it as a hobby. They're burnished oak and bring out the natural woods of my carved headboard and footrest on the bed. An antique I picked up when I went to Bushnell Peak some years ago, about a two hour drive from me. Thankfully, Logan didn't have any issues in making the trek out there to go pick it up for me in his large truck.

Bonnie curls up on the bed with her head resting on her front paws and keeps her eyes on me. "Yes, baby. Momma is going out again." The way she looks at me makes me feel guilty that I've left her all day and will be out for a good few hours this evening. When she was a kitten I tried her on a halter and leash but she wasn't having any of it. I loved the idea of having her come out and about with me like you see some other folk's cats go walking with them.

Half an hour later I have showered, styled my hair into loose curls with the use of my large barrel tongs and applied some peach lip-gloss and black mascara. I've dusted some bronzer over my cheekbones and the tip of my nose and consider myself ready. Now for an outfit. I'm fancying my crisp white shirt that has frills down either side of the buttons, with long puffed sleeves, since it's now cooler outside, a denim skirt and my long, tan cowgirl boots.

"How do I look, baby?" I ask Bonnie who has now closed her eyes. I sigh, so much for a cat girlfriend. I ruffle her head and grab my turquoise fake leather bag on a long chain from the back of my standalone chair in the corner of my room and go back to kiss her on the head. She moves her head slightly then dozes back off.

Outside, it's cool but not too cold so I just take my black corduroy jacket from the metal coat stand behind my gnarled wood front door and sling it over my arm.

"Daisy." I hear a sexy, gruff voice say. I know that voice, I'd know it anywhere even in dark room.

"Deacon." I say and smile at him.

"You're looking might fine this evening."

"Why thank you, Deacon. You look pretty good yourself." He does, in his tight fitting black jeans, a pale blue button down tucked in that stretches across his broad shoulders. His hips taper nicely from his waist. On his feet he is wearing beaten cowboy boots. This man is perfection with his short hair and beautiful eyes. A girl could get lost in those forever.

"Aren't you walking in the wrong direction?" I ask him. Which he is if he is heading over to Logan's for the poker game. Is he blushing? Oh my, he is and he shuffles from one foot to the other.

I grin. He gives me a shrug of those magnificent shoulders of his. "I'm heading the other direction now. Just out for a bit of a walk is all." He says.

Okay, I'm not sure that is one-hundred percent believable since Deacon's house is off the track road nestled in the forest area, not too far from Logan's. "Right." I say. *Going for a walk my ass.*

"I better get going." He says and starts to walk off.

"Yeah, I'll see you later, Deacon. Enjoy your night and leave the guys with some cash to take home." I chuckle. He raises his hand to wave and I shake my head. Strange. Very strange.

I'm thinking his sole purpose was to swing by. I may just be fantasizing here, just because I'd like to think that, doesn't mean it's the case. Anyway, I've got a girls night out to get to.

Chapter 8

D*eacon*

That girl makes me hot under the collar that is for sure. I wanted to pick her up and twirl her around, she looked so damn cute in that dress of hers. Her smile wide and bright, she lights up the sky at night. Just looking at Daisy is like a clear blue sky in the summer. Magical, calming and heartwarming. That sums her up.

I'm looking forward to my poker night with the guys later over at Logan's. I'll get back in my truck now I've had my last glimpse of Daisy for the day. Am I becoming a pervert? I mean, I did drive back to Main Street to see her leave work for the day. Lucky for me she was out later than she usually is.

Man, I think I've got it bad. I've always liked her since we were teenagers but this, now, it's getting worse. I've got no interest in other women even though I see a few over in Copper town but lately I haven't even bothered. My hand is doing the job and a nice warm shower.

On my way back to my ranch, just a two mile drive off Main Street I consider heading over to my folks house. They live close to Daisy and Logan's folks. It's been a couple of days since I have dropped into see them and I could do with some of my mom's special baked apple pie. She's going to be helping out at the fundraiser with Daisy's mom to bake pies and cakes, they're going to make a killing. They always do.

I take a left at the top of main with the mountain view and sprawling forest land in sight. The fall daylight is changing now we're heading into dusk, the blue sky is dotted with pinkish tinged clouds and it sure is pretty. As pretty as Daisy. Damn, I cannot get my mind off her. She is always on it. I wake up thinking about her and I go to sleep thinking about her and then some in between.

My folks house is just up ahead and I can see my mom in her beloved garden, she looks to be pruning some rosebushes. Hearing my truck she looks up and gives me a wave. Her smile spreads across her face. I park up and hop out.

"Deacon, wasn't expecting you this evening. What a nice surprise."

"Hey, Mom." I say as I go over and plant a kiss on her soft cheek. "Couldn't resist coming to see my favorite lady." I tip my hat at her. Mom places a hand on my cheek.

"So good to see you. Come on let's go in. Do you want coffee or a nice fresh homemade lemonade?" Mom also makes *the* best lemonade this side of West Virginia.

"A cold glass of your lemonade, Mom of course." She giggles. "Where's pop?" I ask as I place my hat on the oak dresser she has standing in the wide entrance hall. I am mindful to slip my shoes off knowing my mom cleans almost daily. Where she gets all that energy I have no idea but she's a proud house-lady that is for sure.

"Oh, he's off in his den out back. Tinkering away. You know your father. I'll give him a shout." By that she means she'll call him on his mobile. It still makes me chuckle how these two communicate if they're not in the same room together. For a couple who didn't want mobile phones to begin with, they're now pretty partial to them.

I follow mom into the kitchen with it's large, sliding glass doors that take up the entire back wall. From the kitchen you can see forest land out back. My dad inherited the house from his daddy who inherited it from his. We're from the original descendants of Willowbrook. I find that pretty neat. It's a two floor house that is shaped as an L, with the lounge off the hallway on the right, a small toilet area opposite then down the hallway the kitchen. There is the corridor along the L part that leads to main bedroom suite with a balcony and it's own full bathroom.

Upstairs are four bedrooms each with a bathroom that dad had added on when they decided to have a family. That is my brother, Jefferson who is older than me by three years, he is now thirty eight, and is a lawyer with his offices here in Willowbrook. He is married to Stella who is a stay at home mom, taking care of their three kids. She used to be his assistant once upon a time and though she is a full time mom and housekeeper, she still helps him out working from home when he needs it. It's a win-win for both of them.

Then we have Maxine who is thirty and lives with her husband, Dan. They have two girls and they're as pretty as a picture, Lou-Lou is just a baby around ten months old and Blossom is now four. My sister has her own online beauty shop selling all sorts of organic hair and beauty products. She is one of those successful influencer types, I think that's what you call them. To be honest, I'm not really that versed when it comes to all this online stuff. Hell, I only use my mobile to call someone or send a message, sure I use the internet but as far as all that social media stuff, I wouldn't have a Scooby-Doo.

The fourth bedroom was our playroom, not that we really needed it except if it was a rainy day since the woods out back were always our playground. Dad built us a tree house which is still up, we had a lot of fun as kids playing pirates in that house.

"Deacon is here." I hear mom on the phone to dad. If my mom were to shout out from the back doors my dad would easily hear her, although he could have his pods in listening to an audio book. She makes him keep his mobile on vibrate just in case she needs him and he's lost in another one of his books.

Mom places the phone down and opens the large double, stainless steel fridge and takes out the glass pitcher of lemonade and pours me a tall glass. "There you go, sweetie." Yeah, I know. I'm thirty-five and she calls me all sorts of cute ass names.

"Thanks, Mom. Any chance of some apple pie?" I sit down at the granite island.

"Absolutely. Made a fresh one this morning." She gets out a plate, a spoon and then the pie from the fridge. "You want it warmed up in the microwave?"

"Yes please, and can I have cream on it too, please?"

"Of course you can. I'll make some for your dad." She busies herself away and I have to admire how my mother has looked after herself over the years. She's got a trim figure from all the Pilates and Yoga she does, often dragging my father along too. I know he enjoys it even though he grumbles all the way. They swim together once a week and they are nuts for hiking. These two must be the fittest sixty-something year old's I know.

"Son." Dad's voice fills the kitchen. He comes over and slaps me on the back. My dad is looking good, he has color from the summer and fall days on his face and his grey eyes light up. "Ah, you're only here for your mother's applie pie." He chuckles and goes over to mom and gives her a kiss on the cheek and a small smack on the ass.

"Behave old man." She says playfully. I love that about my folks, how they're still so tactile and display love to one another. It's definitely a relationship that is based on over forty years together, mutual respect and a hefty sprinkling of love and magic. Exactly how I want mine to be one day and a house full of kids.

Which is why I have a large ranch, it's way too big for me right now and the house itself has ten rooms, four double bedrooms with their own bathrooms and a large main suite that sits on the top, second floor. It is spacious and my actual plot size is twenty-three acres. I've a couple of horses stabled that I ride and maybe one day, I'll consider hiring someone so we can run a riding school for the kids around Coppertone and here in Willowbrook who can't afford to have a horse. It'll be great for the community.

"How is work, Son?" Dad asks as he takes a drink of his filled coffee mug mom has just placed in front of him with his plate of apple pie and cream.

"It's good. You know how quiet Willowbrook is, Pop. Not too bad. Some little rascal hooligans got caught trying to decorate the side of the school. A headache of paperwork for us and a slap on the wrist for them."

"Any kids we know?" He asks.

"Nah, from Coppertown. Their expansion programme is going well so we're starting to see some kids coming over who have nothing better to do. We're talking with their Marshal and Mrs. Winters from the school here is talking with their school master to see about offering some of our community services to the kids. You know, try to integrate them some. The councils are talking too. Since Coppertown is only a few miles away it makes sense."

Dad nods. He still has a full head of hair, it's dark with a smattering of grey and I notice a few new ones. "Good idea if you ask me. Those kids need something to do, Coppertown doesn't have too much to offer the kids right now."

He's right, there is the church, a small Main Street, a juvenile hall for them to hang out and a park but they don't have their own baseball playing ground like we do here. Which is mostly down to Logan who was until a few years ago, the sole financer for it.

I finish my pie, it sits well in my stomach. "I've got to be going. I want to head home get changed and then make my way over to Logan's for our poker night. Fancy joining us this evening, Pop?"

"No thanks, Son. You boys have a good game and please don't take all their money." He chuckles.

"Funny, Daisy said the very same thing." I shake my head.

"*And*, how is *Daisy*?" My mom is now very interested.

"She's still Daisy, Ma. No change there."

"I was thinking, that perhaps you could help her out at the fundraiser with her craft stall."

"Mom, I think Sadie from the practice is helping her." Sadie is the nurse at Logan's practice and she's a bit of a crafter too.

"Nonsense, you should offer." I know exactly what my mom is trying to do. It's sweet but I already know I'm a bit too old for the likes of Daisy and she only sees me as Logan's best friend.

"Besides, I'm on dunking again."

Dad laughs. Last year I got saturated but we did make a lot of money since everyone in town had to have a go at dunking the marshal. Nice.

"Well that young girl is going to run off into the sunset one day, mark my words young man." My ma says with a sigh.

I get up and give her a kiss, man hug my dad and say my goodbyes.

Outside it's started to get dark, I hop in my truck and start up the engine. It's time to go and give the guys a thrashing at poker.

Chapter 9

D^{*aisy*} I am still grinning from ear to ear over Deacon being literally outside mine as I stepped off my porch to get into my car. Truth be told, I kind of like it. You all know how much I like him already and one of these days, I'm going to throw myself right at him.

I'd love nothing more than to be held in those large, muscular arms of his and inhale his masculinity. *Hey stop that right now, you hear. You've got an evening out with the girls to go to and having wet panties is not the way to start your night out.* I giggle like a schoolgirl, but you know, if any man is worth a girl's wet fantasies, it sure is Marshal Deacon.

It takes only ten minutes to get down Main Street and take a left at the end down a dirt track road and veer off to the right to see the Lazy Duke's bar. It's an old cabin style building with rustic roofing and a neon sign hanging outside with the name on it.

It looks like it's already busy judging by the amount of cars parked out front. I find a space easy enough though, apply the handbrake, stick my old car in neutral and turn off the ignition. Checking the rearview mirror, I can see Holly walking behind my car.

Quickly I get out. "Hey Holly. Wait for me." I say. Holly, as I've said is Sage's best friend they go back since they were around five, which means I've also known Holly for most of my life since she and Sage are almost ten years older than me. Sometimes, when Sage used to babysit me, Holly would be with her.

"Look at you, would you. *Hot.*" She says and gives me a big grin and a wink.

"In this old get up? You're kidding, right?" I go over and hook my arm through hers. There isn't anything particularly dressy about my bootleg cut, faded denim jeans, my sky-blue halter top with sequins on it and my favorite blue with flowers cowboy boots. I'm a bit cold since the fall evening is brisk. Maybe I should have slung a jacket over.

"With that body, girl you are smokin' hot." She pulls me into her. I chuckle

"Okay, I'll take it."

"I love how you're wearing your hair too. Did you do all that yourself?"

It's only a braid but I pulled out some bits to make it look messy and dotted dried flowers in it that I've fixed with pins. "I did indeed. You like it?"

"It's so pretty. I wish I'd grown my hair after having the kids then I could have been a bit more experimental." She sighs.

"I love your sharp bob though, Holly. It really suits your face and it's so chic." And it is the way it's shorter at the back and dives down below her chin at the front. Her hair is like dark chocolate, rich and glorious. Holly has always been the elegant one, me, I'm usually your shorts and jeans kind of girl. I wear my dresses to work mainly to showcase what I can create for customers, or of course if I'm going on a date. At home, however, I'm definitely a casual kind of girl.

We reach the old barn style door and step inside. Music from the jukebox is playing and I do spy that the mics are on the stage right at the front and the karaoke flat screen. "Looks like we're on for our singing session." I say as we go inside and head straight for the bar.

"Daisy, how are you?" Sandy a guy I dated a couple of times asks me. He's propping up the bar and is looking pretty good. He just didn't do it for me, when we kissed there were no fireworks, the moon was still the moon high in the sky and I didn't feel my toes curl. We had us some fun and then decided that we would be better suited as friends. His folks own the lumberjack yard here in Willowbrook and his sister, Gaynor and his ma run their shop that sells furniture his pop makes.

I lean in and give him a light kiss on the cheek. Holly releases my arm and looks around to see if she can spot Sage, Eliza and Sadie. I've not seen Lottie yet either.

"I'm doing great, Sandy. Good to see you. Have you gotten yourself married yet?" He chuckles, his green with brown flecked eyes dance.

"No way. You know me. I'm just out to have fun. I can't do all those single ladies out there a disservice by taking myself off the market. Not just yet in any case." I nudge him playfully.

"One day some young lady is going to come along and sweep your feet right from under you."

"She already did, only I wasn't the moon to her stars." Aw, shucks. That makes me feel kind of sad because I know he's talking about me. But if he isn't the one, then he just isn't the one.

I want the whole nine yards when it comes to being with my life partner, I want my heart to race, my pulse to quicken, my breath to catch and feel tingling up and down my spine and my toes curling. Sandy is good looking and he's sought after here in Willowbrook, hell even strangers coming in try to hook up with him, but he just wasn't *the one*.

"What will it be ladies?" Abe asks as stands at the other side of the bar. Now he is a man mountain, with his dark, wavy hair that usually hangs to his jawline. Today he is wearing it in a man-bun, his green eyes are like the color of the forest and his tatts are on display with his shirt sleeves rolled up. He looks like he hasn't shaved in a few days since his scruff is longer than normal.

"You lost your shaver or something?" I ask him. Sandy goes back to drinking his beer.

"Or something." He says.

"And your tongue, I'm guessing."

"That too."

"I'll have a bottle of red and a bottle of white wine." I tell him.

"No, make that two of each." Holly interjects. "We're out for a ladies night out remember. We want to let our hair down."

We watch as Abe raises his eyebrows. What is he like, my father? Abe is also best friends with Deacon and Logan, but sometimes, honestly, he could pass as my dad the way he always has an eye on what I'm drinking. He can be over protective to say the least.

"And who is designated driver this evening?" He asks.

"We're going to get a cab back." Holly tells him. "My husband will bring me in the morning to collect my car and we'll bring Daisy over too."

He cocks his head. "And you want four bottles just for the two of you?" Is this is the Spanish inquisition?

"No way. Sage, Eliza, Sadie and Lottie are meeting us. We're just a bit early I guess."

He looks more satisfied with that. "Fair enough. I'll get the bottles ready and have Dawn bring them over. Grab a table over there in the corner by the window. Menus?"

"Yes please, we're eating in tonight." I say.

Holly moves ahead of me as we make our way to the corner table by the front window. It's a bit less crowded than by the bar. Just as we're about to sit down, Sage, Sadie and Eliza come through the door.

"Over here." Holly shouts out. People turn to look. She does have a good set of lungs on her, they'd probably have heard her in Texas.

The ladies come our way and there's a lot of hugging and cheek kissing going on. "So glad we could all make it. Finally." Sage says as she shrugs off her puffer coat, scarf and hat.

"Did you walk?" I ask her only she is dressed up for skiing.

"We did. Much easier than faffing around with cars later. Besides, we're on a drive to be as fit as we can for the wedding and I do need to fit into my gown." She plops herself down on the chair, her cheeks are flushed from the brisk fall air.

Eliza sighs. "Blissful. My feet are killing me." I laugh, it's only a two mile walk from her house to Lazy Dukes.

"Have you ordered the drinks?" Sadie asks.

"Yes and menus." I reply.

"Good, I need a drink or four." She says. Sadie does like her drink but she's good at handling it. Unlike me, I'm pretty much a lightweight when it comes to drinking. Three and I'm giggling, four and I am wobbling, five and I'm definitely a gonner.

Dawn, Abe's new bar girl heads our way with the bottles, behind her is a young lad around eighteen or nineteen who has a tray with the glasses and some menus stuffed under one of his arms.

"Ladies." Dawn says as she sets the bottles down. "Enjoy and don't get too out of hand, especially you, Daisy. I know what you can get like." She leaves us to it and we help ourselves to the wine and start to peruse the menus.

"I think I'm going with the corn, chicken wings, chili dip and some fries on the side." I say.

"I'll have the same." Holly says and Sage nods her head.

"Girls, wait for me." Lottie arrives and kisses me on the cheek, takes off her fleece and sits down next to me.

"We're only just starting." I tell her and squeeze her hand.

"Fantastic. Let's get this show on the road." I hand her a glass of red knowing it is her preference. We all raise our glasses and chink for our ladies night out. It's been a while since we have been out together and boy are we going to let off some steam.

I spot a group of guys at the bar who are eyeing us up, I try not to make eye contact since we do not want any guys hitting on us tonight. Well, Lottie might since she's now newly single again. Holly who is married and Sage to be married are definitely not interested. Sadie, well she only does hook ups so she'll be open to any suggestions this evening but Eliza is married too and wouldn't even dream of it. Although, I'm thinking a bit of harmless flirting wouldn't be such a bad thing, would it?

Chapter 10

Deacon

"What has gotten into you tonight?" Logan's dad asks. And I don't rightly know other than my mind is not on the game nor my hand of cards right now. I've never lost a game well okay, maybe the odd one or two here but this hand is downright awful.

"Ah, nothing. Mind on something else." I say and throw my hand in. "I'm out." I say. Logan raises his eyebrows.

"No way?" He smirks.

"Yes way." I take a swig of my beer. I've been nursing the same bottle for the last hour.

"You're not drinking either, Son." His old man says.

"No, Sir. I'm thinking of heading over to Lazy Duke's in a while see what's going on there."

"And would that be because my sister happens to be out there this fine evening?" Logan chuckles again, his brown with Holly eyes are full of merriment. He's had a couple of drinks himself. To be fair, Logan never gets drunk, he's always stuck at two, the max I've seen him drink is three drinks. Other than when Sage left him here in Willowbrook when he was just eighteen years of age.

He thought they had their futures planned out only she decided to leave for Michigan State to follow her medical career dreams and he didn't follow her. Nursing a broken heart sure did see the bottom of a lot of whiskey bottles and beer bottles. Thankfully, his old man spoke some sense into him and told him that if it was meant to be it would happen, maybe not that year or the year after but that The

Lord had ways. And look at them know. Ten years later and we'll all be celebrating their marriage.

"Don't be ridiculous. I always go to see Abe and have a beer or two. I hear there's a good band on tonight and the ladies are also doing karaoke. I kind of think it'd be fun to go take a look." Is all I'm saying. Logan can see right through me, so can his pop who is smiling.

"Son, you need to do something about this situation. If she is the one then you gotta tell her." He tells me and pats my hand.

"Easy for you to say, only she's ten years younger than me and we're just good friends is all, Sir. You know she's after a man who is more her own age, you only have to see her around town."

"That's just flirting, she's a pretty girl, the boys like her but she needs a man." He tells me. Pats my hand and knocks back his whiskey.

"Okay, who wants another hand or are we calling it quits?" Logan's dad asks. Logan looks at me and cocks his head.

"We'll call it quits, Pop. Besides, I kind of like the idea of going to check on the girls. I heard there were some guys over from Coppertown, you know the new crowd. I wouldn't mind making sure the ladies are okay."

"Tshk, you young guns, you worry too much. Those ladies can look after themselves, besides you got Abe behind the bar, he can handle any man who starts anything in his bar." Logan's dad is right there, you'd have to be a fool to mess around in Abe's bar. The man is a mountain, and covered in tatts.

"C'mon Deacon, let's go check on the ladies." Logan says as he folds his hand of cards too. His pop scrapes the money off the table and gives us a nod. He earned his cash tonight fair and square. Am I sore I lost, yeah a little. That's what happens when you're thinking of a beautiful woman, with golden flowing hair, blue eyes and a smile that lights up the darkest sky at night.

I follow Logan as his dad closes the door behind us to his office. We've been playing at Logan's dad's house this time, we take it turns to host our poker nights. I had headed over to Logan's cabin which is nestled close to mine and came down in my truck giving him a lift. I did have every intention of having a couple of drinks but knew in the back of my mind, I'd be heading over to Abe's bar to check the status out.

I don't like it when I hear there's a new set of guys in town, makes me nervous. We're a small community here, everyone trusts everyone but with the new development over in Coppertown some new folks have been coming through. You can take the man out of the marshal, but you can never take the marshal out of the man as they say.

A few minutes later, I'm in my truck and we're heading over to Lazy Duke's. "Pop is right, you should just come right out and tell Daisy. I have no issues with you dating my kid sister." And there you have it, the word *kid*. It hits the nail right on the head. Daisy is his kid sister, always will be but damn it if I don't fancy that woman something bad.

"Ten year age gap, Logan may not be a lot to some folk but to me it is and trust me, it will be to Daisy. I'm going to be forty in a few years time and she's only going to be heading into thirty. Our outlook will be different, who knows one day she may decide to do a Sage on me, upsticks and want to go and travel the world or something. Daisy has only ever been here in Willowbrook except for your family vacations three times a year. That girl has never gotten on a plane and travelled."

"Aw, Man she isn't like that. Daisy has her business here, she loves Willowbrook, she lives and breathes it. Besides, there will be no taking Daisy away from our folks. You know how much she adores my mom and pop." Yeah, that is true but you never can tell. Whoever thought Sage would decide at eighteen to head off to Michigan, but she did.

"I'll just have to wait some and see, Logan. She has a lot of growing up to do first." I don't want to even think whether she is still an innocent. Shit, I best not think about that whilst I'm sitting next to my best friend, in my truck about whether his kid sister is still a virgin or not. I groan inwardly.

Why couldn't I have feelings for someone else, anyone else? I mean, there are plenty of single women here in Willowbrook, I know several would love to be on my arm, they make it obvious enough.

Logan slaps me on my leg. "It will be what it'll be." He pulls up in front of the bar, we hear the music as we step out of his truck. There are a few people outside by the fire pits smoking, some drinking, there is laughter, twinkling lights on the front porch of above the entrance door and a couple kissing against one of the cars. Your usual at the Lazy Duke's bar.

Logan heads towards the door in front of me and I follow on his heels. He opens the door and enters, there is a woman on stage singing along to the karaoke machine, I hate to say it but I've heard cats sing better, fair play to her for getting up and having herself some fun though.

Then I spot her, with her long hair flowing down her back, some guy has his hand on her lower back but Daisy looks as if she is trying to push him off. The jerk seems persistent to me and is lowering his head so his mouth is close to her ear. I see Daisy trying to pull away. Sage glances up and sees both Logan and myself step into the bar. She glances at the jerk and raises her eyebrows.

Looks like the ladies could do with some help.

Chapter 11

Daisy I glance over my shoulder to see who Sage is raising her eyebrows at, and see Logan and Deacon filling up the doorway. Trust me, Deacon could fill it up on his own with those broad shoulders of his. There is a look of thunder on his face, I frown whilst this jerk who has been trying to chat me up for the last fifteen minutes says something to me.

"What? *No* of course I don't want to go back to yours with you. Are you insane?" I say when my brain engages, for a moment it was lost in the sight of Deacon with his large biceps on display and those tatts that he has running up his left arm. I swear when that man is around I get some kind of brain fog. No wonder the single girls and moms in town all hanker after him.

I try to move from the guy, whose name is Saunder. That sounds like a surname to me but he swears it's his real name. I have been telling him that I'm not interested in having a drink bought for me and that I have no intention of dancing with him or going back to his, but he is persistent like a damn pest. His breath smells of liquor.

"What the fuck are you doing?" Before I know what's happened, I see Deacon grabbing Saunder by the scruff of the neck and pulling him away from me. Oh. My. God. Logan saunters over and places a hand on Deacon's shoulder.

"Hey, Man. Easy."

"Does the lady want your attention?" Deacon asks, his voice kind of mean.

"We were just talking is all." Saunder offers.

"Deacon, are you *crazy*?" I screech at him. "What the hell are you doing? Put him down." The poor guy's feet are only just touching the ground. I can see people turning round to look at us now, great now we have an audience.

"Daisy, are you talking with this man?" Deacon asks, still not letting go of Saunder's shirt.

"Er, no. Yes. I don't know. Not really." Shit, what am I supposed to say that Saunder was being a pest and a pain in the butt. Only, I know Deacon may slap him in cuffs and drag him to his office. Can you do that? No, right? That's not a thing, surely trying to chat someone up isn't a cuffable offence. Being Deacon though, he may decide it is with that stormy look on his face and his dark eyes that look right now like a storm rolling in.

"See, you heard the lady. She wasn't exactly not talking to me." Deacon lowers Saunder so at least his feet can touch the ground.

"I think the lady meant she didn't want you harrassing her anymore. So if I were you, I'd get your shit together, collect your hat if that's yours over there on the bar and get out."

"You can't make me, I haven't finished my drink yet." He retorts. Great, I groan and put my hand to my head. Why can't he just go and everyone get back to their drinking? Us girls haven't even had a chance to get on stage for our karaoke yet *and* we haven't discussed Sage and Logan's wedding yet either. This night isn't turning out quite how I thought it would. At least we managed to eat and fill our bellies. That's a good thing.

"Everything okay here, guys?" Abe is standing in front of Deacon and Saunder with his arms folded in front of his expansive chest.

"Yes, this here guy is just leaving."

"No, I'm going to finish my drink then I'm leaving."

God, I wish the ground would open up and swallow me, all this fuss over a guy talking to me. I don't whether to be pleased that

Deacon is clearly jealous or damn right embarrassed for the display. Thankfully, folks are tired of the show and carry on minding their own business.

"I think it's best you leave." Abe tells Saunder who humpfs but does leave for the bar. He knocks his drink back, grabs his hat and leaves with his tail between his leg.

"And you," Abe says to Deacon. "No more man-handling my customer's. This is a quiet and safe drinking place. I don't need trouble in here. If there is any, I'll deal with it. You're not the law in my bar, Deacon." He turns on his heels and heads back towards the other side of the bar.

"What were you thinking?" I say to Deacon. "I'm a grown woman in my twenties, I can handle myself."

"Yeah, she can." Pipes up Lottie, my bestie always in my corner. I love her for it.

"He looked like he was being a pest to me, and wasn't taking no for an answer." Deacon pulls out a chair and sits down between Sage and Eliza who make room for him. Logan sits down on the other side of Sage, leans over and gives her a kiss on the lips. They're adorable those two. After a decade apart and now back together, it's like watching a couple of teenagers in love. If I weren't so mad at Deacon, my heart would be pooling for them but I am mad as hell at Deacon for embarrassing me.

"He was just hitting on me, Deacon for goodness sake."

"Yeah, well, he had no right."

"Who says?" Now I am fuming at him. Okay, so Saunder what a jerk and I didn't really like him hitting on me, but that was my situation to dissolve not Deacon's and his testosterone. Jeez.

"I say, and you best start listening when I say so."

"Or else?"

"Hey come on guys, break it off." Logan finally interrupts. Lottie is giggling to my side. Sadie and Eliza just look on as if they're watching some kind of comedy show.

"Ah, love birds, so sweet." Eliza says. I raise my eyebrows at her.

"*Excuse me?*"

"You two, like little love birds having a spat."

"We are not love birds, Eliza. Never will be. I'm going to the bar to get a drink. What's the round?" Deacon stands up. Wow, his tone was pretty direct. Fine, I don't care if he thinks like that, I don't want to be the other half of his love bird thing anyway. Stuff him.

"I'm leaving." I get up and grab my bag from the end of the chair.

"Why? We've not had our karaoke yet." Sage is clearly upset that I'm leaving already.

"I don't fancy it, Sage. Sorry, sis-to-be, but Deacon has annoyed me and if he's staying then I'm going."

"Girl, don't be so uppity, he was protecting you. If I had a man like that protecting me, I'd be throwing myself at his feet right now." Lottie says smirking.

"*You* are not helping." I tell her. She pulls me down so I am seated again.

"That's better. Now let's have some drinks, the boys can take us home. We're here to have some fun, sing, dance and talk about the wedding." Sage announces as she raises her glass, we all raise ours too and clink hers. Fine, I'll stay but I'm not talking to Deacon.

Over protective, my ass.

Chapter 12

D*eacon*
   Okay, maybe I over-reacted and Daisy is now pissed at me. I can't say that I blame her but that guy, well he was a jerk. How dare he put his hands anywhere near Daisy. It made me see red, I felt as if steam was coming out of my ears and then some. Man, I was ready to rip his damn head off.

   I'm standing at the bar getting the round in, feeling like a prize jerk. I bet she doesn't speak to me now for days. Great, I'll be the receiving end of the silent treatment from the one and only girl I truly want to be with.

   Abe comes to serve me as soon as he finished with old man Jenkins at the end of the bar, I swear that man is over ninety. Apparently, he reckons a shot of brandy every night keeps the doctor away. He may just be right there. I'll have to follow his lead at some point.

   "Came on a bit strong there, hey Marshal." Abe says as he leans with his forearms on the other side of the bar.

   "Yeah, maybe but it did look like he was hassling, Daisy."

   "That as it may be, that woman can look after herself besides she's with her girls they can all handle a man trying to come on to any of them."

   I don't say anything except order the drinks. "Whatever the ladies are drinking and a couple of cold ones for Logan and I."

   "Coming right up and Marshal, no more throwing your weight around in my bar if you don't mind. I can handle anything that gets out of hand." His eyes are stern and I get what he's saying. We've been friends a long time even though he calls me Marshal, ever since I took over the title here in Willowbrook he hasn't called me anything else. It amuses me since he, Logan and I used to run up trees together, scrape our knees coming off skateboards and the such like, not to mention all the other mischief we'd get up to.

"I'll give you a hand with the drinks. Go sit yourself down. You want a tab?" He asks me.

"Sure, a tab will be perfect. I don't think the ladies are going to be done anytime soon. I'll be on soft drinks after this one since I have the early shift tomorrow and need to have a clear head."

"You got it."

I go make my way back to the table and notice that Daisy is now giving me the evil eye. Fantastic.

"We've `put in our karaoke songs." Sage tells me. "You're singing a duet with Daisy." She looks rather smug with herself. Logan is chuckling. I glare at him.

"I don't think that's a great idea, Sage." Daisy tells her future sister-in-law. "I'm not singing anything with Deacon, he's annoyed me."

Tsk, really? I was saving her from some asshole and this is the thanks I get. Seriously, I don't think I was too out of order, okay so grabbing him by the collar way maybe a little extreme but it'll teach him to hit on women that don't want his attention. Some guys can't take no for an answer and that Saunder or whatever his name is, was one of those type of guys.

"Too late. We've written everything on the paper. Eliza and Sadie are going up with Lottie to sing an Abba song." Sage shows Daisy the paper.

"Yeah but Lottie and I could do a song together, we sound great when we're singing."

"Oh no you don't." Lottie says and wags her finger at Daisy. "I'm going up to be part of the Abba gang. You and Deacon are stuck with each other." She takes a sip of her large wine glass. These ladies could get out of control very soon the amount of wine they're knocking back, I for one wouldn't want to have the hangover that's coming their way tomorrow morning.

I don't mind singing alongside Daisy, I'd do literally anything to be close to that woman. Even though I can't sing, well I don't think so in any case. "So, what are we singing?" I ask Sage who is the master of the list. "And is Logan going up with you Sage only he could sing with Daisy?" Not that I want to get out of being on stage and close to Daisy singing some kind of romantic song, but I know that right now I am not in her good books and the last thing I want to do is piss her off anymore or make her feel uncomfortable.

"Logan's singing with me. We're doing one of our own songs we wrote way back when." Logan places an arm around his woman, they are the perfect couple. I speak for everyone in Willowbrook, when I say we couldn't be happier that after ten years, these two found their way back to one another.

Daisy knocks her wine back and glares at me with narrowed eyes. She looks so damn fucking cute right now, that all I want to do is go over to her and smack a kiss right on those pouty lips of hers. It would be worth a slap in the face. I've not fallen out with Daisy since we were teenagers and I promised to go round and help her with some math homework. I got way laid by a girl named Lucella who was insistent I take her to prom and wouldn't take no for an answer. In the end I gave in because I didn't want to let her down but boy was Daisy mad as hell at me for that one and standing her up for math homework that night.

Naturally she forgave me two days later.

"What's the damn song?" She asks Sage.

"Oh, you're going to love it." Sage giggles. Yep, definitely too much wine there.

"Just tell me already and put me out of my misery." Daisy is sulking like a five year old, she is adorable.

"Lucky by Colbie Calliat." Sage tells her. Logan opens his eyes wide. Yeah me too, only that is a song about being in love with your best friend. Everyone knows that and Daisy looks like she is about to combust.

"I. Am. Not. Singing. That." She folds her arms in front of her chest.

"Too late." Sage smirks and holds her glass for Logan to refill it for her from the bottle of wine.

"Don't be such a party pooper, Daisy. Honestly, it's just a song. Girl, get up there and show them what for." Lottie cajoles her. Nope, not even her best friend is able to make Daisy smile, her face reddens. Oh yeah, damn cute.

Eliza clearly has never heard of the song because she looks confused, and has no idea why it's not such a good idea. I chuckle. Daisy gives me another looks can kill glare. It makes me chuckle even more.

"And the first couple are up." Announces Andy the guy who regularly runs the karaoke here at Lazy Duke's. "Let's give a hand for Marshal Deacon and Daisy." Everyone starts clapping and whistling.

"I'm game, c'mon sulky pants let's get up there. The sooner we sing it the sooner it'll be over."

"Fine." She stomps off and it's all I can do to stop myself from putting her over my shoulder and carrying her right out of the bar and taking her back home to my cabin. This girl is going to be the death of me yet.

Chapter 13

D*aisy*
We're on the stage and I feel suddenly very hot, like scorching hot. Even though I am mad at Deacon for grabbing Saunder like he did, I am kind of zinging a bit being this close to him. I can feel the heat coming from his body, there is only the mic between us and damn if I don't want to run my fingers up his arms. They're so muscular, and his chest is so broad, I'd give anything to be up-close and personal with him right now.

Funny how I can be angry with him, yet long for him so badly. It's not just a longing, it's critical yearning, yes ladies, it is critical. I swear that man needs to come with a health warning, he's incredibly handsome with his close shaved hair that once used to hang to his chin, a few tatts on his arm and I still need to find out what that tatt he has on his back means. I mentioned I saw it a while ago whilst we were having a BBQ at Logan's, it's some kind of Arabic writing.

"You ready, Daisy, darlin'?" He asks as the music begins to come through the screen right in front of us.

"Not really but I suppose I have to be." Honestly, singing this song is going to probably render me to tears. The lyrics alone are so true, okay maybe Deacon isn't my *best* friend but he is my close friend and has been ever since I was a kid, despite the age gap he's always been like one and never treated me just as Logan's kid sister. Well, maybe once or twice but since I was in high school, definitely not.

The music begins to play and the words on the screen come up. We begin to sing the song that belongs to the one and only Colbie Caillat.

> Do you hear me? I'm talking to you
> Across the water across the deep blue ocean
> Under the open sky, oh my, baby, I'm trying
> Boy, I hear you in my dreams
> I feel your whisper across the sea
> I keep you with me in my heart
> You make it easier when life gets hard
> Lucky I'm in love with my best friend
> Lucky to have been where I have been
> Lucky to be coming home again
> Ooh-ooh-ooh, ooh-ooh, ooh-ooh
> They don't know how long it takes
> Waiting for a love like this
> Every time we say goodbye
> I wish we had one more kiss
> I'll wait for you, I promise you, I Will

Oh.My.God if I could stop the lump from forming in my throat I'd be able to hold a better note than I am right now.

Literally, my heart is aching the way I feel for Deacon and the words just make me want to bawl out because I want him to know it's him I love, it's him I want to be with and I know he doesn't see me this way. Sure, he can be over-protective but that's jus this way of looking out for me, and fancying someone like him the way I do, is killing me. Why did Sage have to choose this song?

I know exactly why, because Sage knows how I feel about Deacon as does pretty much everyone in Willowbrook except for thick skulled, Deacon unless he does know but really doesn't see me in the same way. Life can suck sometimes, right?

He's so close to me and singing the line *I'll wait for you, I promise you, I will.* His breath is on my cheek, he winks at me and I almost drown in his eyes and become a puddle at his feet.

His hand touches mine and I zing from my head to my toes, the warmth in my stomach spreads through my body like wildfire. Did he just touch me? Yes, he did. I know he did. It was the briefest of moments but that look in his eyes, that wasn't just any old touch. Was it?

I can't take it anymore, and run off the stage. All the while Deacon the good guy that he is, continues to sing. I swear his voice has just gotten louder and stronger, I run towards the door grabbing my bag off the back of my chair as I hear him belting out,

And so I'm sailing through the sea
To an island where we'll meet
You'll hear the music fill the air
I'll put a flower in your hair
Though the breezes, through the trees
Move so pretty you're all I see
As the world keeps spinning round
You hold me right here right now

I gasp the fresh air as I stand outside, it's dark the sky is lit by the stars and it is such a magical sight it causes me to stop for a second. I can hear cheering from inside, I'm not surprised who knew Deacon could sing so damn well, full of raw emotion that it cuts through my soul. I love that man damn it.

"Hey, Girl." I hear Lottie shout out. "Wait."

"What?"

"You can't just run out like that, what is wrong with you? You both need your heads banging together, honestly we're getting bored of this situation. He clearly has feelings for you, so why don't you make the first move?"

She is standing there with her arms folded in front of her chest. "Because, if he really liked me he would ask me first. You know Deacon, he's just playing the part up there. I don't mean anything to him, I'm just Logan's kid sister. He'll never see me as his woman."

"I'm not so sure about that, the way he was looking at you, Girl we were all swooning. Shit, if I had a guy who looked at me like that, I'd never leave the house. Trust me, Daisy he is nuts about you."

"That as it may be, I am not going to ask him out. What if he says no, I'll feel like such a fool and rumor has it, he is seeing some woman in Coppertown."

"He's not *seeing* anyone, he's a guys he has needs, honey you can't deprive a man of getting it off every now and then. What's he supposed to do?"

I huff and kick the dust on the ground with my foot. I just don't like the idea of Deacon doing it with anyone, it makes me feel so damn jealous, I don't know who he goes to see or what he does, but whoever he spends time with like that, I'd like to scratch their eyes out. It sears in my gut and twists it.

"Well, Honey all I'm saying is you both are so ridiculous. Get on with it already. I'm going back in. Unless you want me to come home with you? I don't mind. I guess you could do with some company, right?"

"No, I'll be fine. I think I'll get changed into my pjs and cuddle up with Bonnie on the bed and read, or sulk." I give her a wane smile.

"Okay then, if you're sure."

I am sure because I do know how much Lottie loves a girl's night out and karaoke and she hasn't even had her turn yet. I know I can be a bit selfish sometimes because I was spoilt being the youngest and all, but I'm not that selfish. I want Lottie to stay and enjoy herself not come to mine and watch me sulk like a five year old.

I nod and give her a hug. "Have a good night, bestie." I kiss her cheek She hugs me back.

"I will but if you need me, call me. I'll be straight there."

"Not going to happen. Get Sage or someone to record you singing and send it over to me." I tell her as I see someone standing at the doorway of the Lazy Duke's bar. It's Deacon, how could I not guess, his frame fills the entire door.

"I have to go." I tell her and start to walk away. She heads back towards the bar, I pick my pace up.

"And where do you think you're going?" His deep husky voice fills my senses.

"Walking home." I continue striding. I'm not match for his long legs, however.

"Not on your own you're not young lady. Now stop so I can pull my truck up and you can hop in."

"No, I'm fine."

"It's not a question, Daisy." I humph and continue to walk.

"Don't make me pick you up and sling you over my shoulder young madam."

"You wouldn't dare!"

"Try me, darlin.'"

I ignore him and the next thing I know, I am indeed over his broad shoulder, my legs being held close to his chest by his strong hands, and my face looking down at his ass. His mighty fine, tight ass I may add. There are worse things to be looking at, let me tell you that.

Chapter 14

Deacon

Can't say I've carried too many women slung over my shoulder, but if anyone thinks I'm letting this little lady take a walk back home in the dark they've got another thing coming. Since she's as stubborn as a mule, she left me no choice.

I chuckle as she hammers on my back with her fists. "Stop behaving like a little brat, Daisy."

"You can't do this to me."

"Well I am and that's that. You should have just walked back to my truck. We're here now."

"I'm a grown woman for Pete's sake." She sounds more like a two year old in my opinion. I guffaw. It dawns on me that she is barely an adult she's only in her twenties and though she has passed the adult threshold since going past twenty-one a few years back, it still seems so young to me.

Shit, I'm heading closer to forty than thirty. "I told you, no woman walks alone in the dark, least of all you, Daisy. Anything can happen out on these back roads."

"I hate you."

Of course I know she doesn't mean that, she is just mad as hell at me. First I got a bit heavy handed with Saunder and now carrying her over my shoulder hasn't helped. It is what it is.

"That's fine, Daisy. You're just het up is all."

"And then some. You're such a jerk sometimes. Do you ever stop being on duty?"

She stands leaning against my truck with her arms folded. I'm surprised we don't have an audience the way she was hollering and kicking. It wouldn't surprise me if I have a couple of rib bruises from where was punching me.

"I'm always on duty, Daisy. You know that. The safety of folks in Willowbrook is my main concern, hell it's probably my own concern."

"You drive me insane. Just open up already so I can get home to Bonnie."

I click the fob and the truck unlocks. "Your chariot awaits, m'lady."

She flicks me the finger, I throw my head back and laugh. Feisty little kitten. I wonder if she's so feisty in the bedroom. Hell, I shouldn't be thinking things like that about Logan's kid sister. Shit, this girl has been my friend forever.

Did I tease her mercilessly when she was a kid? Yeah, maybe a bit but not too bad. As soon as I started noticing she was growing up when she was in high school my whole outlook changed towards her. Do I feel a bit of an older perv right now as I steal glances at her sour looking face? Yes of course I do. Should I? Who knows.

"Drive, already." She huffs and places her arms crossed in front of her chest. I can't help notice how her action pushes her tits up, seeing the swell of them in her jumper. She sure does have nice looking tits, I wonder if she is wearing lacey lingerie or something more like Sloggi. Maybe innocent looking Daisy is a real tiger under that persona.

I'd sure as hell like to find out one day.

"And you can stop looking at me, Deacon." Right, I best stop that.

"Sorry about Saunder. I thought he was hassling you and being a jerk." I turn the engine over.

"He was kind of, you know what young guys can be like."

I do at that, the number of them I've had to deal with over the years and those too that I've seen hankering after Daisy ever since school days. She sure had a lot of guys in tow and she loved it. There's no denying that Daisy did like the attention. I hated it, every single one deserved my fist at their jaw.

"You didn't have to paw him quite like that though."

"Maybe not. I have said I'm sorry, Daisy. Can't do anything about it now."

"And don't ever sling me over your shoulder again." She humpfs.

"Got it. But you were behaving like a brat not getting in my car."

She turns to face me, "Jeez, Deacon I have walked home plenty of times from the bar without any issues."

Has she? I never knew that, I'd neve have let that happen. No fucking way. We don't have a high crime rate here in Willowbrook, if anything it's a pretty sleepy small town but you can still get the odd weirdo and I'm not one for letting women walk home alone. We always make sure the ladies have a ride.

"That wasn't too sensible then was it?" I focus on the narrow road leading away from the dirt track, it's on a bend.

"You treat me like a child. I want you to stop now." She glares at me, I sideways glance at her. Yeah, that's definitely glaring at me. Full on daggers, pointy knives you got it, the lot.

I stop myself from saying anything.

"We'll be at yours in a few minutes. Don't suppose you want to invite me in for a cup of coffee?" What the fuck am I saying? Did I just try to invite myself into Daisy's house. Holy crap. *Get a grip Deacon, Man.*

"Er, no. Not tonight. Any other night sure but you've been such an asshole I want to get out of this truck and calm myself down."

"Fair enough, darlin'."

Daisy turns away and looks on the road ahead, not that she can see too much only as far as the truck headlights will show since it's pitch black and we don't have any street lighting down this section. A few minutes later we're on Main Street. My heart sinks some knowing that we're almost at her house.

I suppose I'm just going to have to work on my age gap issues and also on not being such a jerk when I see another guy sniffing around her. And damn, now I've got to get back in her good books.

"I expect you to be groveling for at least a week before I speak to you again properly."

I chuckle and give her a wink. "That I can do darlin'." I say as I put the truck in stop and hop out to go open her door.

"I've got this too. Thanks." Wow, she is in one this evening. "See you around, Deacon and next time if some guy is hitting on me, I will deal with him. Goodnight, Marshal." She strides up the path that leads to the steps to her wrap around porch.

I stay watching to make sure she gets in okay and wait for the lights to go on. A few minutes later I get back into my truck scratching my head and raking my hands through my hair.

Not sure I can let Daisy handle any guys that hit on her, I'd have to break their fucking necks. Just seeing Daisy with another man makes me get out of control.

I watch as she closes the curtains in the downstairs window and know she is safe and put the truck into reverse and drive back to my own cabin.

It's warm inside, I had left a few logs on the closed in fire to keep the chill off. I pour myself a two-finger whiskey and knock it back. That woman kills me, literally. She is so damn fine and so sexy it's unbelievable. The way her tousled blonde hair hangs around her shoulders, that smoldering smile of hers and the way her eyes light up like stars in the dark sky.

My dick twitches, and here we fucking go again, I can't control the way I feel about her. It begins to throb and ache just imagining what Daisy would feel like underneath me, how she might look stripped naked to just her lacey panties and bra. It's no good, I need to head off to the shower and jerk one off thinking about her luscious lips wrapped around my cock, taking me deep into her throat and allowing me to shoot my come in her mouth.

All thoughts of our age difference are gone as I let the warm water sluice over my body, one hand resting against the wall in front of me the other on my throbbing dick as I give myself long strokes, holding myself tight. My balls tingle and I am ready to shoot, jeez it's like being some kind of hormonal teenager all over again.

Chapter 15

Daisy

Bonnie mooches around my legs and wraps her tail round one, she purrs away as I stand in my kitchen and pour myself a nice cold glass of water, the wine I've been drinking is making my head a bit woozy and I don't want to wake up with a headache.

"C'mon sweetie, let's get ready for bed." I pick her up and snuggle her head under my chin and carry her into my bedroom where I set her down on the bed.

Does Deacon infuriate me? Tonight he did. Picking me up and throwing me over his shoulder, honestly. Although, okay, I liked it. Butterflies flutter in my stomach. It definitely did something to me and now all I want is to be in his arms and feel his lips pressed against mine.

Warmth creeps up my core and I can feel myself getting wet just thinking about his broad shoulders and the way his hips are narrow, I'd give anything to be intimate with him. This crush has been going on for more than ten years, it's shocking and you'd think I'd have grown out of it.

Yet, every year that man becomes more and more handsome, he's the devil that's for sure with his sultry eyes and the way he can make me swoon in a heartbeat. Feeling his hand on my legs to secure me over his shoulder, the heat that radiated off it was enough to make me dizzy on a whole different scale.

Now I want him in my bed doing all sorts of dirty things to me. Bonnie cuddles up on the end of the bed content that her mommy is back home safe and sound.

I undress and think sod it to the shower, I'll have one in the morning I only had one before I went out and slip into my pj shorts and tee shirt and get myself in the bed. What I'm going to do is read only I am way too distracted by Deacon to even focus on the words on the page.

What I'm feeling is aroused, him throwing me over his shoulder was so primal and manly. I've never been hoisted up like that before and even though I was mad as hell at him for embarrassing me the way he did in the Lazy Duke, I can't help that my body is on fire for this man.

I lay my head back against the pillow and put my book down and close it, there's no way I can concentrate besides I feel so turned on that I'm considering getting my damn vibrator out and seeing to myself.

The thought of Deacon kissing my lips and giving me fluttering kisses down my neck and along my collar bone, makes my stomach clench and my clit begins to throb. Damn it. I want that man so badly. The thing is, how on earth am I going to get him?

I know he sees me just as Logan's kid sister but I swear he likes me too. I wonder if I was a few years older or he was a few years younger if he'd have the same issues. Sage told me that apparently he's worried about the age gap, well I'm not. It's only about ten years, it's not like he's fifty or anything and even then that works for some folks. Okay, maybe not for me but he's not even forty yet.

My hand makes its way down my stomach and I feel as my nipples bud and stand to attention. I swirl my finger round one and squeeze it, instantly I feel the heat coming up from my lower regions and clench my legs. Oh fuck it, I want to get myself off so that's exactly what I'm going to do.

Lazily, I glide my hand down under my shorts and my sheer lace panties and begin to stroke my clit. I'm so wet already just thinking about Deacon and how he'd feel riding me good and hard. I bet his dick is huge, it'd probably be a tight fit and hurt but I'd be willing to find that out for myself.

I circle my clit with my fingers and caress it with my thumb. With my other hand I manage to open my bedside drawer and pull out my bullet vibrator. Yes, I have several toys but right now I want my bullet, I love how fast it goes and gets me off real quick which is what I want right now.

If Deacon were here with me at this moment, I'd take his swollen dick into my mouth and run my tongue up and down his shaft, flicking his engorged head with my tongue and tasting his salty pre-cum. I groan. Belle doesn't move, she's fast asleep.

Placing the vibrator against my clit I press the little button and it hums into life. Fuck me, it feels so good as I massage it around my clit and dive it in and out of my soaking pussy. My breath catches as I imagine myself straddling Deacon, feeling his dick inside my pussy and raising his hips up and down. I think about grinding myself on him getting my clit off until I can feel the waves start to roll through me. I scream out as I orgasm over my fingers and my vibrator, calling his name.

It was intense, I've not had an orgasm like this for a while and least ways not such a quick one. It's all that damn pent up sexual tension. Sated, I lay my head back against the pillows and wait for my breathing to regulate and close my eyes.

I wonder what it'd be like to lay in his arms after sex and inhale his fragrance, to feel his heart beating under my hand, to feel warm and secure with his strong body next to mine. Sleeping together and waking up together would be a dream come true.

Now all I need to do is think just how I'm going ot make that happen. Because wanting him like this is killing me, it has done for the last ten years ever since I was in high school. I don't want another man, he has totally ruined me for anyone else. And, there is no way I am taking any chances with Deacon finding another woman. That would literally kill me, seeing him around Willowbrook with anyone else.

My mind races with things I can conjure up until it dawns on me that I need to get him alone with me somehow, I fantasize about us being stuck in a lodge with just one bed like in those damn romance books. He'd not be able to get away from me, oo I am liking the idea of this now how do I make something like that happen?

My mind whirs away until finally, I fall asleep. The seed is set. I am going to get me my man.

Chapter 16

D *eacon*

"That didn't go too well last night, did it Bro?" Logan says as I tuck into my pancakes at Bluebell's wondering if Daisy will be in this morning or if she's nursing a helluva hangover. I'm going with the hangover. Perhaps I ought to go and check up on her, that's what a good friend would do.

Lottie comes in with Sage, they aren't looking too clever themselves, but then the ladies did manage to put some drink away. They slide in next to Logan and I.

"Hey, Deacon. Saw you throwing Daisy over your shoulder in the car park last night. How did that work out for you?" Lottie asks with a playful smirk on her face.

"Not too well, I dropped her off and was told to get out of there."

"I'm not surprised, a lady only likes that kind of action when she's getting some."

That almost makes me choke on my pancake. Honestly, these younger girls have no shame, they're so open about sex that it makes me blush. Yes, a grown man like myself who has been round the block and then some, blushing.

"You okay?" Sage asks. I nod. Babs approaches the table.

"What can I get you ladies?"

"I'll have two rounds of pancakes with extra maple syrup, and a very strong coffee please, Babs." Sage requests.

"And I'll have the waffles with scrambled egg and bacon strips, and second that on the strong coffee please." Lottie chips in.

"You ladies have a hangover?" I ask raising my eyebrows at them. Lottie sticks her tongue out at me. "Have you spoken to Daisy yet this morning?" I ask her.

"Nope. I did message her, she's got a hangover and may not open the shop up today." She plays wit the napkin holder. Sage grabs her hand to make her stop.

Logan pushes his empty plate aside, "that was delicious. So, the fundraiser, we're all set?"

"Just about. I've got mom on the bake sale with your mom, Daisy and Sadie are doing craft stalls, you're on the band and Deacon is on the dunking machine." Sage tells him. That makes me groan, I'd almost forgotten I said I would do it again this year. Great, my favorite thing – not, is to have balls thrown in my direction which upon contact with the board make me fall into the water beneath.

"Maybe I should go check on Daisy. See if she needs anything." I say absentmindedly. All eyes are on me, Logan's eyebrows are raised.

"You think that's a good idea, you're in her bad books? You can't manhandle a woman like you did and expect her to open the door to you the next day." He informs me.

The thing is though, if Daisy isn't opening up today and stays at home to nurse her hangover, I won't get to see her and I just can't help but want to see that pretty face of hers and her enigmatic smile. Although, I doubt today she has a whole lot to smile about.

"How are the wedding plans coming on, what did I miss last night?" I ask as I wait for my coffee to be refilled by Babs who has just bought the girls' plates of food over.

"Well, you missed quite a bit actually. Logan and I have decided rather than having separate pre wedding parties, that we'll hire a cabin up in the mountains and we can have a get together all of us. Feel free to bring anyone you like, Deacon since we'll be mostly couples." Sage is clearly excited about this and to be honest it sounds a great idea.

"Except me, I don't have any plus one and whilst I'm thinking about it nor does Daisy." Lottie chips in.

"Ah, right. I though you were sort of seeing that fella from Coppertown. Has that all fizzled out now?" Sage asks as she looks at Lottie.

"I wasn't seeing him seeing him, we were you know just hooking up from time to time."

"Too much information, stop right there, Lottie." I tell her before she goes any further.

"I could bring him though, I don't want to be the only one without a plus one." Lottie looks as if she is deliberating it, she'll probably end up bringing whoever it is the ladies are talking about.

Sage nods. "Perfect. Eliza and her husband are coming, Sadie said she is going to be bring Tyler, her on-off fella. So, that just leaves you and Daisy, Deacon." She has a weird grin on her face.

"Ladies, Logan, I have to go to the station." I get up and leave a twenty on the table to cover my breakfast, first I need to go round and check in on Daisy. I kind of feel bad for throwing her over my shoulder last night, Logan is right, I shouldn't have done that.

On my drive over, I ponder on whether this is a good thing or not, but at the very least I should apologize to her. I stop off at the pharmacy and buy some Ibuprofen just in case Daisy doesn't have any in and some chocolates they have in one of the aisles. All girls love chocolate, right?

I wait outside a few seconds after I've knocked on the door. I know she's in there since her car is on the car port, unless she has decided to walk to the shop maybe to clear her head.

"What do you want, Deacon?" I hear from the other side of the door.

"To say I'm sorry about last night." Silence.

"Okay, thanks. You can go now."

"I brought you some Ibuprofen and chocolates. You want them? How are you feeling?"

"I'd feel better if someone hadn't thrown me over their shoulder for the whole world to see and made a fool out of me. You do know someone has posted a picture of that on Instagram, right? With comments about how the Marshal was heavy handed with one of the Willowbrook community members." Silence. I shuffle.

"I'm truly sorry, Daisy. Will you just open up please?"

"No."

"Please."

Silence then, "and the worst thing is I look awful, it's not even a good picture of me. Good job they didn't get the ass end."

I suppress a chuckle, okay it's not that funny but if that's all she has to worry about then she can't be feeling too hungover this morning.

"Leave the pain killers on the porch and those chocolates I can see you have in your hand. I'm still not talking to you."

"I'll catch you later, Daisy. If you need anything be sure to give me a shout."

"Not happening you disgraced me in front of everyone in town."

I chuckle. "I heard that, it's not a laughing matter, Deacon. It's embarrassing as hell. What will my customer's think? They're going to think I'm a disorderly drunken woman."

"I'm sure they won't. Everyone in town loves and knows you, Daisy. Besides, you are entitled to let off steam every now and then."

"Goodbye, Deacon."

I step back after placing the Ibuprofen and chocolates down on the porch as requested and head off to my truck. As I get in the cab, I see her slender arm coming through the slightly ajar door and grab the chocolates first then the pain relief. The door quickly closes. I can't help but laugh, that girl, she's really got my heart and soul.

And one day soon, I'm going to come right out and tell her.

Chapter 17

Daisy

I wait until he has gotten back in his vehicle and left, not before checking out that mighty fine, tight ass of his. I am mortified about last night and do not want anyone to see me. My phone beeps, why does it have to be so loud? And why did I have to drink quite so much?

Hey girl, did you hear from Sage yet?

Nope why what's up?

She and Logan are having a weekend cabin for us all to go to with them for their pre-wedding get together.

Oh, isn't she having a bachelorette party?

No, they discussed it last night, she's not bothered about strippers and going to a club she said she'd rather have us all go to a cabin and we can all chill out. Logan will bring his guitar

Sounds amazing. When is this, only they're getting married in a couple of months and I know Logan and she are really busy with the fundraiser and all?

We're all going next weekend, she booked it last night at the bar?

Wow, that was quick she doesn't waste anytime.

You know what Sage is like, Daisy. Once she's got an idea in her head that's it. Oh by the way, Deacon will be going to since he's Logan's best man.

Right, of course?

BTW, how is your head this morning? Mine is through the roof, wish I hadn't drunk so much last night.

That makes me chuckle at least I'm not suffering alone.

It's pretty bad but I have to get to the shop and open up. I just don't think I can face anyone coming in especially not after being flung over Deacon's shoulder. What a sham and so embarrassing.

Girl, it was funny. Damn I wouldn't mind him throwing me over his shoulder anytime soon. He should have carried you straight to his cabin and onto his bed. That'd sort you both out once and for all.

Lottie, you're not helping right now.

Gotta go, I have to be at work myself soon. Catch up with you tonight over hot chocolate and a corny Netflix movie, how does that sound?

Sounds perfect, you can stay over at mine, we'll have our own quiet girls night in with our pjs on.

Wait, invite Sage see if she can come that way we can talk about the wedding, we didn't cover much of it last night other than Logan has got his band playing and the cake is organized. Your mom is making it.

I thought she might be, mom is an amazing baker and it'll be to die for.

I know, right. Can't wait for the wedding.

Me neither.

Love you

Love you too, Lottie

I place my phone down and set some kibbles in Bonnie's bowl for her before heading into my shower. Everyone loves a wedding but this one is special, ten years apart and now getting married again, it's the thing that romance books and movies is made of. It makes me smile, even though my head hurts so bad.

Thirty minutes later and I feel a bit more human, and after my second coffee. Bonnie is purring loudly for me to let her out. That reminds me I need to ask Logan to come over at some point and put the cat flap in that I bought about six months ago. I keep forgetting.

I open my shop bypassing a stop off at Bluebell's, yeah I am ducking and diving from seeing anyone who may have been at Lazy Duke's last night and seen the car park spectacle. I want a quiet day working on the prom dress for Janice. I also need to make time with Sage to discuss the bridesmaid dresses, I've made the mock-ups and we all need to have a fitting. Tying that woman down around the practice, the fundraiser and everything else she fits in can sometimes be hard work.

Settling myself down with Janice's dress, I reach over to my mobile and put on one of my favorite playlists, it's mostly country music and hum away as I run the gorgeous green fabric through the machine.

It's not long until my stomach starts growling, damn it, I really ought to have had breakfast and I do need to get hold of Sage to find out about the weekend cabin thing. There's nothing for it, I need to close up for lunch and head over to Bluebell's or maybe I could go to the Italian down on Main Street.

I opt for Bluebell's I can't hide out forever. As I close up, I decide that since the sky is a beautiful cloudless blue the fresh fall air will do me good to have a small walk. Cruising along the road I spot Deacon's work vehicle. "Hey darlin'. How you feeling?"

"Okay thanks. I'm still not talking to you." I yell out and hurry along the sidewalk. Next thing I know he has parked a little way ahead of me and is jumping out of his vehicle. Damn if he doesn't look fine in his cargo pants that are tight and hug his muscular thighs and narrow hips. He should be arrested by the law for looking so good.

His smile is arresting as he walks towards me. "C'mon now, Daisy don't be like that. It was for your own good."

"Says you."

"Why are you being so stubborn and huffy? Let me buy you a coffee at Bluebell's."

"I can by my own coffee."

"That you can, but I'd like to buy you one. What are friends for hey, if they can't buy each other a coffee?"

"Don't try that friends bullshit on me, Deacon. You were out of order last night. Everyone saw and probably my panties too."

He chuckles, it's deep and throaty and why does he have to be so sexy when he chuckles too? His skin around his eyes crinkles a bit but adds to the character of his face. I can see he hasn't shaved, I am a sucker for a few days old stubble. It suits him, makes him look all rugged and handsome.

"Hey you two love birds." I turn to see his sister, Maxine heading our way.

I tsk. "Hi, Maxine. How are you? Where are the kids?" I ask as she comes over and gives me a quick hug.

"At playgroup, I thought I'd take myself for some coffee and pancakes and then do a bit of shopping. I want to check out the new boutique further up on Main Street. *Bonita's*. Have you been there yet?"

I shake my head, to be honest I haven't had a chance with making up the bridesmaid dresses for Sage's wedding and the prom dress for Janice. It's been full on for the last few weeks.

"You want to come join me?" She asks. Deacon coughs.

"You say something, Deacon?" Maxine asks and raises her eyebrows at him.

"Daisy and I are going for a coffee, Max." He tells her with his hands on his hips.

"No we're not." I interject. "I'll have that coffee with you, Maxine and come and check the new store out. I hear the owner is a Spanish lady?"

"Sounds perfect. Deacon, we'll catch you later." She gives him her best sisterly smile but I can tell he isn't too impressed now that

Maxine has literally hijacked me from under his nose. Serve him right for throwing me over his shoulder last night.

Although, okay, I'm not going to lie, just thinking about it sends tingles up and down my spine and makes me want to clench my thighs together. Holy crap.

We settle ourselves in the diner, Barb comes over and takes our order. I go for a stack of waffles with syrup, blueberries, eggs and bacon. So? I'm hungry I skipped breakfast.

"Wow, you must hungry." Maxine says grinning. Her auburn hair glints as the fall sun comes through the large glass windows, we're seated by one and it couldn't be a more gorgeous day. The trees that line the sidewalk outside are displaying colors from russet, to orange and vibrant red. Maxine's hair is definitely the right shade for fall and it's all natural. She's *so* lucky.

"I have a bit of a hangover, it got out of hand at Lazy's last night."

"Ah, girls night out I gather?"

"Yeah, to discuss Sage and Logan's wedding only we did more drinking than talking then there was karaoke and I had to duet with Deacon." I place my hands over my face and groan.

"That must have been awesome, you both have great voices." She lifts her coffee cup that has appeared, to her lips. I peek between my fingers, her eyes are on me.

"No it was *awful*, your brother had just grabbed some guy called Saunder by the neck. All the poor fella was doing was talking to me."

She laughs and almost splutters coffee everywhere. "That doesn't sound like Deacon, but when it comes to you, he sure does do some strange stuff."

"Don't I know it." I sigh.

"And how are the wedding plans coming on? Deacon hasn't told me too much except he is best man and of course I have my invite."

"We're all headed to a cabin next weekend with the guys for a pre-wedding get together."

"Oh wow, that'll be amazing so no bachelorette party for Sage then?"

"No, she said she didn't want one. They've got so much on her and Logan with the fundraiser for the baseball club and then we've got Thanksgiving too."

"Busy time of year. I'm so pleased I ran into you though. I have a small favor to ask."

She sets her cup down, "sure shoot. What can I help you with?"

"Well here's the thing. I know Deacon wants to open at some point a riding school for the under privileged kids, I mean he has the space and he's mentioned it a few times now only with his work and all, he hasn't really got the time to coordinate anything and look into it properly. I've been doing some of the research first and reaching out to the authorities, but he needs a few more horses too and I wondered if you would come along with me to a horse auction."

She looks kind of like she's up to something but I can't put my finger on it.

"A *horse auction*, me? Honestly, Maxine I don't have a clue about what horses are good to buy. I mean, you know I can ride, I've been riding since I was a kid but to purchase a horse I wouldn't know where to start or what to look for."

"Don't worry about that, it'll just be nice to have you around. We don't get to spend too much time together nowadays, with your business and everything."

I do think this is a bit out of the blue and I'm wondering why but when she puts it like that, then maybe. I mean we haven't caught up properly in a while and Maxine was always looking out for me when I was younger. She's about eight years younger than Deacon which puts her at thirty and just a few years older than me.

"I'd like that, okay. I won't be much help but sure, I love horses. When are you going?"

"Saturday."

"This Saturday?"

"Yes, you in?" I quickly run through what I've got on, I mean I have chores at home to do, shopping you know the usual things and I wanted to drop in and see my folks but hell, I can do that all on Sunday.

"Absolutely." She pats my hand like she's just performed some kind of miracle and I still have that little gnawing in my stomach as if Maxine is up to something.

Chapter 18

D*eacon*

I can't get my mind off Daisy. "You okay?" My deputy asks. I nod and shuffle some papers around on my desk.

"You sure about that, only you don't seem to be here and I've been talking to you for the last fifteen minutes or so?"

"Huh, what were you talking about? Sorry, I've got shit on my mind."

"You don't say. Coffee?"

"Yeah, a strong one. Thanks." I watch as he goes over to the machine and makes the coffees. Aroma fills the small front office as he does. I do have a back office but I like it out front, I have company for a start with my crew here in the station and the windows allow for views to Main Street and the small green area across the road.

"Heard you threw Daisy over your shoulder last night. Did you take her home?" He asks, I glare at him, like it's any of his business.

"She wouldn't get in the vehicle and she'd been drinking. What's a guy supposed to do?"

"I guess that's pissed her off some. You two are good friends, right?"

"*Were*. She's not talking to me right now."

"I can see that." Curtis says.

I raise my eyebrows at him. "I don't think you understand, I wasn't about to let her walk home alone in the dark with alcohol inside her. What did you think I was going to do? She was already blowing steam out of her ears because I dragged some guy up by the collar. Saunder I think his name was." I do remember his name, I remember every detail about the jerk who had his hand on Daisy, the same hand I'd quite happily have chopped off.

"So I heard." He sets my coffee cup down.

"Word travels fast around here." I mutter and lean back in my chair. "Better than any telephone exchange if you ask me."

Just as I speak, Lacey our ladies man of the police force with his jet black hair and emerald green eyes comes sauntering in. "Yeah, apparently that Saunder guy is pretty damn pissed off." He says and sits down at his desk, leans back and puts his feet up.

"Get your feet off the table, Lacey. This isn't your mom's lounge. And I doubt she'd have allowed it in any case." He does as he says grumbling.

"I don't care if he's pissed off or not. He had his hand on Daisy and from the look of it, it wasn't welcome. I was just upholding the law." This causes Curtis and Lacey to guffaw. "What is so funny?"

"You, Deacon that's what is so funny. Hell, we all know you're smitten with that little lady. If it were me I'd have already got her between the sheets." I growl at Lacey. The thought of that womanizer with Daisy in his bed makes my blood boil in a second.

"Don't you go anywhere near Daisy. You here me. She's off limits and that goes for you too, Curtis." I glare at him too.

Curtis holds both his hands in the air. "Not me, Deacon. No way. I have my own girl now."

I raise my eyebrows. "Since when? You're as bad as Lacey over there, I'm surprised you two haven't picked up any nasty diseases yet." They flick me the finger, what are they some kind of double act now?

"Since a couple of months ago, I've been keeping it quiet. You know her. Taylor the girl who works behind the counter in the hardware store." Ah, that rings a bell.

"Pretty thing with red hair, curly hair, right?" I ask.

He nods his head. "That's the one and lips like cherries." Okay, so now he looks dreamy. He's got it bad. I throw a paperclip at him, as he blushes.

"Man, you're so pussy whipped." Lacey comes out with.

"You'll be next." I tell him.

"Nah, not me. Never. My folks divorced when I was a kid and I've seen what it does to folks that getting hooked up shit and married. I'll be single for the rest of my life." He folds his arms in front of his chest.

"Then you're going to be a lonely motherfucker." I tell him. My phone beeps, I check to see who the message is from. It's my sister, Maxine.

Hey Deacon, I'm going to the horse auction on Saturday. You fancy coming? I checked your roster with your assistant, she says you're not on duty.

I think about it, I mean I could do with looking at some new horses if I want to get the riding school/retreat off the ground. I keep thinking about it and talking to my folks and Maxine about it, only I've not got very far. I know Maxine is doing all the paperwork for me right now and she said she'd be up for helping me out. I've also got to hire a new ranch hand, my guy Philips is moving to be closer to his children in Florida. So much to do, so little time.

Sure, why not. What time?

I'll swing by and pick you up around nine and we can have breakfast at Bluebells.

I'll check see if Logan wants to come and Sage. They're looking for a couple of horses for themselves.

Next time, let's just go on our own for this one. I frown at my screen, that's not like Maxine at all. She's usually up for Sage doing anything with us.

Sure, np. Whatever you say. I'll catch up with you on Saturday. And Max, thanks for helping me with this. I really appreciate it.

Np. You owe me.

You got it.

We end the conversation. "Right, guys let's go on patrol. Curtis, you stay here and man the office." I stand up, down my coffee, place my hat on and head for the door with Lacey behind me.

As soon as we step outside, a young woman stops in her tracks. She blushes as Lacey gives her one of his winning smiles. I groan, the man just cannot help himself.

"C'mon Romeo. Let's go, get in the damn truck." He does as he's told. I like Lacey, he's a good guy as is Curtis. They've worked under me for the last few years and we make up a good team. I know they've always got my back and off duty we hang out together sometimes.

"I spy with my little eye, something beginning with D." He says from the passenger seat.

"What are we like five again?" I ignore him.

"Nah, but you'll want to see this." He motions his head to his right. I see Daisy on the sidewalk and if it isn't that jerk Saunder standing right next to her. Without hesitation, I brake hard and jump out of the vehicle.

"What did I tell you last night? You stay the hell away from Daisy."

"What the hell, Man we're just talking."

"That's already too much." I try not to yell at him. Meanwhile, Lacey hangs one arm out the truck and watches with amusement.

"Just step away from Daisy." I tell him.

"I've done nothing wrong, *officer*." I don't like the way he says it, but I can't exactly arrest him for anything. Seeing him so close to Daisy makes me see red and I want to punch him in the jaw. I have to clench my fists beside my legs.

"*Marshall* Deacon. If you so much as do anything, I swear to God, I will not be responsible for my own actions." Daisy shouts at me. Lacey begins to laugh. A few people are looking at us as they pass by. Her hands are on her narrow hips, her eyes are flashing angrily at me and I swear, all I want to do is carry her off into my truck, throw her on the back seat and kiss the anger right out of her body.

What can I do? I'm stuck between wanting to rip Saunder's damn head off and not pissing Daisy off any more than necessary. Maybe she *actually likes* him? I hadn't considered that.

"C'mon old man." Lacey shouts out the truck window. "Let's roll. Leave the lady and her beau in peace." I turn and glare at him, what did he just say, beau? I swallow hard, like that's going to contain my anger at this moment.

Okay, so I get it. They're just talking. It's a free country and all that, Daisy can speak to whomever she likes but it doesn't mean I have to be happy with it.

"Just go do your job, Deacon." She grabs Saunder by the arm and leads him away. Leaving me staring at her swaying ass as she walks with her arm threaded through his.

"Did you fucking see that?" I ask a laughing Lacey. He chuckles.

"Oh, Man. You've got it so fucking bad."

I punch him in the arm. "Shut the hell up." I turn the engine on and pull off the sidewalk where I planted the truck fuming, and thinking of all the things I want to do to Saunder right now, which extends from thumping him one to locking him in a cell for the rest of his life.

Chapter 19

Daisy

The last couple of days have passed in a blur. I finished the prom dress for Jeannie, she was over the moon with it. It was lovely to see her so happy and I am sure that when James, her prom date comes to pick her up, he is going to fall in love with her all over again.

The bridesmaid dresses for Sage's wedding are coming along nicely and I just have a couple of alterations to do for Lottie who has lost a bit of weight, she needs to be careful there it's not as if she has got any to lose, but she has just started running and Pilates again and things are changing with her body. She looks amazing regardless, that girl could wear a sack I swear and still look hot.

It's nine in the morning on Saturday and I'm about to head over for ten to meet Maxine and go off to the horse auction. I've never been to one before so I have absolutely no idea what to expect. Other than of course, a whole lot of horses. I love horses and sometimes have been out riding with Deacon on his land. Usually, he lets me ride his Appaloosa, Mitzi who is around four years of age and as docile as a butterfly. She is a dream to ride and having ridden since I was a kid starting at the Buckner's school for riding on their farm, I know at least how to handle a horse.

I am excited to go to the auction and maybe I may find a horse that needs a loving home. Oh, wait one. I've kind of fallen out with Deacon that puts the brakes on a bit. Only, I would ask him if I could keep it at his place, he has more than enough land and stables. I bite my lower lip as Bonnie rubs her head on my shins. I bend down and tickle the top of her head. Right, I guess I need to make up with him if I am considering buying a horse. I'd love to have one of my very own but I have absolutely nowhere to put it. Unless I ask Logan and Sage.

Yes, that can work. They have plenty of space and a stable block for four horses, I remember Logan telling me he and Sage wanted to buy each other horses as wedding gifts. I wonder if he and she are coming along today. I grab my mobile off the counter and shoot him a quick message.

Are you coming to the horse auction today it's in Bottom Creek.

I don't have to wait too long before I receive a reply.

Not today, Sage and I are going to Yellow Creek in a week's time for the horse auction. Why?

I am going with Maxine and thought you'd be going along to since Bottom Creek since it's not too far away.

Can't today. I've got the fellas coming over to help me build the stage for the band and the pillars for the walk from the cabin to where the stage will be.

Ah, right. Okay. Wait, pillars?

Yes, pillars. Don't ask. Sage has decided that she wants pillars evenly spaced along the walk from the cabin to the stage where we will be married, she wants to have flowers draped off them and fairy lights so at night it'll look pretty.

Aw, that sounds amazing. She's got such vision.

Yeah, and of course I'd do anything for Sage.

You're a good man to her, Logan. She's going to have the best day ever.

I hope so, that's the plan.

Okay, I'll catch up with you later. Excited to go to the cabin next weekend with y'all. Oh yeah, so I was going to ask, I totally forgot with wedding talk and all, if I see a horse I like can I keep it at your place?

Of course you can, we've got plenty of space and Sage will love tending to it when you're not around.

Thank you soooooo much.

Catch you later, Daisy. He signs off and leaves me some kisses. I am now over excited like a five year old being told they're going to Disneyland. I clap my hands and pick Bonnie up, hugging her to me and smother her head in kisses. She wriggles to get down. I laugh and put her back down on the floor where she scampers off. No doubt to hide from me.

I check the time, it's already nine thirty, shoot. I better get dressed out of my pajamas and into some clothes fit for a horse auction. It's chilly now fall is here although there is some sunshine but marred with a few grey clouds here and there.

From my closet I pull out some trusty old Levi's, my blue cowboy boots and a vest top. I move to my drawers and find a pink t-shirt to pull over before grabbing my navy cable knit cardigan off the back of my door. Throwing my satchel over my shoulder I consider myself ready to go meet Maxine at Bluebells.

As I walk, since it's only down on Main Street and about a fifteen minute walk, I whistle and hum random tunes. Most of them made up. Seriously, I am that girl who knows all the tunes to numerous tracks but cannot remember the lyrics. It doesn't matter to me, I'm happy in any case.

As I enter Bluebell's the door chimes, I inhale the smell of pancakes, waffles, bacon and coffee. It makes my stomach growl, I knew I should have eaten breakfast this morning.

"Over here." I turn to the voice and see Maxine in the corner by the far window. I squint my eyes then narrow them further, what the hell is Deacon doing here? Okay, I need to chill out a bit, it's a diner, he has every right to be here. I can cope with that. Honestly, though I ought to forgive him for being an ass the other day and launching me over his shoulder but then he started on Saunder again in the street. So, maybe not. I am still mad at him.

"Hey Maxine." I say ignoring Deacon whose lips are upturned in that smirk he has going on.

"You made it. Fantastic. Do you need to eat before we head off only I'd like to get a good spot?" She says, full of enthusiasm. I ignore my stomach pleading me to feed it, after all I can get something at the auction and I've had two coffees already.

"I'm good. Ready to go when you are. By the way, I'm looking out for a horse for myself." Deacon raises his eyebrows.

"Where are you going to keep it?" He asks, playing idly with a napkin.

"At Logan's. I would ask you because your slightly closer, but I'm pissed off with you right now." He grins.

"And what sort of horse are you going to buy?" For goodness sake, what is it to him? Why doesn't he just leave already? Oh, I forgot, Maxine and I are leaving.

"I'll know when I see it. Come on Maxine, let's go." She chuckles, grabs her purse and comes round the table just as Deacon stands and puts some notes on it.

"I thought we could all go in my truck." He says. That stops me in my tracks.

"What? I thought it was just Maxine and I going?" He grins. I want to slap him now.

"Sorry, Daisy. Maxine invited me to come look at some horses for *my* stables." Right, okay, yeah, so they are his stables and he should have a vested interest in what sort of horses he will have but honestly, I could do without being close to him. Just as I huff, the door opens and in comes Saunder.

He takes one look at me and gives me a wide grin and tips his hat. "Good morning, Daisy."

"Morning, Saunder. How you doing?"

"I'm all the better for seeing your mighty pretty, fine face this morning. You're like a ray of sunshine on this almost overcast day." He is still grinning.

"Let's go." Deacon says gruffly and nudges me forward.

"Why thank you, Saunder. That's so kind of you to say."

"I said let's go."

"What has gotten into you?" I snap at Deacon.

"Me? Oh, nothing. We've got an auction to get to, there's no time for shooting the breeze with the likes of him." Deacon jerks his thumb in Saunder's direction.

"Well, I happen to like him. So there." Yes, I know I'm acting like a child but he is driving me too it, I swear.

"I'll catch up with you later, Saunder." I say as I move it along to the door and hear Deacon mutter.

"Over my dead body." I humph, yes well, we'll see about that won't we.

Chapter 20

Daisy

When we arrive at the auction place it is *busy*. There are people literally everywhere. "Parking is tight, right?" I say. Maxine and Deacon both nod.

"Sure will be. It's best to get to these things early." He says not taking his eyes from in front, as he looks for a spot. "Over there." He tells Maxine.

We park and step out of the vehicle. The aroma of bacon and bbq fills my nostrils. My stomach churns again, why am I so hungry? I just ate not that long ago. But the smells are mouthwatering.

I see some pretty handsome looking cowboys pass by, mm, maybe I'll have to bag me one. It makes me smile, Deacon glares at me his eyes narrow as he watches me watching the two hunky fellas that have just walked passed me. One tips his hat. "Let's go." Deacon says and takes my arm. I shrug him off.

"I do know how to walk, thanks Deacon. Stop acting like a jealous brat."

"Me? You've got to be kidding. I'm not jealous. Why would I be jealous?"

Right, exactly why would he be jealous, we're not dating? Oh yeah, I forgot I'm his best friend's kid sister and that is just how he sees me. More is the shame.

"Stop it you two, will you." Maxine pipes up as she throws her shoulder bag over her shoulder and starts to stride to the main entrance gates. There are so many girls too, all wearing tight jeans, shorts even though it's cool at this time of year and some with their butts hanging out. I glance at Deacon. He doesn't seem to notice, unless of course he is doing a good job of not checking them out.

My cheeks flush. Why do I care who he looks at? It's nothing to do with me but it does make me have a pit of fire in my stomach. Dammit this crush I've had on him since high school is getting out of hand.

"This way. Let's go through. Are you excited, Daisy?" Maxine turns to glance at me.

"Sure am. I can't wait to see the horses. What happens to the ones that don't get sold?" I ask as we show our tickets and go through the five bar, iron gates.

"You don't want to know, sweetie. Some are kept for the next auction wherever that may be, some are left out to pasture and others." I stop her right there by putting my right hand up.

"I don't want to know, you're right." You see, I'm partial to animals, always have been. At one point I wanted to be a vet but then I liked the idea of being a fashion designer, hence opening my own business in Willowbrook and all sights of being a veterinarian flew right out the window. That and I don't think I'd have been able to cope with having to put animals to sleep and losing them when they got sick.

Deacon strides in front, I see a couple of girls looking at him and nudging each other. They're giggling. One has very blonde hair, yeah, it doesn't look too natural to me and large breasts which she isn't covering up too well in a crop top. I mean, a crop top in this weather. It's a sunny but brisk day, not the height of spring or summer even. There, my little jealous green monster has raised its ugly head again.

"Ladies." He tips his hat at them. It angers me, why couldn't he just bypass them and have ignored them. I huff. "Something up, Daisy?" He asks as he turns to me.

"Nope."

"Good. Glad we're settled on that. How long is this charade going on for where you're not talking to me?"

"Forever."

"So adult of you."

"Guys, give it a rest." Maxine interjects. Honestly, you both need your heads banging together. "Come on. Let's go grab some seats and wait for the auction to start." She pushes her way in front of Deacon and makes for some seating right down by the front. I trail behind her and Deacon goes behind. "Here will be perfect." She sits herself down three seats in. Leaving Deacon and I to have to sit next to one another, since there is a burly looking fella sitting on her other side.

"Can't you sit between us?" I ask her. She looks at me like I've grown a second head.

"For goodness sake, no way. Deal with it." Wow, that affronts me a bit, I didn't realize that Maxine could be so, well, direct. She grins. Ah, I see, she is using subtle manipulation of the situation. Now I know why she has invited me not because I had even thought of buying a horse but to get Deacon and I in one place, close together at the same time.

"Sneaky." I say and plonk myself down next to her.

Deacon sits down next to me, his legs wide apart and I can't help but look between them at his crotch. Heat intensifies within me. I catch him watching me with a smirk on his face.

"Anything you like?" He grins. I could slap him here and now. I don't.

"You have got to be kidding me." I fold my arms in front of my chest and stare in front of me waiting for the horse auction to begin. Only, it's very distracting because I can feel the heat from his strong thighs against my own legs. The seating isn't exactly wide spaced to say the least. My stomach has butterflies floating around as I move my leg just a fraction closer. What the hell am I doing?

He is still smiling then winks. I flick him my finger discreetly. "You're so childish." He whispers in my ear sending a heat wave through my entire body, causing those nice kind of shivers up and down my spine. His warm lips just brushing my ear. I lean into him and inhale his woodsy and shower fragrance. I have to stop from inhaling because right now, I just can't get enough of him. Even though I'm still mad at him about Saunder and whole carrying me of his shoulder thing. But oh my, being this close to him is heavenly.

"And you're not." I retort. He chuckles, his head goes back and dammit even his Adam's apple as it bobs up and down is so sexy. His skin is smooth and tan, his strong, square jawline has just enough stubble on it, that gives him that extremely rugged and sexy look. My fingers are itching to touch it and stroke it. Instead, I unfold them from across my chest and place my hands under my thighs, you know, just in case I do something downright stupid like run my fingers across his chin.

The auction starts with the host welcoming us all and telling us to have a good time and to be generous with our bids. I hope I find the right horse for me today, I can see myself riding through the fields and forestland trails of Willowbrook. Sitting side by side with Deacon on his horse as we ride off into the sunset, holding hands. Right, I seriously need to get a grip. For a start, I know Deacon has a woman he sees every now and then in the other town.

He moves in his seat, his arm brushes mine and the heat intensifies in my body. Has he also just moved his muscular thigh closer into mine? It feels like it. Warmth pools in my lower stomach and between my legs. I wonder what he'd feel like being over me, cupping the back of my head in his hand whilst he kisses me. I cross one leg over the other and squeeze my legs together.

If only.

Chapter 21

D<i>eacon</i>
I know what I'm doing opening my legs slightly and feeling our thighs touching. Am I pervert, an old pervert? Maybe but dammit I am so attracted to Daisy. Always have been and always will be. I do notice, however, that she doesn't move her leg away. I can feel the warmth emanating from her body.

Maxine smiles at me. "I knew this would be a good idea, the three of us." I raise my eyebrows. She winks. Maxine has always been a bit meddlesome in my love life.

Back when I was about fourteen, she tried to fix me up with Patsy Jenkins who was in one of her classes. Patsy was a pretty girl, always gregarious and outgoing, she played every sport going and was mighty keen on horses. She used to come and ride with Logan, Maxine and I but she doesn't wasn't my kind of girl. Sure we got on as friends, only Maxine kept on pushing us together, she'd invite us to the movies then do a disappearing act, then there was the time she told us to meet her for pancakes at Bluebell's and came out with some baloney that she had a stomach bug and had to dart back home and go to bed. Only, when I got home later that afternoon, not standing Patsy up because I'm a nice guy, Maxine was busy reading a glossy magazine and painting her nails, *and* eating a bowl of ice cream. Stomach bug my ass.

The host begins to announce the first horse. "Good day ladies and gentleman and welcome. First up, we've got number one-one-three a beautiful Tobiano Paint colt, weighing two-hundred-fifty pound, light brown and white with a good lineage. The mother is a distinguished registered Paint Quarter horse, broodmare."

"Oh my gosh, how adorable." Daisy gushes. Her face lights up, her blue eyes dance and I swear I've never seen her look so happy. Her hands clap together. Maxine smiles and raises her eyebrows.

"I think she's going to be out of our league." I whisper to Daisy, leaning into her catching her fragrance that fills my senses and does something to my dick. I place the auction magazine over my crotch.

"You can afford it, Deacon." Maxine pipes up.

"And what do I want with a colt? I need a couple of more mature horses for the riders. I don't have time for a colt you know that Maxine."

"Don't give me that, Deacon."

"Starting the bidding at one thousand dollars." He announces. Maxine raises her hand. I pull it down.

"What are you doing?" I hiss.

"Bidding."

"Are you insane woman?"

"No, but somebody would love her." She nods towards Daisy who is enraptured by the colt standing in the paddock area. I have to admit it's a fine looking colt and with a good lineage I could easily breed with it.

"Two thousand." The host shouts out, I look around scanning to see who has just bid.

"Two and a half." Maxine yells out. Daisy swings her head round to her, those blue eyes like large buttons.

"Is she seriously bidding for it, I mean that's a lot of money?"

"It's not for that particular colt to be honest, Daisy. But when Maxine gets started there is no holding her back."

"I mean, it's adorable and I'd love it but it is way out of my bracket. I think I'll have to wait until the older ones come out." Her shoulders sag a little. Damn, it pulls at my heart.

"Four thousand." I hear a man's voice and look around, I see a big burly fella with a ruddy face holding up his hand, he's wearing an old cowboy hat that has seen better days.

"Four and a half." I shout out. What the *hell* am I doing? I don't even want the colt. I mean don't get me wrong it's a fine animal and will grow to be a shining horse, no two ways about it, but I need horses for the riders and the kids, not a colt. Maxine shoots me a look and grins.

"What?" I shrug. Daisy is staring at me wide-eyed.

"I didn't think you wanted a baby horse." She eyes me suspiciously, I could drown in those baby blues of hers, her pink, full lips are just asking for me to kiss them.

"I changed my mind." I tell her and shrug my shoulders. Her lips turn up.

"Okaaay." Is all she says. I can feel the tension building now the bidding for colt starts to pick up.

"Six thousand." WTF? Who is bidding that high? Maxine and I both swing our heads round. I can't see who has just bid but it's not the big fella who bid earlier.

"Seven." I yell. Daisy starts to fan her face. I need to fan my face. I am bidding way out off my radar, I had budgeted for two horses no older than fourteen to start with for five grand tops.

Maxine is holding her breath, then I realize I am too. "Going once." The host says. I wait feeling strangled, if someone bids now I'm going to personally find who it is and punch them in the face. Nobody is getting this colt, not now I know Daisy has fallen in love with it. I saw the look on her face the moment the little thing was brought out for us all to see. She melted and pooled, the little sigh that left those damn beautiful lips of her said it all.

"Going twice." I hear some shuffling in the seat behind me and whispering. My hands clench, my hands are sweating. *Please don't let anyone bid.*

"Sold to the gentleman over there." The host directs his pointer to me and everyone close by turns and claps.

"Deacon, you feeling okay?" Maxine asks and puts a cool hand to my head.

"Nope."

"What came over you? Seven thousand for a colt?"

"You started it, don't even go there with me."

Daisy grabs me and hugs me and plants kisses all over my face. I guess she's talking to me again then. All it seems is forgiven. "I can't believe you've just bought a colt. Oh. My. God. Deacon, that's fucking insane." I smile what else can I do? I want her to have the damn thing, it's not for me.

"He's all yours, Daisy." I say. Maxine looks at me as if I have sprouted two heads and just been beamed down by Scotty and his crew.

"What? Are you serious? You can't spend seven thousand on a colt and give him to me. No way. I can't accept it." She stutters, tears welling in her eyes. I want to brush them away, even though I know they're happy tears.

"I can do what I like with my money. You can't afford it. Don't tell me you didn't want the little fella."

"You've got me there, the moment I saw him I fell in love with him but seriously, Deacon that's just too much. I'll never be able to pay you back."

I wave my hand. "Don't worry about that. You'll have to come and take care of him, that's your responsibility."

"Thank you so much, I don't know what to say. I'm just." She starts blubbering, I don't do girls blubbering very well. It makes me feel uncomfortable. I shift in my chair as the host begins to auction the next horse.

"You are such a soft ball of fur." Maxine tells me. I grunt. I'm definitely *not* a soft ball of fur.

"I think I've spent my cash for the day." I murmur instead. "Let's go speak to the folks to organize the transportation and get out of here. Unless you and Daisy want to stay?"

"No way, I want to get Dreamer home." Daisy says. It fills my heart knowing that I've made her entire day, it feels good to do something amazing for her, even though we are still well and truly in the *friend zone*.

"*Dreamer?*" I raise my eyebrows.

"Yeah, he looks like a Dreamer and he's my dream. Deacon, thank you so much. Logan and Sage are going to be so jealous."

"Dreamer it is then. Let's get organized so he can be home at mine later. You'll need to come over and take care of him, give him a brush. I've got a warm blanket for him. He'll go in his own stable next to Mitzi and Magic. They'll soon be best friends."

"I'm so excited to go see him." Daisy is up like a shot, Maxine pushes past me.

"A step in the right direction, Deacon." She whispers as she passes me. Yeah, a huge fucking expensive step. But fuck it. It got Daisy speaking to me again and we're back to being friends, even though it was a pretty extravagant way of going about it. I care about Daisy more than I probably ought to and I am sick of fighting it.

Chapter 22

Daisy

"He did *what*?" I watch as Lottie's cupid bow mouth makes a big O, her dark, curly hair is bouncing all over the place as if it has a life of her own as she springs up and down on the sofa in my lounge.

"I know, right? I can't believe it. I am still pinching myself."

"Who the fuck does that? Jeez-us, Girl that man has just stepped out of some romance book. And you and him are still just friends, are you sure about that?"

"That's the one." I say as I add some ice to our neat lemon Vodka's. Neither one of us like to spoil a good Vodka. It's nice and chilled, I'd sat it in the fridge for thirty minutes before Lottie came over.

As soon as I was back home, after I got dropped off I couldn't wait to message her. "I've got to go back to Deacon's at some point this evening to see the colt, feed him and give him some tender loving care. You can come with me."

"Let's reel back first Daisy. You're not getting out of the line of questioning that easily. He fucking bought you a colt for seven thousand dollars? That is insane, I mean INSANE."

She is very loud, I've never seen her quite so excitable. I am grinning from ear to ear. "Don't ask me what came over him. He said he wasn't interested in getting a colt that he needed more aged horses and then the colt got brought out and I swear I fell instantly in love with it."

"But who does that for just a friend? You know he likes you, *likes* you, right?"

"Sure, everyone likes me." I try to play it coy.

"Don't you try that on me. He seriously likes you, the kind of I want to fuck you, like you."

"*Lottie*." I screech as I hand her the glass shot glass with the one ice cube in it. She knocks it back and places it on the coaster on my sofa table. "Please don't say things like that. We're just friends."

"Just friends, horseshit. You get wet panties just thinking about that man. I bet he gets a boner looking at you. I bet, he jerks off in the shower with images of you in his mind." She starts to laugh. I knock my drink back and go back to the kitchen with her glass and refill them both.

"Just bring the bottle over, it's not like we're not going to get a bit tipsy tonight. We could have a few here then go to the Lazy Duke." She now stretches out of my small sofa with her legs hanging off the ends.

"No can do. I told you, I have to go over to Deacon's to see the colt."

"Has the colt got a name by any chance? Tell me everything about him. I bet he's so damn cute."

"The cutest. Here this is a picture." I hand her my mobile. "I took loads so scroll through them." She gasps and makes aww noises and generally is taken with the colt as I am. "I called him Dreamer."

"Yeah, that suits him. He looks so dreamy. Fuck, though Daisy. I cannot believe that Marshal Deacon went and bought you a damn colt just because you were fawning over it. So, is there some payback?" She chuckles. I smack her on her bare legs playfully.

"No, there is *no* payback."

"Ah, but I bet you'd love to pay him back with that mouth of yours."

"Lottie, behave. Honestly, so I like him. But that doesn't change a thing, We're good friends. He sees me as Logan's kid sister, the one with braces and pigtails who just hung around with them all the time. Besides, he has that lady friend over in Copper Town. What's her name?" I furrow my brow trying to think of her name. Lottie tops us up again, I'm on my third shot. I need to take it easy if I'm to get to Deacon's. Er, how am I going to get there. I won't be able to drive. Drat. I'll have to call Logan. No way I'm calling Deacon to come fetch me.

Being close to that man makes my panties wetter than standing in a rainstorm. Bonnie comes and jumps up on my lap. I fuss her ears. "Molly is her name." Lottie offers. "He's not serious about her, daresay she'd like him to be, but you know he only goes there when he you know, needs to express himself." She is now giggling. Someone has got to stay off the shots.

"Lottie, I do have to get to Deacon's later. You want a pizza or something before I go? Or, do you want to eat and then come with me? I'll buzz Logan see if he can pick us up. We've had three shots and can't drive."

"Pizza sounds good. And yes, I have to come and see Dreamer and Deacon. I mean that man is pure sex on legs."

"Honestly. You're not helping."

"I know I'd like to help myself to him. You're one lucky lady for him to have the hots for you like he has. So, when are you going to give into him and have wild sex with the man?"

I clench my thighs, just thinking about Deacon's hard cock between my thighs sends a shiver up and down my spine. "Have you got goosebumps? You have. Oh. My. God. Daisy."

"Lottie stop it now. Right, no more Vodka for you." I place Bonnie on my bestie's stomach so I can go fix us a pizza and put it in the oven. I make sure I take the Vodka bottle with me.

My phone vibrates. "Hey, Girl it's your *boyfriend* calling."

"I don't have a boyfriend."

"You know who I mean."

"Deacon?"

"The one and only."

I smooth my hair down, like he can see me through a mobile and feel ridiculous for doing so. Lottie hands me the phone and goes back to stroking Bonnie who is lapping up the attention.

"Hey, Deacon."

"Did you still want to come over this evening to see, Dreamer? Only, I can feed him, put a blanket on him. He's settled in well in his stable. Mitzi and Night have nosed with him. No issues. All good this end."

"I was thinking to come over, I've just got Lottie with me. Can I bring her?"

"Sure, no problem. It's okay if you don't want to. I can take care of him."

"No way, I want to spend time with him. I've just had a couple of shots so I'm going to ask Logan to come pick me up."

"I can come get you. No problems and Lottie. I'll drive you both back afterward."

"Hold on a second, Deacon whilst I check with Lottie."

I hold my mobile to my chest. "Lottie, Deacon can come get us. You still want to come?"

I watch as she cocks her head to one side, and has this weird look on her face. "You know what, I've got my nails to paint instead this evening. I tell you what. You let him come pick you up and you go over on your own."

"What? Why? I thought you wanted to see Dreamer."

"Er, no. I'll be gooseberry in the middle. Besides you never know what may come of it. You two, alone, near the horses, stables, hay." She giggles and wriggles her eyebrows. I launch one of my easy pillows at her from the chair next to me and stick my tongue out at her. But, she does have a point. I mean, something could happen, right?

"Hey Deacon. Sorry to keep you waiting like that. You can come get me." We hang up and I am not going to lie, I am already over heating thinking about being close to that man again with his broad shoulders, popping biceps and God only knows what's between his legs.

Chapter 23

D*eacon*

My heart is racing, what was I thinking buying her a damn colt? How could I resist the way her face lit up, her hands on her heart and those big eyes of hers as she saw him coming out into the ground. Maxine had given me that knowing look of hers, the one that says *I knew it*. Yeah, well.

I watch as Daisy comes out of her place, she's wearing jeans that look like they're sprayed on her lean legs and I am betting her ass is real high, damn it my dick twinges. *Not now*. She gives me a brief wave.

"Hey, thanks for coming to get me, I had a couple of drinks with Lottie."

"Where is Lottie? I thought she was coming with you?" Not that I mind, I mean having Daisy all to myself for an hour or two, is the best thing ever. Okay, I intend to not hover over her when she is with Dreamer, it's not like she doesn't know anything about horses. Daisy was always at ours riding when we were younger, my folks always had horses and my granddaddy. Logan has had horses for as long as I can remembers, you know she knows her way around a horse.

"Er, she decided she had something else she needed to do." That sounds pretty ominous. I am wondering if Lottie has ditched her best friend for a reason, a meddling reason more than likely. Lottie can work in mysterious ways that is for sure.

"How is he?" Daisy asks as she snaps the seatbelt in.

"The same as when you saw him just a few hours ago. He is settled in, my two seem okay with him. We'll know more tomorrow when I let them out into the big paddock."

"You'll keep an eye on him though won't you. Only, I've got to go to the store and finish off the bridesmaid dresses. I've only got an adjustment to do for Lottie's."

Is she rambling? It sounds like it, maybe Daisy is nervous sitting in the truck with me. It makes me smile. My palms are sweating, what is going on with me? I am a grown man in his mid thirties, not some young kid going out on his first date.

"I'll be with them. You don't honestly think I'd let him go out first time unattended. Come on, Daisy you know me better than that." I try to keep my eyes on the road ahead and not on her breast which are looking perky in her tight green sweater. She smells of perfume, floral essence, I wonder if she has just put it on for me. I mean, she wouldn't freshly spritz herself to go see a horse. Would she? Who knows how a woman's mind works, especially Daisy's.

"Thank you, Deacon. I still can't tell you how over the moon I am that you bought him for me *and* keeping him at yours. I thought I'd be taking him to Logan's." I want to tell her, that if I could, I'd pick the moon right out of the sky and place it on the palm of her hand. I stop myself before something stupid comes right out of my mouth. I have to remember that she is ten years younger than me, whatever the spark is that keeps igniting between us, it's probably some kind of mild flirtation. No one as feisty, outgoing and as beautiful as Daisy would want to date an older man like me. She deserves to be with someone her own age, who isn't going to be hitting nearly forty.

"Told you, he can stay at mine for however long you want him to. No need to move him to Logan's." We pull off the road along the track, my truck handles the dips and stones well, it's built for it. The track leads to Logan's cabin in the woodland and then a short distance further, to mine. We always said, growing up that we wanted to practically live in each other's pockets and yeah, I guess we do now. We still have our privacy since there are trees between us and land, but if we fancy a beer together, we can just walk the five minutes to one another's places.

"We're here." Daisy is practically jumping up and down in her seat. I wish she wouldn't do that, it's giving me all sorts of funny ideas, imaging her bouncing up and down on my lap. God help me, this woman is making my dick want to be released from my tight jeans. I knew I should have worn baggier ones, not these that are fresh out of the wash.

I pull the truck up and the handbrake on, kill the engine and watch as she jumps out of the truck like a bat out of a hell. It makes me chuckle, she sure is excited to see Dreamer.

Her arms are around his neck as she stands on the stable side of the his door. His eyes are big and brown as they glance at me walking towards the two of them. "Can you see how friendly he is? Look his head is over my shoulder." She sounds like the young woman that she is. It makes my heart melt. I take in her slender frame, her high ass and groan inwardly, I have got to stop thinking about Daisy like this damnit. Being so close to her as I stand on her left hand side is making me feel dizzy with her scent and closeness. I want to reach my hand out and touch her soft and delicate hand.

Shit I have got it so bad for her.

Chapter 24

D^{*aisy*} We are standing so close I can smell his woody aftershave, his forearms are big and the veins pop, and that is without him even moving them although he is idly playing with his truck keys.

I want to reach out and feel his scruff on his chin, it's pretty damn sexy I can tell you that much. "He's going to become a fine horse, you picked well." Deacon tells me, all the while keeping his eyes on Dreamer.

"I don't know that I really picked him as much as literally fell in love with him the moment I saw him." Dreamer is still resting his head over my shoulder. I kind of feel bad that he is taken away from his mother, maybe he had been a while back. Who knows.

"Do we know what happened to his mother or anything, you know like a back story?"

Deacon shakes his head. "No idea, I can find out for you if you like." He glances at me, my breath hitches as his blue eyes making me pool, wondering what they'd look like when aroused. I bet they go a smoldering dark blue. I feel myself flush. Dreamer moves away and nudges my face before making his way back to his hay feed.

"I bought him some junior feed too. It's over there." Deacon moves his head and I can see a gigantic bag of feed in the corner of the stables. His black horse, Lady Night his black magic Arabian horse whinnies. "Ssh girl, don't be so jealous." He moves away from me to stroke her nose. I instantly feel cold, okay not cold as in freezing cold but his heat is removed from my side. I liked it. I can feel myself slightly wet from being in such close proximity to Deacon.

"Thank you, Deacon for everything. I can pay you back for the feed. Dreamer will take a little longer."

"Told you, he is a present."

"He's a pretty huge present in terms of presents, Deacon. Don't you think?"

"Not really." He doesn't miss a heartbeat but keeps his eyes now on Lady Night. "If you like someone you gift them and besides, how could I leave him there? I wanted to make sure he is with someone who is going to love him, take care of him and give him the best start in his life journey. Couldn't think of anyone else better than you, Daisy."

Oh, wow he is making me swoon. Just the sound of his deep and gravelly voice gets me. Butterflies are whizzing around like crazy in my stomach and I am pooling with a capital P.

I move closer to him. Dare I touch him? What would he do if I placed my hand on his? Frankly, I think I've had enough of this growing up nonsense where he sees me only as Logan's kid sister. It's not like Logan has ever scared Deacon away from me with that whole *she's off limits* kind of bullshit. Or has he? No, surely not Logan. I can't imagine him ever doing that with Deacon.

Deacon has always had a clean, good reputation. It's no secret he sees someone every now and then in Coppertown but he's discreet enough. I only know because Lottie told me some time ago and when I asked Logan if Deacon had a steady girlfriend, he'd told me no but that he has a girl on a casual basis in the next town. Fair enough I suppose, I mean it's not like I've never dated any guys.

Although, Saunder could be in the running. Okay, that's a lie. I like Saunder he is an honest guy maybe a bit too cocky for my liking. He's broad and good looking, a real rancher and I bet some girl is going to take his hand some day but it won't be me. I know it's mean to confess to, but I was only using him to try to make Deacon jealous.

I think I managed it. I inhale deeply as Deacon nuzzles Lady Night's nose. He doesn't move. Maybe he isn't aware how close I am to him now. I check on Dreamer, he's content munching away and then I stand right next to Deacon. His body tenses.

I move my hand onto his left hand which is on the stable door, his other hand is caressing Lady Night's face and neck. Am I jealous, can you even be jealous of a horse? No, but I sure as hell wish that big hand was stroking my face and neck. My panties are getting wetter, my stomach is in knots. I've never been a forward kind of girl before, but hell they say there is a first time for everything, right?

Deacon doesn't move his hand, the electricity is pulsing through my body like some kind of fire. The connection is out of the world, my heart is racing my mouth is dry and my clit is aching. It's been a while since I've had sex, months as it happens.

"Daisy, what are you doing?" He asks and looks at me, his pupils larger than before. "Don't do anything you may regret." His voice is a growl, I like it the sensation of warmth shoots through me. Those eyes, they are intense.

Slowly I move even closer and face him, he remains with his side to my front. I push into him. "Daisy, I'm warning you not to do anything, I won't be able to control myself." His voice is now a rasp. I kind of like that I am undoing him. Me, little Daisy undoing the marshal here in Willowbrook. It is one helluva turn-on.

"I don't want you to control yourself, Deacon. That's the whole point." He humpfs at me. "Let's be wild. I know you like me."

"Such a tease." He mutters. Am I? Okay, maybe but I am bored of waiting for this gorgeous man and he is all MAN not doing anything about our mutual attraction. Sometimes you gotta just take the bull by the horns. My panties are already wet.

He lowers his head down and turns more towards me. I move my body up against his hard stomach and chest and raise my head. He lowers his a fraction, our lips now just millimeters apart. I can smell coffee on him. Tilting my head backwards I wait for him to lower further so our lips can join. I am dying to have them on mine, I want to taste him, feel his wet tongue inside my mouth, teasing me. My breath quickens, my heart races more, and my clit I am telling you, is literally aching. I want to feel his fingers hook inside my tight jeans and find that warm place and delve right inside me.

"Daisy, last chance to tell me to stop." His voice is low, growly and so damn sexy.

"Hey anyone in there?" Deacon jumps back as if he has just had boiling water poured all over him.

He coughs. The arousal still evident all over his face. "Yeah, hey Logan." He shouts back. I hear steps coming towards us. Deacon moves further away and goes to stand at the next stable by his Appaloosa horse, Mitzi.

"There you are, thought I might find you here too, Daisy." Logan has a big grin on his face. "Thought I'd come check out this colt you've got yourself. Wow, he is something else." He stands with his hands on his narrow hips. I hope he cannot tell how flushed I am. It's not exactly dark inside the stable area since Deacon has lighting up.

"Yeah, isn't he just. Couldn't resist getting him for Daisy." Deacon informs him. Logan pats Deacon on the back.

"Well, Daisy you've got a lot of hard work in front of you, taking care of him and breaking him in when he's a bit older. How old is he and what did you call him?" I am still in shock from my almost kiss and Logan coming waltzing in. Cockblocker, honestly sometimes I could slap my older brother. He is totally unaware of what he has just come between. Argh.

"I called him, Dreamer. He's two."

"Nice. He's going to be a beauty no two ways about it." Logan turns to Deacon. "You want to have a beer? I've walked over. Sage is on the phone to her mother about wedding arrangements, then she's going to firm up the bookings at the cabin week after next. You still coming aren't you?"

"Sure." Deacon replies. "I'll be there. Wouldn't miss your joint stag and hen night for anything. It's going to be fun."

"Yeah, to be honest I am looking forward to the actual day of the wedding and then our honeymoon. This stress is killing me."

"Behave, Logan." I say. "You're not doing all the planning, Sage is."

"Hey, I'll have you know I've been invovled with cake tasting, caterers and I am making her a platform out back to be married on with enough space for the band to play after the ceremony."

I roll my eyes, does he have any idea how stressful planning a wedding is. Sage has had to choose a dress, bridesmaid dresses, flowers, napkins, table covers, invites, balloons you name it she has done it. And whilst working full time at the practice that is now busier than before since they are taking in more patients from Coppertown and a couple of the other neighboring towns.

Logan pokes me in the stomach like he used to when we were kids. "Don't you roll those babies at me, Little Sis."

"Stop calling me that, we're grown up."

"You'll always be Little Sis." He chuckles, the skin around his eyes crinkles. He's a good looking fella my brother but calling me Little Sis, is going too far. Especially in front of Deacon. It'll make him run a mile from me.

"I'll have a cold one with you, Logan. Daisy?"

"No, I think I'll head home. Lottie can come get me so you can stay here with Logan." I tell him and whistle for Dreamer to come back over to me.

"Wait, did you come here with Deacon? Sorry, Bro. We can do beer another time."

"No, honestly, it's fine. You stay here and I'll message Lottie to come get me."

"Are you sure, only I am happy to take you home. Logan will be fine for half an hour by the time I get you there and come back myself."

"Yeah, no big deal." Big Bro says.

"It's *fine*." I don't want to be in the truck with Deacon on my own now, I feel embarrassed that I came on to him, and we were interrupted. Honestly, I want for the floor to open up so I can slip down into it. As I pull my mobile out of my back pocket, Dreamer is at the stable door. I give him a big hug and a kiss. "See you soon, Baby. I'll be back early in the morning."

"You want me to come get you in the morning?" Deacon asks. Logan starts to chuckle, I glare at him.

"What?" He asks. Like he doesn't know what. He's outright having fun at our expense. I feel exasperated and irritated on top of embarrassed.

My fingers move quickly over the mobile. Within seconds Lottie shoots me a message back to tell me she's on her way. "No, I'll drive myself, it'll be early, I am thinking I need to be here around six so I can spend time with Dreamer, give him a nice brush down then head back home for a shower and get ready to open up. We're having the fundraising last planning meeting tomorrow over breakfast at Bluebell's aren't we?" I ask of Logan.

"Yep, can't believe it'll be the last one before the event. Looking forward to it as usual. It always feels good to be doing something positive for the kids in town."

"Sure does." Deacon nods his head. "Right, let's go back to the cabin and I'll get us a couple of beers." I give Dreamer a huge, tight hug and a kiss again on the nose and follow behind the guys.

"So, are you growing a beard for the wedding or something?" I ask Logan noticing how it looks like he hasn't shaved for a week.

"Yeah, Sage likes a bit of scruff so I thought I'd oblige her. Personally, I'd like to shave the damn itchy shit off my face."

Deacon laughs, I watch as his Adam's apple bobs up and down, it's sexy. How can an Adam's apple even be sexy? Trust me, his is.

Lottie honks her horn fifteen minutes later, I leave the guys to their cold ones and hop in car. "Hey Girl. Did you have fun? Hey, wait why are you so flushed?"

"Just drive please Lottie and get me home."

"Did you and Deacon get it *on* in the stables? Please tell me you did."

I slap her leg playfully. "Nope." I pop the P. "I wanted to though. Lottie I was this close," I press my thumb and forefinger together leaving the tiniest of gaps. "and then Logan showed up, out of the blue." I slap my hand to my forehead.

Lottie laughs. "Better luck next time, maybe during the weekend away, you could slip into his room. That'd be something." Her laugher ripples through the car. Only, I don't think that's such a bad idea.

Chapter 25

Deacon

What was I thinking? What the HELL was I thinking? She's Logan's kid sister, she's ten years younger than me. But damnit, I want her, my dick wants her and I just couldn't stop myself. I don't know where it was a good thing or a bad thing that Logan came in when he did.

Only, I know for sure I would not have been able to stop myself. The way she smelt, her lips so close to mine, I could smell the peachy lip gloss or was it strawberries, maybe a mix of both. Her fragrance. I could see the stark arousal in those blue eyes of her. My dick was aching in my pants, to have her and be inside her wet pussy. I bet she was as slick as anything.

"You okay?" Logan asks as he takes a seat on my back porch. I hand him the beer.

"Yeah, miles away."

"Sure was a nice thing you did there for Daisy. She gets by with her seamstress business and is going into design, but she doesn't make a lot of money. Enough for a decent living but not for a horse."

I shrug my shoulders. "It was the least I could do. She's always helping out with my horses since I have had them. That girl loves them and they love her. She's my best friend too, well except you. We've grown up together. Daisy is like my kid sister." Who the hell am I trying to kid. *My kid sister.* I am such a liar since every fiber of my body is not thinking of Daisy being anything like a sister. No siree. More like a woman, with her pert tits, her high ass and her glory between her legs.

If Logan knew what kind of dirty thoughts were and have gone through my mind about Daisy, he'd probably kick my ass all the way to China and back. I take a long drink of my beer. It feels cold and refreshing as it slides down my throat.

"So, you ready for the big day, Bro?" I ask him. His long legs are stretched out in front of him. He nods.

"You bet I am. I've waited a long time to get a ring on Sage's finger. Ten long years. I never thought I would see the day if I am honest. When she upped and left me all those years ago, the way my heart broke, it was the saddest day of my life. Then seeing her around town on her short visits back and with that dick, whatever his name was. I mean, they were never suited."

"Turned out to be a jerk if you ask me. Who would leave Sage and go to London for a fellowship? He could have done that here, right?"

"Rumour has it that he is back, didn't work out for him. One of Sage's friends mentioned it. Maybe he was homesick or something."

"Or maybe he thinks he can have Sage back." Logan shoots me a look, his eyebrows raise to his hairline.

"I'd like to fucking see him try. Over my dead body. Sage is mine now and in just a few weeks, she will be wearing my wedding ring. No man is taking her away from me again."

"Glad to hear it, Logan. You are right, you have waited a long time for this. I'm looking forward to the wedding, everyone is. It'll be one hell of a do."

We sit in silence for a while looking out to the darkness with the stars above us and the moon shining brightly. It's a beautiful night, crisp fall air surrounds us, I can hear the nightlife amongst the trees. "So, you going to ask my sister on a date anytime soon? Only, it's no secret."

I take another long drink of my beer before answering him. "Honestly, I don't think she'd be interested."

"Are you kidding me? You see the way she looks at you, always has done and hanging off your every word."

"There is a ten year age gap, what does Daisy want with an old man like me?"

"Hey, less of the old man. We're the same age, and there is nothing old about me."

"If you say but being around Daisy makes me feel old. She's young and vibrant and so full of energy. I think maybe it's an infatuation with her, nothing more. The moment she saw me in the morning she'd run a mile. When I am fifty and much older, she will still only be young forties. That matters to me."

He shuffles his feet, then crosses one leg over the other, his right knee at a right angle on top of his left leg. I mirror him. It's comfortable.

"You worry too much, Deac. Trust me, that isn't just infatuation. I reckon she loves you."

"Pretty strong word that, Love. You know it conjures up all sorts of images, wedding bands, babies, back yards with toys in it, you know all that stuff. What if I am not that kind of man?"

"You are that kind of man. Besides, when Sage and I have our children you are going to be a Godfather."

"Seriously, me?"

"Yes you. Why ever not? You're my best friend, Deacon. I couldn't imagine asking anyone else."

"Thanks, Man. That means a lot to me. Is she pregnant?"

"Who Sage? No way, I'm just saying. We've already discussed it and we decided we want you."

"I don't know what to say. That's huge."

We sit in silence again, me thinking about Daisy and whether or not we could make it work with the age gap, but she is so young to me. The way she talks, the music she likes, we're a million miles apart. For God's sake she is a Taylor Swift fan, I am not. She likes pink and bubblegum stuff, a true Barbie girl. I am more a Bruce Willis, Mark Wahlberg kind of man. Although they do say opposites attract.

But being nearly forty and Daisy not even thirty, it still leaves a weird kind of feeling in my gut.

"Have you got your best man speech ready? It better not be filthy or embarrass me." Logan says as he chuckles.

"It's ready don't worry, as for embarrassing you, I wouldn't be telling any truths that no-one already knows about."

He humpfs. "Well, it's been nice having a cold one with you, Deacon. You meeting us all for breakfast tomorrow, last run down before the fundraiser. Those little kids are going to love it. I know I'm excited about it."

"Sure am. Will be at Bluebell's nice and early. Although I am looking forward to it, I don't relish being dunked again like last year. I was soaked through and cold. Hopefully, we'll have more sunshine this year."

"The forecast is good, you'll be fine. If not, you can always get my sister to warm you up."

"Logan, don't even go there."

"Just saying, Bro. I kind of like the idea of you being my brother-in-law. I think it'd be pretty neat."

"Yeah, maybe. But you're running away with yourself. I have a lot to think about. There's definitely an attraction there, but seriously I still think I am way too old for a young, free spirited woman like Daisy. I hear she wants to go to Paris and to Milan for some of her fashion design courses. We'd be apart before we even start and what if she meets some young Italian. I can't tie her down before she's even lived her life. Daisy has never stepped out of Willowbrook, well not on a flight that's for sure and especially not to Europe. It's a big world out there, Logan. I can't clip her wings before she has had a chance to fly."

"That's honorable but still think you should get in there first. Besides, you can travel with her. That's what planes are for, they seat more than one person." He chuckles.

I finish my beer and stand to go see him out. "Stay seated, I can see myself round to the front. Enjoy the rest of your evening and give some thought to asking my sister out on a proper date instead of trying to sex her in the stable next time."

Jeez, I want the ground to open up and to fall right on it.

Chapter 26

D^{*aisy*} It's the hen-stag party weekend and I am nervous because I am going to have to face Deacon and spend two whole days with him being in close proximity. I don't think my pussy or my heart can take it. I mean the last time I was so close to him, I was itching to strip his shirt off and feel his pecs under my fingers. Heat rushes to my face.

Bonnie knows something is up since her small cat basket is out, she probably thinks she has to go on a vet visit hence why she is staring at me sitting on the sofa with a glare to her eyes. "Okay baby, mommy isn't taking you to the vet. We're going to a cabin up in the mountains. You'll love it." She still glares at me even though I am using my most soothing voice. My phone rings, I know it's Lottie when I hear the *Man I Feel Like A Woman* coming from it, it's Lottie's favorite track and she is nuts for Shania Twain. Who isn't?

"Hey Girl." She drawls into the phone.

"Hey yourself."

"You looking forward to being up close with Deacon this weekend?" She laughs, I do not find it amusing. Especially not with a whole bunch of our friends being around. I am pretty convinced that Logan caught us being so close because the last few days he keeps dropping hints. First off he told me that there was nothing wrong with a relationship where there was a ten year age gap. That one made my jaw drop to the ground, then he winked and went about his day. Luckily, at the fundraiser meeting over breakfast at Bluebell's,

Deacon had not arrived. Sage gave Logan a punch in the arm and told him to leave it alone. Still, my face flushed bright red.

"There will be enough of us for me to avoid him. Honestly, I can't control myself near to him so I think it's best I stay away from him. I will hang with you and Sadie most of the time. Besides, we have different things going on from Logan and the guys, right?"

"Of course we do but there are some mixed activities."

"Remind me, I've been so engrossed in the last minute touch ups to the dresses and getting my stall ready for the fundraiser that I haven't looked over the agenda properly."

Lottie sniggers. "Are you laughing? What in heaven's name is so damn funny, Lottie?"

"There is a treasure hunt and you are paired up with Deacon." She is almost in hysterics.

"Deacon? Why Deacon. Why not you? Who set this up?"

"I expect Logan and Sage. Maybe you two just need a bit of an extra nudge."

"You can't nudge someone who is stubborn as a mule and we all know he is a mule."

"Ah, but a cute one. I mean, his ass is like you want to bite it."

"Lottie." I say with warning before she goes any further. "Anyway are you bringing, what's his name." Sometimes it is hard to keep up with Lottie and she changes her guys like most of us change our panties. She is an out and out fun girl, not one who wants to be tied down. Not yet anyway.

"Nah, coming on my own. That way if I see someone in the next cabin I won't feel like I can only look and not touch." She chuckles.

"You are incorrigible, Lottie. Shame on you."

"Tell me you don't want to touch Deacon and feel how strong his..." I cut her off right there.

"Do not utter another word." I tell her and scoop Bonnie up and place her in the carrier. She's a good kitty and doesn't scratch, she's used to the carrier, I take her most places with me that I can. To be honest, Bonnie and I have never been apart except when I run errands or go to work and have Logan's dog, Hector with me.

"Biceps, I was going to say. Damn, Girl where is your mind today?"

I humph, "are you nearly ready we can swing by in fifteen minutes, just need to load Bonnie and my weekend bag into the car."

"I am ready as I'll ever be. By the way, did you see the new fireman in town?"

"What, no of course not. I've been busy. Who, is he handsome?"

"You bet he is, tall, dark, swoony something out of an Elsie Silver book. I'm definitely going to get me some of that." She howls with laughter and I have to admit I cannot contain myself either. Lottie is a scream.

"Bonnie and I will see you in a few minutes, Lottie and go change your panties after drooling over the latest male addition to Willowbrook." Laughing we both hang up, I shake my head and grab my weekend bag, make sure I have unplugged everything in the kitchen and lounge and head out.

I have butterflies swarming in my stomach just at the thought of seeing Deacon again. He never made it to the fundraising breakfast meeting, something came up at the station, adolescents from Coppertown and graffiti I think it was. I've kept long hours adjusting the bridesmaid dresses and am finally done and ready. Let's hope none of us drastically lose weight or gain a few pounds because these dresses with their fitted bodices are literally made to measure.

I place Bonnie's carrier on the back seat and strap her in with the seatbelt running through it, fling my bag in the boot and seat myself driver's side and pull off my drive.

Lottie is already standing outside her place waving as she sees me driving up. I wonder who dressed her today, usually very stylish she is wearing a garish pink ensemble. A puffer coat with white fur trimmed hood, pink matching puffer type boots, pale pink jeans tucked in and Lord only knows if she is wearing pink underneath.

"Are you going all Barbie on me?" I try to hide my smile.

"I happen to know that Fireman Boy likes a bit of pink." She licks her pouty lips.

"He's hardly likely to see you here outside your front door, Lottie. Honestly, get in the car. Please tell me you are not wearing pink underneath."

"I am. Actually, he is going to be at the cabin."

My head does a ninety degree swivel, "run that by me again."

"I said he will be at the cabin. Turns out he is an old friend of Logan's. His wife passed away three years ago and he has a young girl, Logan invited him said it'd be good for him."

I let out a breath. "You are not going to try to come on to him are you, Lottie. Please tell me you won't. And how do you know this? What happened to seeing someone at the other cabins?"

"Well, if you kept up with the local gossip at Bluebell's like I do and overhear your brother talking to Sage and asking her if he should invite his friend, then you'd know a helluva lot more."

I roll my eyes. "Some of us, Lottie do not live in Bluebell's diner." It's now her turn to roll her eyes at me.

"Is Deacon bringing anyone?" I ask trying to pretend I don't care whether or not he is. She lets out a rip roaring laugh.

"Oh, Girl. You are so predictable. I knew it." She slaps her thigh with exaggeration. "I just knew you were going to ask. Damn, I wish I'd run bets on it with Sadie, Sage and Eliza." That makes me stick my tongue out at her.

"Nope." She pops the P. "He isn't bringing anyone. He's all yours girl. Don't waste it."

I try to ignore Lottie making fun and keep my eyes focused on the road to Logan and Sage's cabin. We're all meeting there then transferring to his and Deacon's trucks for the trek up to the mountains to the Shoehorse resort and cabins.

Secretly, I am pleased to hear that Deacon isn't brining anyone, it makes my stomach flutter and brings a sense of joy to my heart. I have brought some new lingerie with me, you know just in case.

Chapter 27

Deacon

"Will you stop pacing up and down. You are going to wear this old rug out. It's already worn out." Logan is grinning from ear to ear as he stands in the cabin he and Sage have rented for the pre-wedding event, with a large, steaming mug of coffee in his hand. "You want some whiskey in that coffee you are there nursing?"

"No, damnit. Leave me alone."

"Don't be so tetchy." He grumbles.

"Guys what's going on?" Sage appears looking amazing in a wrap around dress the color of russet leaves, it looks like a velvet fabric and a moss green cardigan. I hardly see her in anything else other than jeans, but she looks good.

"Nothing, he is badgering me."

"Why?" She asks her eyes wide glaring at Logan.

"Because he won't sit down and relax. I bet it's because Daisy is on her way." He chuckles. I could throw a cushion or something at him only it'd knock that coffee out of his hand and Sage would end up clearing it up.

"Just pack it in Logan and behave. Honestly, can't you act your age for a second?"

"Nope, not when I know Deacon is in a dither about Daisy. I swear it's kept me amused for nearly fifteen years."

"I have not had the hots for your sister since she was ten, you damn pervert you."

"Okay, ten years then. I know you started liking her when she went through her change at school, I mean you couldn't take your eyes off her. One minute she was Daisy with the braces and braids, then she was Daisy with straight, sleek hair, no braces and that crazy smile of hers." He is right, Daisy does have a crazy ass smile, her face radiates, she is like an angel and those blue eyes of her sparkle like sapphires.

"Just stop, okay. I am not nervous."

"Go do something useful, Logan please, like chop some wood." Sage tells him and nudges him to the front door of the cabin.

"Why can't Deacon do it?"

"What are you twelve now?" She stands in front of him with her hands on her hips. Yeah, these two are made for each other. I am kinda jealous if I'm honest, they have this amazing relationship, found each other again after so long and you can just tell they will make it until one leaves the other to go over the rainbow. It's a perfect match.

I chuckle. "And you," Sage glares at me now, "can go take your bag upstairs into the bedroom second on the left up the stairs."

"Don't forget Ryle is coming now too. Do we have enough room?" Logan asks her wiggling his eyebrows and trying to put his arm around her. She pushes him off gently. "I hadn't thought of that. To be honest, I booked only for Eliza, Sadie, us, Deacon and Daisy." She pauses as she looks at her fingers she is counting on.

"Shit."

"What's up?" I ask seeing her concern and the way she is biting her lower lip.

"Fuck. We need five rooms without Ryle and we have four masters. How could I get it wrong? Shit. This isn't good."

"Lottie can share with Daisy, right?"

"Oh. My. God. This is a nightmare. Lottie and Daisy could share then what about Eliza or Sadie and now what about Ryle? This is a cluster fuck up. How could I do something so stupid."

"Hey, calm down." Logan puts his arm around her. "It'll be fine. We can sort it out when everyone arrives."

"Yeah, but how could I even forget about Lottie too?" She hangs her head down. Logan lifts her chin and places a kiss on her lips.

"It'll be okay, Sage. There is a large sofa and we can double folk up." She nods but I can tell she is mad at herself for getting this wrong.

"For a start, Deacon can share with Daisy." Logan lets out a loud laugh. Sage punches him in the arm and I am about to wring his neck.

"Going out for some fresh air before everyone arrives." I say and place my mug down on the mahogany, square coffee table that is between two large tan sofas. I will leave Logan and Sage to discuss stuff between them. Share with Daisy? He has got to be kidding me, right? Daisy will have a fit and I don't think I would be able to control myself with her hot little body in the same room as me, let alone the same bed as me.

Sure, in the past growing up I've shared a tent with her but we were kids and now, well let's just say things are a different right now. I fancy that woman, I yearn for her body and her touch. I shake my head and close the door behind me to be greeted by Daisy's car pulling up. Lottie jumps out first, wow that's a lot of pink. She isn't going to get lost anytime soon, this girl looks like a homing beacon.

"Like the color pink, Lottie?" I grin at her. She gives me a big hug.

"Good to see you too, Deacon. Is Ryle here already?"

"Ryle, do you know him?" I ask her bemused, he is new to town, how on earth would Lottie even know Ryle?

"No, but I'm going to get to know him. See ya." She heads for the front door leaving Daisy standing by the car chuckling.

"Can you help me with the bags, Lottie seems to think I'm her butler or something now."

"Sure." I walk towards her and follow her cute ass round to the boot. She pops it open and leans forwad. Man, I shouldn't look at how round and pert her ass is. It makes me twinge. *Get a grip, Deacon, Man. She's Logan's kid sister, she's ten years younger than you old man.* But my dick is not listening to my head, it seems to have ignored that memo like an A+ student.

She hauls a large bag forward. "Lottie's I take it?"

"Yep, here." She moves aside so I can reach in the trunk and grab the bag. I smell her fragrance, it's a blend of lavender and lemon, it smells might nice and fresh. I want to nuzzle into her neck to smell her some more.

"Thanks, Deacon. I can manage mine and Bonnie's carrier."

"You brought Bonnie?"

"Absolutely I did. She won't be a problem, she'll find a space to curl up and stay put most of the time. You know she's a good little girl." This is true. Daisy sometimes takes Bonnie to her shop where the black and white cat snuggles and curls up on her favorite window seat cushion, sleeping or watching the world go by.

I take the case to the cabin steps, lift it up as I walk up the four steps leading to the porch. Another vehicle turns up, it's Eliza's sedan and I see the shock of pink hair that belongs to Sadie. At least everyone is pretty much on time. Sage has got a lunch organized for everyone and got to the cabin extra early with Logan to make sure everything would be perfect.

Logan's band are also arriving and staying in the next cabin. Then I see a black truck bowl up and make out the large frame and dark haired man sitting behind the wheel. It's Ryle.

"Hey, Deacon. Long time no see."

"That's for sure." I put the case down and watch as he strides up the steps two at a time and pulls me in for a man hug. Daisy's jaw drops to the ground. I feel a stab of envy the way she is checking him out. I raise my eyebrows at her, she blushes and busies herself with Bonnie's carrier.

"Good to see you, Man." I say and open the door. He has a large, black travel bag slung over his shoulder. As soon as we open the door I see as Lottie's eyes pop like saucers and her lips separate. Damn this man is a pussy magnet if ever I saw one. Ryle is a nice guy though, he lost his wife not that long ago and this is his first time and away from his kid, Summer I think her name is.

Lottie makes no small thing of being impressed by man mountain Ryle with his dark hair and ice blue eyes, she twirls her hair around her finger. I roll my eyes. Daisy comes in behind me with the carrier and her over night bag.

"Here let me help you with that and take it to the room." I say. Our fingers touch, electricity pulses straight through my lower arm, and straight to the top. Surely she must have noticed it too.

"I got it." She sets the carrier down as Eliza and Sadie enter.

"Can we close the door so Bonnie doesn't make a run for it." Daisy says. Eliza closes the door. All of a sudden with us all filling the space, as large as it is, the cabin feels small. I can only smell Daisy and feel her closeness, I think it's getting hot in here.

"Great everyone is here. Fantastic." Sage claps her hand. Logan grabs Ryle in for a man hug.

"Glad you could make it, Man."

"Yeah, me too." Ryle says.

"Right before we have lunch we need to sort out the rooms. I have to confess I have made a bit of a boop. We've got four rooms, the master for Logan and I so leaving three rooms. Eliza you will want a room on your own and Geoff. That leaves, Sadie, Lottie and Daisy, Ryle with only two rooms left."

"I can share with Ryle." Lottie says way too cheerfully. Ryle looks like a scared rabbit and coughs.

"It's cool, I'll sleep on one of those sofas." He says.

"Yeah, I can sleep on the other one. " Lottie offers not missing a beat.

Ryle shifts from one foot to the other. I shoot him a sympathetic look. He rolls his eyes.

"I'm not sleeping on a sofa." Sadie comes out with, "definitely not next to Ryle he'll probably snore and wind. No thank you." She places her hands on her hips.

"Okay, so Sadie can have a room and share with either Daisy or Lottie. Deacon you want to sleep on the other sofa?"

"Yeah, I could do that."

"Oh wait, so why doesn't Ryle then have the last room and I can sleep down on the other coach?" I swing round to stare at Daisy. Is she insane? She can't sleep anywhere near me, no way.

"Don't be daft, let us guys sleep on the sofas." Ryle says.

All hell breaks out whilst Lottie and Daisy try to vie for a sofa.

"Get us some drinks would you, Logan." I say. Whatever happens, I need to make sure I am not in the same room as Daisy because I swear to God, my dick won't be able to contain itself.

Sage claps her hands. "Enough. This is what is going to happen. Eliza and her husband will have room 2. Deacon needs a room and he can share with Daisy. Lottie you will share with Sadie. Ryle sorry you have the short straw for the sofa."

"No problem I am a last minute addition, sorry to muck your plans up." I feel for him he's such a good guy.

"You haven't I am pleased you are here with us, it means a lot to Logan that you are here, Ryle. Please don't think like that." He nods at Sage's words.

Why is she putting me in with Daisy? What the hell is going on here. I glance at Daisy who is grinning like the cat who got the cream.

God help me. I'm going to have to slap a restraining order on my dick.

Chapter 28

Daisy

Oh wow, I am almost beside myself. Me and Deacon, one room, one bed perhaps, this could be all my dreams rolled into one. He looks very uncomfortable almost like he is squirming. Lottie shoots me a look and grins. Ryle looks from her to me. He looks like he is squirming too, I bet he is since Lottie has made no bones about the fact that she'd like to be jumping his bones tonight. I try not to guffaw. Sage appears mildly stressed, "come on let's crack the drinks open." I say, she needs something to take the edge off.

"Drinks, we're having lunch first and it's a maximum of one glass of wine or a beer each. Logan has got logs to bring in, the guys can help bring all your luggage in, you need to settle Bonnie down and then we're all going for a walk and a treasure hunt." Sage exhales.

"A treasure hunt? Oh, I don't think I am up for that." Sage almost glares at Eliza.

"It's not a massive trek, Eliza you can manage it." Eliza's husband chuckles.

"She isn't really one for walking unless it's to the corner shop are you, Dear?" She shoots him a look that says *shut it*. I chuckle, nothing will phase me today since I have the knowledge that Deacon and I will share a room.

"Er, is there a spare bed in the room?" Deacon asks out of the blue. Sage furrows her brow.

"Oh, for goodness sake, Deacon. You have known Daisy since she was a kid, behave yourself. I am sure for a couple of nights you two can act like adults. Stuff a pillow between you. I fucked up what can I say?" She raises her hands in the air then huffs out to the back of the cabin where I assume the kitchen is.

Logan shrugs his shoulders. "Wedding stuff, you know how it is guys." I pick my jaw off the ground, only Sage is usually pretty unflappable and has everything under control, but then I guess she hasn't had to try to plan a wedding before on top of all her other commitments and she sure does have a lot going on with work, fundraisers, looking after her and Logan's horses, running a clinic for teenage girls who have gotten themselves pregnant. It's exhausting just thinking about all the things Sage onboards one after the other.

"Right, I am going out to fetch the logs in. The rest of you can sort everything out in your allocated rooms. Deacon come give me a hand please after you take Daisy and Lottie's bags up. Ryle, can you help Sadie and Lottie with theirs please?" Logan sounds authoritarian all of a sudden, go bro. Ryle nods.

"Sure, no problem."

I walk through the open space, with its high vaulted wood beam ceiling, take a look out of the floor to ceiling windows on either side. The day is bright and sunny, the perfect fall day. I follow Deacon towards the wooden stair case checking out how tight and high his butt out. He sure must work out an awful lot. He's built mighty fine. He takes Lottie's big case up under one arm, the strength of that man. I wonder what it'd feel like for him to swoop me up in his arms and carry me to our bedroom tonight.

Oo, it makes me all warm and fuzzy just thinking about it as a rush of heat purrs its way up from my lower regions to my stomach. I clench my thighs together. He checks over his shoulder. "I hope you're not checking my ware out."

"Who me?" I blush, he caught me dammit. Lottie sniggers. I push her gently as we go up the wide staircase. At the top the railing goes round to the right, in front of us are three wooden, large doors and two at the far end of the corridor. "This way, Lottie, Sadie." He says and shows them to their room. "Here you go, I'll let you ladies get settled in and meet you with the others downstairs." He glances behind me and sees Eliza's husband with their luggage.

"Let me give you a hand." He says to Eliza's husband.

"Thanks, I think Eliza has packed the kitchen sink and the bath tub." He jokes.

"Which one is our room, hunk?" I ask Deacon. He rolls his eyes at me once he has placed Eliza's cases in the room allocated to them.

"This one." He points to a room at the end of the corridor which is also flooded with light from the sky lights and a side window. It sure does look pretty being able to look up and see the blue sky today without a cloud in sight. It's going to be a cold night but I know just the man who can keep me warm. I blush again thinking about Deacon and what he has hiding in his pants.

"Daisy." His voice brings me back to the now.

"Yes, coming." I'd like to be coming all over his cock. I follow him to the pine distressed door and allow him to open it before stepping inside. It's a large square space with sliding doors at the far end, which appear to lead onto a balcony. I walk towards it and take a look. "Wow the view of the mountains is breathtaking."

"It sure is. As you can see there is a sofa in here." I take a glance around and see it. A tiny little two seater made of a patchwork fabric with a blanket to match thrown over the back of it and a couple of scatter cushions. Next to it stand a small, round table with a 1920's lamp on it. Quaint. I love it.

"And *your* point is?" I raise my eyebrows at him.

"My point is, that is where I will be sleeping, Daisy." He has his hands on his hips, his narrow hips that show off just how broad and muscular his shoulders are. From the kid in High School, Deacon sure has grown into a fine looking man, I notice the stubble on his square jaw, it's sexy as hell. His voice is gruff.

"Don't be ridiculous it's tiny. You can sleep in the bed, just see how big that bed is and comfortable." I throw myself on it and pat the side by me.

"Forget it, Daisy. I am not getting in that bed with you."

"Relax will you, Deacon. I'll put some pillows between us, only I think it's going to be chilly this evening, I may need you to warm me up." There goes the eye roll again, as I smile sweetly.

He appears a bit hot under the collar, now he has his arms folded in front of his chest. "I don't think so."

"Why, are you scared of me?" I ask him, tilting my head to the side. Am I flirting with him? You bet I am.

"No, I'm scared of what I might do." His voice is deep and gravelly, it zings my entire body in an instant as butterflies erupt in my stomach and I feel wetness between my legs. This without him even touching me, but his eyes and the way he is looking at me, I can tell with his pupils now increased in size that he wants me as much as I want him. And I still haven't forgotten how close I was to him in the stable, nor how we were about to have a passionate embrace.

"Really? Is that so? Well then maybe we should do something about it."

"Don't tempt me, Daisy. I swear just don't even go there."

I cannot wait for tonight, It is a good job I have packed my finest lingerie. Having to share a bedroom at Sage's insistence is the icing on the cake.

Chapter 29

Deacon

"Deacon you and Daisy will be on one team." Sage tells me as I raise my eyebrows. What is with the whole pairing me with Daisy? Not that I mind, to be honest I was kind of hoping I'd be paired with the girl who has held my heart for the last ten years or so. Only, isn't Sage being a bit obvious or is she trying to meddle? Who knows, but I'm not complaining. Daisy huffs and places her hands on her narrow hips and blows a strand of hair off her cute face.

"I wanted to pair with Lottie." She says belligerently, I scoff. She glares at me.

"No, Lottie is pairing with Sadie otherwise Sadie doesn't have a pair." Sage confirms.

"What about Ryle, I could go with Ryle?" Lottie offers. Holy smoking, this is such fun watching the girls all trying to vie for Ryle, well at least Lottie. There is no shame in her right now. Ryle rolls his eyes, he's done that at least four times and I am beginning to lose count.

"What about you and Logan?" I ask. "How is that working?"

"We're not taking part since we came up with the clues. Eliza will be with her husband, Lottie will pair with Sadie, Ryle is helping Logan with wood now and sorting out the band and acoustics for the band later. They still have some touches to do to the bandstand." Sage explains.

"Easy way out." I say, and catch Daisy looking at me. I wink at her, she blushes.

"Okay, I guess being with Deacon isn't so bad." Daisy says and licks her bottom lip. It makes my stomach fizz, is she giving me the come on? I'd like to fist her hair, pull her head back and kiss those luscious, cherry lips of hers. There is definitely a glint in her eyes.

"Here are the clue sheets, do not lose them."

"What does the winner get?" Daisy asks Sage.

"You will receive a bottle of champagne and a box of Molly's Fudge." Logan steps in.

"Oo, I love Molly's fudge." Lottie says licking her lips.

"Me too." Sadie says. "Right, Lottie we've got to win this, besides, I never lose a treasure hunt."

"And guys, mobiles stay here, there will be no cheating. Everyone reconvenes at the cabin for lunch in ninety minutes." Sage hands out pink pieces of paper with fancy, italic kind of writing on in dark blue. Very feminine. I take the piece of paper only to have it snatched from my hands by Daisy.

"Mm, this smells beautiful. Where did you get these fragranced sheets from, Sage?" She asks smelling the paper still. Fancy shit, fragranced paper, it seems almost old fashioned.

"Hoogan's. He ran up my invitations for me and place settings. They all match."

"Beautiful." Eliza offers, her husband just hangs back, I am guessing Eliza wears the pants in that house.

"First clue," Daisy begins. "Getting the first clue will be a joy. Look for it where you would put your toy?"

Lottie begins to chuckle. "What kind of toy, like a vibrating toy?" Daisy and Sadie start laughing. I roll my eyes and Sage glares at them.

"Obviously not a vibrating toy. Girls, keep it clean, *please*." She implores. Logan guffaws.

"Toy box. Only where in this cabin would there be a toy box?" I ask and look at Daisy who is giving me *come to bed eyes*. Shit, she's doing something to me, my heart is melting and I can feel my dick wanting to spring into action, only I'm wearing tight jeans and can't be doing with having a hard-on in front of everyone.

"A bedroom. Come on Deacon let's go." She grabs me by the hand and starts to head up the stairs, we're followed hot on our heels by Lottie, Sadie, Eliza and her husband.

"See you guys later." Logan calls out as I watch him pull Sage in to him and kiss her. I love how they are together, their whole relationship and being together says it all, *forever*. Happiness is looking at those two that is for sure.

"Quick let's take a look in this room?" Daisy says eagerly.

"Hold on, shouldn't we ask to go in one of the other rooms, I mean it will have personal belongings in it?"

"Nah, no-one will mind."

"You can go in there." Lottie calls up with Sadie right behind her. Daisy swings open the first door and takes a glance around.

"It's a double room like ours, doubt there'll be a toy box in here."

"Maybe we should check our room first, only I am pretty sure there was a wooden chest in there." I know for a fact there is. Her hand feels warm in mind, electricity is pulsing right through my arm. I want to touch her more and pull her into my chest and kiss her, to inhale her shampoo on her hair. I'm wild for this girl and it's intense being so close to her, holding her hand.

She dashes down the corridor to where our room is and flings the door open. "Yes, over there by the window." She makes a dash for it and quickly opens the box. "It has toys in it and a pink piece of paper." She reads the next clue.

"Twist me and turn me and look into the ? this is where you can see your face." Daisy starts to squeal, I've never seen her so excited about anything, well except when she knew that the fowl was hers. "It's the lake, the lake. Come on, hurry up."

"We heard that, bet we get there before you two." Lottie shouts out. I groan, really, treasure hunts are so not my thing.

"On second thoughts, Deacon we could just stay here." What did she just say? She is looking between me and the bed. My heart begins to race, it's thumping so hard it could easily leap right out of my chest.

"Daisy, I told you before not to tempt me. If I start something with you, I don't trust myself to be able to stop."

"Good, maybe it's just what you need." Her voice is flirtatious. Jeez-us this firecracker is killing me. One of us has to remain sensible, even though I am struggling with that right now. How on earth am I going to cope with us sleeping together tonight, I have to remain strong? I cannot get entangled with Daisy. I want to start a family, I want a forever girl like Logan has Sage. And Daisy, well Daisy is still young, she will want to roam free and be wild not tied down to an old man like me. But hell, to feel her moving up and down on me, riding me like she wants me, her hair falling all over her shoulders. I groan. What's a man to do?

Chapter 30

D^{*aisy*} I am holding my breath as I wait for him to respond. Will he give in or not? That is the million dollar question only the way my clit is throbbing right now and how wet I am just looking at his broad shoulders and the way he tapers down to his narrow hips, I am hoping he says *forget the treasure hunt*.

"We can't. Everyone will know and I like to be discreet Daisy."

"You just don't want me do you, Deacon? I felt for sure you do though." Is my bottom lip pouting? You know what I think it is.

"Of course I want you. There you go, I have admitted it. But.." He rakes his long fingers through his hair. It looks sexy as does his stubble that's at least a few days old. I bet it feels all soft.

"But what? Don't be so chicken." I get up and move towards him. "Forget discreet, hell the whole of Willowbrook is waiting for us to finally get it on." I inch closer he stands with his legs hip width apart and his arms folded in front of his chest.

He doesn't move, I'm so close I can feel the heat radiating off him. I stand on my tip toes as he grabs the back of my head with one hand and forces my mouth onto his. Wild. Oh. My. God so fucking wild, I am *finally* kissing Deacon. My childhood crush, the boy that has grown up to be such a fine looking man and filled out perfectly, like one of those GQ models. He's everything I want and then some. His lips are soft, warm and squishy, did I just say that? Oh my. They are, it's like falling into a warm bed after a hard day. His tongue eaes open my lips and slides inside as he presses me closer into him, firmly holding the back of my head. I can feel his hardness through his tight jeans as it presses into my stomach.

That would be the stomach that is all a flutter with butterflies, literally hundreds of them going nuts in there, warmth creeps up from my lower regions and swarms through my body like a tidal wave. My heart is racing, my breath catches and then he places a hand on my lower back and draws me in even closer. I can feel the blood rushing to my ears.

His tongue finds mine, he tastes of beer I kind of like it. Would I ordinarily like second hand beer? Not on your life but on Deacon, it's damn good. Our tongues find each other and tangle, the pressure on the base of my spine and the back of my head is doing things to my body, electricity is running through me, the connection is like nothing I have ever experienced before. He is literally taking my breath away. This is no friendly kind of kiss, no way. This is all encompassing, the way he is searching and exploring me tells me this man wants me just as much as I want him.

I can feel my heart thudding in my chest, I bet he can feel it too. His warmth envelops me. "Hey guys where are you at?" I hear Logan's voice. "Ten minutes til Sage serves up. Meat is on the BBQ don't be too long. Where is everyone at?" I can hear footsteps. Deacon pulls away as if he has been scorched.

And I want to thump Logan one, I mean seriously? This is the second time he has cockblocked me and I am not one bit happy about it. That man has got *the* worst timing in the world.

"Sorry, I went too far. I didn't mean for that to happen." Deacon says only I can see from his dilated pupils that he is lying. Of course he wanted me just as much as I wanted him.

"Rain check on this, Deacon." I tell him as I give him a peck on the lips and sashay my way out of the room.

"What were you doing in there?" Lottie asks me giving me a holy shock as I come out of the bedroom. Then she sees Deacon coming out after me. "Er, did you two just?"

Deacon grins, "no we didn't. Get your mind out of the gutter, Lottie. Honestly." Why is he denying it. Don't worry, I'll be putting Lottie very straight later on before bed of how amazing my first ever kiss with Deacon was.

"There you are, jeez guys I thought we'd have to send a search party out for you both." Logan appears at the top of the stairs. I raise my eyebrows as I take in Lottie's messed up hair, why hadn't I noticed it before and Ryle coming out of a bedroom tucking his shirt in?

Wow, that is fast-tracking moving if ever I saw it. Only, hold on, didn't he keep rolling his eyes earlier? I place my hands on my hips and glare at Logan then at Lottie.

"What y'all waiting for? Food. Come on." Logan claps his hands, like doesn't he even guess what has been going on. I mean my bestie is a little flushed as no doubt am I, Ryle is grinning like a cat that got the cream and Deacon and I are standing way too close for just friends. I can feel his breath on the back of my neck, my instinct tells me to turn round and shove him back into the bedroom where we came from.

"Let's go." Ryle says. "I'm famished."

"I bet you are." I tell him. He raises his eyebrows at me. Lottie sniggers. "I suppose you are famished too are you Lottie?" She continues to giggle.

"Tell you all about it later, bestie." She marches down the stairs swaying her hips still dressed in those ridiculous pink leggings and sweater, okay they're not ridiculous but she does look a bit too Barbie right now.

"Lottie," she turns briefly. "Your leggings are on inside out."

"Fuck me." She checks and can feel the label on the outside at the back. Deacon guffaws, Ryle rolls his eyes and I bend over double laughing so much I could almost piss my own pants.

Chapter 31

Deacon
It is not easy to walk with a boner and try to go undetected and even worse I am not able to stuff my hands down my pants right now to rearrange myself. Thankfully, the girls and Ryle are distracted with Lottie and her on-back-to-front leggings. Well I have to say it didn't take Ryle and Lottie long to become acquainted. Good for them, life is too short in my opinion.

Daisy shoots down the stairs giving me a glance behind as she lowers her eyes to my crotch. I groan, Ryle shoots me a look but has the decency to act as if nothing is up. So I think until he says, "guess someone else had the same idea." He chuckles and heads down the stairs bypassing a flaming red Lottie who is now going back into a bedroom to get herself together. Not a bad idea.

But let me tell you, being pressed up so close to Daisy was intoxicating, the fragrant smell of her, the way her lips met mine, the softness and her tongue as she willingly gave it to me, surrendering herself. I have no doubt in my mind how amazing she would feel pinned underneath me with her legs wrapped around my waist and groaning my name. This is doing nothing for my hard cock situation, I need to get my mind off Daisy and her perfect body, the way her chest rose and fell, feeling her breasts pushed up against my chest. Oh, Lord I am in trouble and everything I promised myself I would not do with Logan's kid sister, I have just gone and broken the rule book.

I try to think of my next shift at the station, run through my domestic chores list at home, anything else but Daisy and her pert ass, the way her breath caught as I bit her lower lip and whispered into her ear. I told her I wouldn't be able to restrain myself, she is willing and eager. Okay, so I need to think about washing my truck or maybe the horses that I need to get on and ride when I'm back, wait what about the ins and outs of the riding school set up. Yeah, that'll make my raging hard-on go down some.

"Deacon are you coming?" Logan shouts up. Before I can answer, Lottie appears out of the bedroom with her leggings on the correct way.

"I bet he'd like to be." She yells back and sniggers as she races in front of me down the stairs.

"Not funny, so not funny, Lottie." This is what I mean, her and Daisy are so young, youthful, it reminds me of when Logan and I were just in our twenties, everything was funny and we had smart mouths too. Maybe I still do, but I don't use it quite as often.

Downstairs, Eliza and her husband are sitting at the island, Eliza is tossing the salad in a large wooden bowl, her husband drinks from a beer bottle. Sage glances up. "About time, what took you so long." She glances from Lottie to me.

"Hey not what you're thinking." I say as I hold both my arms up in the air, my hands facing her. She raises her eyebrows.

"Ask Ryle." I shoot at her. Logan almost spits his beer out.

"What?"

"Nothing, Man." Ryle says as he shoots me a look that distinctly says *keep it shut, Bro*.

Lottie goes to hug Daisy and gives Bonnie cat a stroke under her chin. "Where's Hector?" I ask to diffuse any further thoughts that Lottie and I could have been getting it on upstairs. Daisy on the other hand is sitting at the island with a large glass of white wine smiling as if she is the cat that got the cream. Bonnie goes over to her and jumps on to her lap. She fusses her cat, it's adorable. I watch as she strokes Bonnie's head, her long, slender fingers. Thinking how amazing they would feel gripping my cock. Shit. *Stop thinking like that, Man. Everyone is going to notice a boner in your pants.*

"He's with my folks for a couple of days." Logan replies.

"Who won the treasure hunt then?" I ask knowing full well it could only be Eliza.

"Well obviously not Lottie and I." Sadie pipes up also holding a large glass of white wine. "Since Lottie disappeared upstairs with either you or Ryle." Say it as it is girl I am thinking.

"Not with me, told you. I definitely have not been anywhere with Lottie." I say in my defense.

Lottie giggles and goes to Ryle and gives him a kiss on the cheek, he blushes. So he should, he's been here back in the group for five minutes, okay maybe back in Willowbrook a few days more but you get what I am saying and already he has caught himself a girl. Lottie is totally unabashed, he wraps an arm around her waist and pulls her into him.

"Wow that didn't take long." Sage comments and looks at the pair of them. Logan grins and raises his beer to Ryle.

"Kids these days." Eliza says with a cute smile on her face.

"I'm not a kid." Ryle says which is true. He is the same age as Logan and I, which gets me to thinking he doesn't seem to be phased about the age gap thing at all. So, why the hell am I? Is it because I feel older? Is it because I've been around the block and then some? Is it because my ways might just be a bit wild and forward for innocent Daisy. Not that I think she hasn't had sex before, she told me already she isn't a virgin. Now I want to smash whoever face it was that she gave her V-card up to.

My gut clenches, my stomach knots. What the hell is happening to me? Am I jealous? Me, Marshal Deacon jealous of some high school kid who probably had Daisy's consent to take her. Holy cow this isn't good. I wipe my head with my hand.

"Right, let's all go out the back. We've set the chairs and tables up whilst you guys were all misbehaving upstairs. By the way to answer Sadie's question it was team Eliza that won, of course." Sage informs us.

Eliza smiles broadly, good for them, I can only imagine they haven't gotten up to much shenanigans' for a little while. She turns and kisses her husband, adorable.

Logan lets Sage go in front holding the salad bowl, Eliza follows with some glasses, Lottie and Daisy grab bottles of wine, Ryle takes the cooler of beers in one hand and a platter of meats with the other. Logan follows up the train with a cheese board and crackers. Sadie takes a plate cake in each hand.

"Wow this is so pretty." Daisy says as we all get outside and she is right. The wooden pagoda is strewn with fairy lights casting a yellow-orange glow across the sanded wood deck, it's like something out of a fairy tale. There is a small stand set up with mics, drum kit and the electric guitars on their stands. "You guys *have* been busy." She says, her voice is enchanting, I want to kiss her there and then. To fist her hair and draw her lips to mine. It's all I can do not to stare at her and hang off her every word.

"I love it." Sadie says and places the cakes on one of the tables. "When are the band coming over?"

"Just gave them a call to let them know food is ready. The main meat is already on the BBQ. Let's tuck in."

We all sit at the tables, Daisy comes and sits right next to me and shuffles her chair up. I feel the heat off her body. She squeezes my leg right at the top of my thigh and brushes her thumb over my groin. My eyes almost pop out of my damn head. She grins wickedly at me and licks her lips.

Fuck me. What's a guy to do? No doubt sharing the room tonight is going to be difficult in trying to keep my composure.

"I can't wait for later." She breathes into my ear. My dick instantly stiffens, she chuckles and brushes it with her thumb again. I try to move her hand but she is clutching on to my leg like a vice.

"*Daisy*, I keep telling you, once I stop I will not be able to stop. You deserve better."

"I deserve you."

"I'm not how you think I am in bed, Daisy."

"Great, I can't wait to be under your control."

Jeez-us.

Chapter 32

Daisy

Oh my, you should have seen the look on Deacon's face, it was a picture. I almost feel sorry for that poor man, I know he is caught between a rock and a hard place so to speak. It's obvious he wants me and I couldn't be more obvious if I tried to be with him.

The band is striking up and Logan is taking to the stage. I know he's going to belt out one of his love songs for Sage. Apparently, he has been writing some new material. His voice is deep and rich when he begins to sing, his words flow. It's a song about his childhood sweetheart, who got away but came back and things weren't easy for a while, but he won her heart.

Honestly, the words are bringing a lump to my throat. I catch as Sage looks on at him, it's beautiful. Their love is what I want and preferably with Deacon. Even if he thinks he is too old for me. He is watching me watching Sage and Logan, I can tell from the corner of my eye. Lottie turns and gives me a glance and cocks her head. She is dying to speak with me, but I also know she doesn't want to leave Ryle's side, who has got an arm slung round the back of her chair. She sure didn't waste time getting cozy with our new firefighter in town. It makes me chuckle.

Deacon sitting so close to me is making me catch my breath, I could fan my face right now. I mean it's fall, we're high up in the mountain area so strictly speaking it's not that hot right now in the early evening which it is right this moment, but I am hot. Very. Hot. His presence it making butterflies swarm freely in my stomach.

YOU HANG THE MOON

"Nice song." He leans in and whispers into my ear, the sensation oh my god, that sensation makes my body alight. I am so ready for this man like never before. Sure, I've had relationships here and there but they were all kids from High School, not a masculine brute of a man like Marshal Deacon. He's always been mannish, you know what I mean. Broad shoulders, his scruff that he rarely shaves even though I know for a fact he gives his guys at the station flack for if they don't look shaved.

Sage, Eliza, Lottie and Ryle clap when Logan is finished. He extends his hand for Sage to head up to the make-shift stage where his band are waiting for her. "How about my beautiful lady, you come up here and sing a song with me for our good friends and family." She doesn't hesitate as she takes his hand and goes to stand next to him. They make me swoon, the way he wraps his arm around her tiny waist. Logan bends his head down to kiss my future sister-in-law and truly, I could not be happier for a better sister-in-law than these two. Oh, and what about when they have kids. I am hoping they have a whole brood, I want more nieces and nephews. I hardly get to see my other brother's kids since they don't live close to us at all and with his travelling for his business for long periods of time, my sister-in-law travels with him. They usually have stay aways from six months to two years.

"Aww, isn't that the cutest." I turn to say to Deacon, he is leaning back on his chair, his legs kicked out forward with his ankles resting one on the other. It doesn't go unnoticed by my eager eyes that it looks like he has a fairly sizeable package between his legs. I fan myself. He shoots up his eyebrows just as Sage begins to sing. It's one of their earlier duets which they wrote when they were in High School together, called *He is just a boy and I am just a girl*. It's a cute song and I still think they should be releasing their stuff on their own YouTube channel.

"Something getting you all hot and bothered, Daisy?" Deacon asks me, his lips upturned.

"No. What on earth makes you say that?"

"Oh, just the way you're checking me out between my legs and fanning your hotself there."

"So, you think I'm hot then do you?"

"Everyman in Willowbrook thinks you're hot, Daisy. I'm no different." My body literally zings, he thinks I'm hot. Ooo, I feel girlish like a fifteen year kid knowing that a senior thinks she is hot and sexy.

"Is that so. Maybe I just want one man in particular to think I'm hot, Deacon."

"Maybe he does already. What do you have to say to that?"

I am blushing furiously, I am playing with fire here. Flirting with Logan's best friend and all. Not that I bet, Logan would have anything to say about it. He's not really the possessive big brother, okay sometimes he was when I had started to bloom. Yeah, maybe. But I'm pretty sure he'd have no issues with Deacon and I hooking up. Only, I'm not just after a hook up but Deacon might be. After all he's in his mid-thirties and hasn't settled down yet. He has never mentioned wanting to or having kids and I definitely want kids. At least four of them. Two boys and two girl, even though I know it doesn't always work that way, honestly, I'd be happy with whatever the good Lord gives me.

"I'd say that's a good thing because I only think one man in the whole of Willowbrook is hot." I pronounce.

"Really and who exactly might that be, Daisy?" Is he for real, he's putting me right on the spot. He chuckles as his arms are folded in front of his chest. Sage is really belting the song out now with Logan. Lottie turns again in her chair, is she checking up on Deacon and I? Little minx I bet she is. I poke my tongue out at her.

"Childish." Deacon says. Instantly, I feel silly for doing that I mean it just highlights that even though I'm in my very early twenties, compared to him I probably come across as some kid.

"She deserves it." I smile at him.

"You didn't answer my question." He says watching me closely, I want to fan myself again. He's making my panties wet the way his eyes are on mine, he runs his tongue over his lower, full lip. He is a man-tease.

"Do I need to tell you, Deacon?"

"I'd like to know who my competition is, Daisy." He chuckles. I swat him on the arm.

"You." I breathe.

"I didn't hear you." He says. I glare at him and toss my hair over my shoulder. He grabs it with one hand and fists it as he brings my face so close to his, I can smell the beer on his breath. He brushes my lower lip with his thumb.

"Tell me again so I can be clear on that."

"You." I manage to say as my breath catches.

"I think you're extremely hot Daisy and there are things I'd like to do with you that no other man has ever done."

Did he really just say that? Am I panting? I think I'm panting. I catch Lottie giving me a sly wink and focus my eyes back to Deacon's. His forehead rests on mine. "But I won't."

He lets go of my hair and I almost collapse and pool into a puddle right there at his feet.

"I want you too. I want you to show me and teach me all the things I've never experienced." Whoa, aren't I the bold one? Where has this come from? It's not me, but this man is making me do and say things I'd never do or say before.

His lips are upturned, I bite my lower lip. "I want everything you've got Deacon."

His eyes are dark, his pupils are large I can see them even with just the fairy lights on and the candle lit on our table. "I can't go there with you, Daisy. Once I start, I'll never be able to stop. You will be my addiction."

My pussy is begging for him, my thighs clench together. "That's exactly what I want Marshal Deacon." I can see between his legs, that he's got a raging hard-on bulging in his pants and I am itching to take it in my hand and feel him in my fingers.

Deacon shakes his head whilst I am thinking, we'll see about that. He won't be able to resist me. Will he?

Chapter 33

D*eacon* Whoever would have thought that sweet and innocent little Daisy would be so bold and upfront when it comes to letting me know exactly what she wants. And where do I get off on being so bold back, but I can't resist. The words keep tumbling out of my mouth like there is no filter. Where Daisy is concerned there is no damn filter. Did I seriously just tell her that I want to show her things nobody else has? Fuck. I rake my hands through my short cropped hair. Yep, I did. That was me, the one and only.

She bites her lower lip, I raise my hand and run my thumb along it. She lets her tongue come out between her pouty lips and sucks on my thumb. A bolt runs right up my forearm and into my pants it feels like. My dick is straining, I swear it's going to explode any moment. How can one woman do this to me? She is unravelling me just by having the tip of her tongue on my thumb. Shit. What would she do to me if her lips were wrapped around my manhood?

"You guys okay over here?" Logan is by our table, his eyebrows raised. I am mortified, I mean his sister is practically fucking my thumb and she is most definitely eye fucking me right now.

"All good." I cough and try to adjust myself on the seat without giving away that I have a raging hard-on going on right now. Daisy swings one leg over the other and glares at Logan.

"Are you the checking police, only everytime I seem to be too close to Deacon you appear like a puff out of nowhere?" Her cheeks are still flushed, no doubt from me whispering in her ear about the things I could be showing her.

"Just checking. You're still my kid sister, Daisy don't be forgetting it."

"How could I ever, Logan?" She huffs and folds her arms in front of her chest. Logan glares at me.

"Unless you're going to do something about it and not some damn fling or anything, then leave it."

"Don't call me an *it*." Daisy's eyes are even narrower than a feline cats can get. Logan glares back at her. Honestly, I didn't think there would be such an issue so now you can see exactly why I was trying my darndest to leave Daisy the hell alone.

"A word." Logan says to me and cocks his head towards the back of the cabin away from the tables and folk.

"Excuse me a moment please, Daisy." I say as I stand and follow Logan toward the cabin.

"Listen, it's no secret that you like Daisy and she likes you. It's been brewing since she was in High School. My sister has always been carrying a torch for you. I get it, I really do. But you don't want to settle down, you're seeing that woman in Coppertown and I worry for Daisy. I'm her elder brother, you know I care about her. I don't want to see her getting hurt." I take in what he is saying and to be honest if I had a kid sister and especially one that was ten years younger than the man she had her sights set on, I'd be having the same conversation with the dude.

"I understand, Logan. I haven't seen my lady friend in Coppertown for a couple of months now. In fact I haven't been seeing anyone." I tell him. He doesn't need to know that my dick and my hand have become pretty damn close lately. Why did I stop seeing her? Truth is, I don't particularly care anymore for seeing someone for just sex. Maybe I've grown out of it after all these years of emotionless sex. And of course I do have feelings for Daisy. They run deep, I can't deny that anymore and to hell with it, I don't want to hide it anymore.

"I have a deep respect for Daisy, Logan. She means more to me than you will ever realize. To be honest, I have been keeping my distance out of respect for her. She's young. She has her whole life ahead of her, I don't want to get in her way. I'm not getting any younger and I may want a family of my own. Saying, I don't want to settle down isn't the case anymore. I want what you and Sage have got, what Eliza has with her husband. Maybe it's time I started to put roots down so to speak and have the woman and the babies."

He looks at me and cocks his head. "About fucking time, Deacon. I never thought I'd hear you say the words."

"Well, if I'm honest I had to figure it out for myself and I've tried to my darndest to stay away from Daisy but she's like a light attracting me, and I'm dealing with the whole age gap thing. It's on her to be honest, maybe I'll just be a fling for her, maybe she just wants to know what it is like to be with a more experienced mind. Who knows with Daisy, only for me, I want the whole nine yards."

Logan slaps me on the back. "In that case you have my blessing. You know, though you're going to have to go through my old man, right?"

"That scares me some." Not that their father is a scary kind of guy, but it'll be an absolute first for me. Laying my intentions on the line.

"Let's just see where this goes first, no need to get your father involved. It's Daisy's call now. Nobody else's. If she wants me for the long haul then of course, I'll speak to your father, but if she is just after a fling well then it'll be my heart that gets torn apart."

"That bad, eh?"

"Something like that, yeah. Never thought I'd feel this way about a woman. Honestly, your kid sister, she's gripped my heart and has spoilt me for all the other women out there. In my opinion, that girl sure does hang the moon. If I could get it and give it to her, I would."

"Best of luck then, Deacon. I won't stand in my way, but..." There's always a but, right?

"If you hurt her, you will have me to answer to and I won't hold back." I nod. There is no way on earth that I would want to hurt Daisy. It's going to be me that gets hurt if she only wants me for a fling. I'd happily lay my heart on the line though for Daisy. I'd practically do anything.

"Let's get back to the party. We have a cake to cut that mom made specially for tonight." I follow Logan back, Daisy glances in our direction as I take a seat back down next to her.

"Everything okay?" She asks. Damn she looks cute with her wide eyes and slightly upturned nose. I lean into her and place my arm around the back of the chair.

"It will be."

"Does that mean you're going to succumb to my feminine charm?" I chuckle.

"I'm all yours, Daisy. Do as you will."

Chapter 34

D*aisy*

The shivers that are running up and down my spine and the tingles from my head to my toes, which are curling in my boots, are tipping me over the edge the way he talks to me and his warm breath grazes the side of my face.

"Hey guys, are you coming to dance?" Lottie asks as she stands up and grabs Ryle's hand.

"I'm not much of a dancer, Daisy." Deacon tells me.

"I'll show you then, line dancing isn't that hard, you can do it. Hell anyone can. Come on let me show you my moves." I am flirting like a wild cat with her tail in the air and you know what? I don't give a damn. This man has practically told me he is all mine and that I have the biggest, brightest green light ahead. Do you all know how long I've been waiting for this? It's like all my Christmases have come at once, like I've been given all the birthday cake and don't have to share it. I mean, some girls want rocks and diamonds, they want the stars, the moon, they want the earth to be shifted for them and then some. All I've ever wanted is to have Deacon and it looks like finally my dream is going to come true. I am literally, I tell you, *literally* tingling with anticipation.

"Okay then, Buttercup lead the way." *Buttercup*, ooh I like that it sounds so sexy coming from his lips. I grab his large hand, he tucks his fingers around mine and I notice how perfectly I fit in his hand. Like our hands were meant to be united from birth. I know I'm a huge sap right when it comes to Deacon but honestly, have you not had the hots for some one since you were a kid?

Lottie and Ryle are already on the makeshift dance floor, the band are playing one of their own country songs, it's up tempo and Sage is flinging her arms around over her head. It makes me smile to see her totally lost in the moment, normally she's pretty serious though not as serious as when she came strolling back into Willowbrook some six months or so ago, I'm telling you that girl had a serious attitude back then and was the grumpiest woman I've ever encountered. She had this thing about avoiding Logan who wasn't about to let this woman slip from his fingers again. That man has the patience of a saint, but look at them now. He reaches his arms around her waist and pulls her into him so her back is against his chest and nuzzles into her neck and causing her to turn and kiss him. It's romantic, they are romantic and making me swoon.

Lottie is already showcasing her moves and Ryle is doing a good job of keeping up with my minxy friend, those hips are swaying and her booty is doing it's thing. I chuckle as Deacon steps onto the platform and pulls me close into him in one swoop. Oh wow, my hands make contact with his broad, taut chest. He is rockard and I cannot wait to run my hands up and down his naked body later when we get back to the room.

I'm already wet at the mere thought of him being so close and personal with me. He tilts my chin up with his thumb and forefinger. "Show me what you got then Miss Daisy. I can't wait to see these moves." I can feel he is stiff in his pants. That's gotta be obvious right? He forces me in closer using his other hand on my lower back. I am swooning like a damn fangirl and my legs feel as if they're about to buckle under his touch and closeness.

He swishes me out away from him and releases my hand as I watch him tuck his thumbs into his jeans belt and start to tap his toes and my word I am absolutely blown away. *Can't dance my ass.*

Rockinghorseshit. This man can move like sex on legs, I mean my mouth is open my jaw is on the ground and I am drooling like a teenager. Marshal Deacon is a wet panties dream for every girl out there. I catch Lottie clapping and giving me a wink.

Oh, boy Deacon is making my stomach flutter, my chest is rising and falling like the devil in a furnace. I have to fan my face. Deacon gives me a goofy grin. "Moves Daisy. Get to it Buttercup." His words, that drawl, the sex in his voice I clench my thighs together. He steps closer all the while not letting his moves down.

"You getting all wet in your panties Buttercup?" I almost want to launch myself at him, throw him back and straddle him right this second. How can one man be so damn HOT?

"I'll show you Deacon what moves I've got and you'll be fanning yourself in seconds. Watch me go, big boy." He smirks and gives me a grin. I start to move, my feet moving fast and in with the music. Deacon nods his head as if he is impressed. Lottie claps from behind and Eliza and her husband are cheering me on. I fly through the track, enjoying every minute of it. The band change track but keep the tempo up, now I'm right in my rhythm. Deacon comes and stands behind me, his fingers dig into my hips, my ass is right against his groin. I can feel his hardness and begin to move my hips against him.

"Don't make me explode in my jeans, Daisy. You want to ride this stallion later don't you Buttercup? Nice and slow, easing on it, riding it up and down." Fuck, I want him to rip my panties down right now and show me what he's got. I swear if I weren't out here with folk around, I'd be on him like a cat in heat.

"You're a big tease, you know that Deacon." I gasp and groan as he moves so I can get a nudge of his hardness through his jeans.

"Me? Well, I don't seem to be the one pushing their ass into my groin right now. But let me tell you, Daisy you sure got some moves."

He chuckles in my ear as he presses deeper into my hip bones. It feels delicious and sends a flood of heat and intensity through my core.

"You guys are going to need to get a room. "Lottie says as she steps forward with Ryle in tow.

"Hush your mouth." I tell her. She giggles and grabs Ryle's hand to go towards their table.

"You want a drink cool you down some, bestie." She is not funny. Although a drink does sound like a good idea, and actually so does a might freezing cold shower. He has got me all streamed up and then some.

"I'll have a drink." I tell Lottie as Deacon lowers his head. I can feel his warm breath against my skin.

"I'm going to show you things no other man has, Buttercup. Are you ready for me?"

Fuck. What? "I was born to be ready for you Deacon." He throws his head back and laughs.

"That might well be true my Buttercup."

Chapter 35

Deacon

This girl shakes me to the core, my whole body zings and is on fire for her. Now she wants to have a damn drink and all I want to do is fist her hair, pull her sweet cherry lips onto mine and throw her over my shoulder, into the cabin, up the stairs and on to the bed and have my wicked way with her.

"You want a drink too, Deacon? You look might heated up yourself. Must be all that dancing." Lottie giggles. Ryle raises his eyebrows at me.

"I'm good, Lottie thanks." She nods and heads over to the big metal crate packed with ice that houses the beers, to the side are buckets with white whine in on the wooden table, dressed with fairy lights around it and some bottles of red wine.

"You having fun, Bro?" I ask Ryle.

"Yeah, it's good to be here. Hanging with you and Logan, couldn't be better."

"Glad to hear it. It's good you have yourself stationed at Willowbrook, we missed you for a while." It was a long time that we missed Ryle. He moved away about eight or nine years ago now, then got married had the kid and well, it's a sad story about his wife. I don't even know how I would feel if something were to happen to Daisy. I think my heart would crumble and I'd not be able to breathe.

Lottie comes back and hands a glass of white wine to Daisy, a beer to Ryle and has a red wine for herself. "Let's go sit. Come Daisy you can tell me about your evening." She giggles. Girls, right?

I give Daisy a stern look, her eyes are open wide and her lips are parted. I bend my head down so my mouth is on her ear. "Don't be long, my dick is aching for your pussy." She lets out a low moan.

"And I want to run my tongue along your slit and bite on your aching clit. I bet it's throbbing right now isn't it, Buttercup?" Yeah, she is biting her lower lip now and blushing. She's actually gone past the blushing stage and straight into beetroot.

"Come." Lottie's insistent voice comes from the table behind us.

"Don't forget Buttercup, don't be long. Otherwise, I'm going to have go take a nice warm shower and let the water trickle down my body as I take my cock in my hand, fist myself and pump my cock until I come all over my fingers." Her eyes pop wide open.

"Oh, Daisy I told you I was no good for you. I'll ruin you Buttercup." She drinks some of her wine, her eyes like saucers.

"Good, that's exactly what I want Deacon." Daisy tilts her chin up as if I haven't shocked her with my dirty, filthy mouth. And winks at me. Well, I'll be damned this girl has got some spunk, I'll tell you that. Only, I know those guys she has been with have got nothing on me, I'm a real man. I know what I want and how to give to a woman, selflessly. It's my pleasure to make sure that Daisy is totally content when I am finished with her and I want to take my time with her and over her sweet body. She is as ripe as a peach.

Daisy bites her lip. "I'll be with you soon. Why don't you go and chat with Ryle and Logan."

I pat her ass, she jumps. "Daisy, come on will you already." Lottie pulls on the back of Daisy's top. As much as I like Lottie, I am personally thinking right now she is a little cockblocker. My dick is straining in my tight jeans, it needs to be unleashed and inside Daisy's tight, wet pussy.

Daisy goes to sit with Lottie. Ryle gives me a knowing look. "Hear you want to set up a riding school for the kids." He opens the conversation.

"Yes, it's kinda coming along. I have a couple of horses and we went to the auction the other day and picked up a couple more. I bought Daisy a colt. She is in love with it." Ryle chuckles.

"I can see that. All girls love a horse. Man, I cannot believe our boy Logan is getting married to his childhood sweetheart. Sure has been a road for those two." Ryle shakes his head.

"Sure has. They deserve this though. I'm over the moon these guys are finally with each other. It's like their journey has come full circle. He's had such a bad time when his wife died and then Sage coming back in to Willowbrook, well it's been a windy road for them. But look at them now." Am I sighing with contentment for them? I think I might be. It's awesome to see my best buddy happy, the look on his face as he looks at Sage, it's like she hung the moon or something. I can tell his heart is bursting with pride for the woman that stands by his side. All these years, ten years apart and now together, finally. If love stories and romance books are anything to go by, these two deserve a feature.

"I'm ready." Whoa, Daisy is in my face out of nowhere. Nothing shy about her this evening.

"I guess that means we're going for a stroll then." I take her small hand that fits perfectly in mine. The band plays some slow track as we begin to walk away from the folks and leave the party behind us. "Didn't you want to stay for cake?" I ask her as she holds tightly onto my hand. I love how her tiny one fits inside mine like we were made for each other.

"I'd rather have my cream another way, Deacon." I almost choke. Little Daisy has grown up and it seems she has a dirty little mouth on her.

"What's up, Deacon? Not so innocent now am I? I told you, I'm all woman." I chuckle.

"Is that so, Daisy? And I'm going to corrupt you in a million different ways when I finally get you up in that bedroom."

"I'm ready for you, Deacon." She says with full confidence. Damn, she is sexy. Not only does she look like a vision with her long, flowing blonde hair all over her shoulders, her full lips smiling and her eyes gazing up at me, but she is confident and bold.

As we reach the cabin, I turn to her and rest one hand behind her head at the base, with my other I trail my fingers down her face to her chin, tilting it up that my lips can meet hers. "You are the most beautiful woman I've ever met." Daisy whimpers at my touch as I caress her jaw with my thumb, her body presses against me and my dick swells in my jeans.

Our lips meet, my tongue glides across her lips. She parts them to allow me entry and damn she tastes of heaven and wine. A murmur passes as I delve my tongue further into her mouth. "I've waited so long for this Deacon. I am so ready for you." She is breathless, I can feel her racing heart beating against my chest.

"You sure about this, Daisy? You can back out. I understand. I mean, I'm ten years older than you. You can have any man you want." We pull apart, our heads resting together. Her hands firmly on my broad chest.

"No way. I want you Deacon. I've wanted you since High School. I don't care about the age gap not at all. You're the only man for me Marshal Deacon." She smiles, my heart flutters. Yes, it actually flutters. What the hell is going on? My heart has never fluttered for any woman.

With one swoop I place my arms beneath her legs and lift her up. Daisy hooks her arms around my neck and rests her head on my shoulders. "If you want me to stop at any time you just tell me okay, Buttercup."

"Sure, but I'm telling you Deacon, I won't ever want you to stop." I kiss her waiting mouth and head inside with her in my arms, through the kitchen area and the open plan living space and head straight for the stairs.

As soon as we get to the bedroom, I manage to open the door, step inside and kick it closed with my right foot behind me. The bed awaits us. Gently, I lower Daisy down. Her head splays out over the pillows, she looks like a vision from heaven, an Angel sent here to me. She looks so young and it scares me half to death how much my mind, body and soul wants this woman.

"Tell me what to do." She says and fuck if that doesn't almost send me over the edge.

"Take your clothes off, Buttercup. Slowly and tease me." She groans as I stand at the edge of the bed watching her slide out of her jeans. I give her a hand by helping to pull them off. She wriggles until they're finally down. Why do girls wear these clothes so damn tight, surely they can't be comfortable?

I help her to sit up to remove her top until she is just in her lacy bra and panties. "Fuck, Daisy you are so beautiful." Her skin is tan and looks as soft as silk. My dick strains. Slowly I unbuckle my belt and remove it from my jeans then undo the buttons and let them slide down. Daisy licks her lips. She is so sensuous.

I pull my top over my head and discard it on the floor by my feet. "Are you absolutely sure about this Buttercup because once I start, I don't think I'm going to be able to stop?"

"Yes." She nods, her eyes are hooded as I watch her taking in my broad shoulders, my flat stomach and the bulge in my boxers.

God help me, I am going to lose my shit just looking at her. How am I going to stop myself from coming in seconds when I touch her?

Chapter 36

Daisy

The way he is looking at me right now and the desire in my eyes makes me feel like I am the only woman in the world and the most beautiful woman alive. I am so desperate for him and the way he is teasing me by kissing my thighs and circling his thumb on my clit is literally, driving me insane. I am breathless, this man is a God.

"You are so beautiful, Daisy. I'll never stop telling you." He looks directly into my eyes and I can see something else. Is it deeper than just attraction and lust? I know that the way my heart is racing and banging in my chest that what runs through me is more than an attraction to the gorgeous, handsome very masculine Marshal Deacon. It always has been ever since High School when he started to fill out to be the man he has become. My eyes have only ever been on him, probably, no definitely the reason why I have never settled with anyone nor wanted to.

"Do you want me now, Daisy. I am ready to explode you are making it very difficult not to like a horny teenager." His voice is gruff and husky. Damn it makes me tingle all over.

"Yes, don't make me wait any longer. Deacon, I've waited half my life for you, now is *not* the time to wait." He lowers his head between my legs, his warm mouth touching my core, electricity bolts through me, I roll my eyes back and run my fingers over his short cropped hair. It's surprisingly soft, I anticipated it would be coarse but nothing about this man is.

Deacon licks my slit and enters a finger inside me, my hips buck up at his touch, I am close to orgasm all this tension and teasing each other, all the flirting it's almost sending me right over the edge. I hold back as best I can because I don't want him to think I'm new to all of this. Which of course I am not, but to be honest, I've never really had anyone between my legs like this. The guys I have dated before, well they were just selfish now that I think about it, and only in it to get themselves off. Have I ever really had a true orgasm except for when I've used my toys? Probably not.

He lazily runs his tongue up an down, my legs grip his face not caring at this moment whether I am suffocating him or not. "Take what you want, Daisy. Don't be shy." He murmurs and the vibration is too much for my hyper-sensitive lady bits. This is divine, I could feel like this forever. Dammit I want to feel like this forever. Maybe Deacon only sees this as a hook up. I haven't thought that far for now I'm going to ride with it and do as he says. I don't feel embarrassed with his tongue on my clit, his fingers working their magic inside my wet pussy. He sucks on my clit, the pressure is something else entirely as he continues to work his finger then slides another inside. He eases it in, and I realize how tight I really am.

"Damn, Daisy you are tight, so fucking tight." I move my hips faster bucking up with every stroke of his tongue, the pressure is mounting, heat rolls up my stomach and I can feel the first waves of orgasm about to take over my body.

"Scream my name, Daisy. Scream as loud as you like. Be a good girl for me and let me hear it drip off your tongue as you let go." He works magic, his fingers with just the right amount of pressure, his tongue working away on my slit and his lips tugging and teeth nipping at my swollen, aching clit. I bring my fingers up to my breasts and begin to roll my budding nipples between my fingers and my thumb. They ache, they need to be touched, they are literally begging to be squeezed. He looks up.

"You are one sexy woman, that's so hot watching you play with your titties like that. You're driving me over the edge, Buttercup." His voice, his words, I am there as the wave burns right through me and I release with such an intensity that my legs grip his face even tighter as I ride him with abandonment not caring about anything except chasing this wild orgasm. As I come I cry out his name not even caring if anyone can hear me. My breathing is heavy. Deacon kisses me between my legs gently, then strokes my thighs which are trembling.

"Deacon." I breathe.

"I know, Daisy. I know." He kisses my mount and all the way up my stomach to my breast which are all a jingle-jangle. Fuck this is intense. Then he trails his lips up my sternum to my collar bone, to my neck and jaw and finally resting on my own lips. His feel like soft squidyy pillows, I allow his tongue to enter my mouth.

"You are beautiful, Buttercup. The most beautiful woman I have ever known and you taste damn sweet like sugar and honey. I think you may just be my new addiction, Buttercup."

I groan into his mouth, feeling his hardness on my stomach. "Are you ready for me, Daisy? Can I put myself inside you now?" Like he needs to ask but it makes my heart flood with something, just the mere fact that he is so considerate and not taking me because he can. It's tender the way he kisses me and looks at me, his eyes are soft and warm. There is definitely something more there, but I can't identify it. All I know is this man is making me feel like I hung the moon.

I nod. "Wait, I need to put on a condom." Shit, I forgot about those pesky things. Even though I have been tested and on the pill, I know it is for the best. After all not everything is one hundred percent safe. Deacon rolls off gently nipping at my collarbone, sending a shiver down my body and grabs his pants off the floor.

Watching, he removes the condom from the back pocket and uses his mouth to tear it. "Let me." I say just before he kneels to put it on himself. "Sure?"

"Sure." I take it from him and grab his swollen cock, I admire the veins that pop all over it, damn this man is HUGE. Like, will he even fit in me, how will I accommodate a cock this big.

"I'll go in gently and slowly." He tells me as if reading my mind. I gulp because I've never had something so huge presented to me before. His balls look high and tight as I slide the condom on and sheath him. "Damn Buttercup, your touch is featherlight, I could easily spill everywhere just with your touch."

Deacon lowers himself propping up on his elbows so as not to squash me with his weight. I feel the tip of his engorged cock at my entry and tremble with anticipation. My breathing is shallow and his breath catches as his head touches the outside. "Shit." He murmurs. "I'm going to explode."

Slowly, very slowly he begins to slide inside me, I wriggle my hips some to try to accommodate him and feel myself stretching. It hurts a little but it's minor compared to the divine feeling as he moves in inch by inch. "You feel so good." I manage to breathe out as I suck in each time he moves deeper inside.

"You okay, Buttercup?" I nod. Of course I am okay I am fucking loving the way he feels inside me. He stops everything to make sure I have him. "Am I hurting you?"

"No. You feel amazing. Please don't stop Deacon, I want to feel you make me come all over your cock."

"Dirty mouth, huh?" He waggles his eyebrows at me.

"You can talk." He chuckles, the skin around his eyes crinkles. I want to kiss him, he senses it and brings his full lips onto mine, my heart is flying out of my chest, I feel as if I am floating on a cloud. The intimacy it feels almost too much as I wrap my arms around his head. I am breathless as Deacon begins to move slowly rocking his hips, I raise my ass a little bit and wrap my legs around his waist to allow him deeper access.

"Daisy." His voice is warning. "Hold on a second do not move. You will make me explode in seconds." I chuckle. Wow, to have this effect on him is powerful, you know what I mean. I try my hardest not to move, it's not easy when your entire body wants to be unleashed and run like the devil with a crucifix in its face.

Deacon begins to move faster, his hips are rocking forward and back, I raise mine to meet him, we find our rhythm, I grip on tighter with my legs around him as he rests on one arm, his bicep bulging, fuck it is so sexy and his other arm he places under me, grabbing my ass and lifting me higher. Oh, wow the friction on my clit against his lower abdomen is sensational, it is exactly what it needs. I grind and buck as he pounds faster and deeper into my needy, wet pussy.

"Are you going to come for me like a good girl, Buttercup? I am close to the edge." His voice whispers into my ear, his breath warm.

"Now, Deacon please now. I'm so ready, I'm......" I can't say anything else as he runs on me like crazy every thrust filling me up, diving deeper into me. My head rolls to the side, my eyes to the back of my head and my hands dig into his shoulders. Yeah, he's probably going to have some nail marks on his soft, tan skin. But I don't care as I grip him like a vice and scream out his name for the second time.

"Fuck. Fuck. Fuck. I'm coming, Buttercup come with me." I don't need him to tell me but this passion takes over and I am crashing, I thrash and buck and grind until my orgasm washes all over my body feeling Deacon pumping his come inside, his pulsing cock feels like heaven on earth. White lights flash in front of my eyes and I swear to God I am seeing fireworks.

Intense
Earth moving
Fireworks

Deacon lowers himself and kisses my lips. "You okay, Buttercup. Sorry if I went a bit wild there I couldn't hold back any longer." I smile at him, he looks peaceful and beautiful with his upturned lips and eyes that would melt your heart.

"I loved how wild you got riding out on me. I can do this all night long with you Marshal." He chuckles and nuzzles my neck.

"That Buttercup is what I intend to do. But first, let me get rid of this condom and get you a warm cloth. You'll be a bit sore." He makes me swoon how caring he is.

I watch as Deacon stands, removes the condom and heads into the bathroom where I hear him run the tap. He comes back with a navy washcloth that is warm to touch as he places it between my legs. He holds it there for a few seconds, my heart is pooling and melting. Deacon bends his head down and kisses my shoulder. "You are one beautiful, amazing woman, Daisy. I've never experienced anything like this before."

"Me neither, Deacon." I don't want to ask what it really means for now I want to be only in the moment with this beautiful man who is taking care of me after sex.

"I've got this." Placing my hand on the cloth that is soothing between my legs. Not that I mind the delicious ache between my legs right now, no way I am loving it.

He releases and comes to lay on the bed beside me, his arm under my neck and pulls me into him. He is warm and smells masculine and of sex. It's my new favorite fragrance, Marshal Deacon will fill my senses for eternity.

Chapter 37

eacon

D Damn my heart is still racing, Daisy has got me doing summersaults and all sorts of things. I swear I had fireworks go off and bright white lights as I released with her moving against me, her hips moving with mine as one. The way her pussy grabbed me, tight and needy. As she lays in my arms, one of her arms stretched out across my chest, her breathing slow and gentle and murmuring like a kitten when it is dozing off, fills my entire being with something. I don't know what because trust me, I have never felt anything like this before.

But the way we were together just now, that was all together a new experience for me. I have never been so turned on by a woman, never taken to such heights or felt a release like that. The earth felt as if it had moved. I look down at her and my heart literally bursts, it explodes and the fierceness in my chest to take care of her and protect her is so strong it scares the holy crap out of me.

She's soft, gentle and so damn small compared to me, the way she fits in my arm her head on my chest giving off sighs of contentment, my chest is puffing like a bear. "You okay, you need anything? A damp, warm cloth?"

She sighs and places a kiss on my chest. "No, I'm all good for *now*." Her voice is full of innuendo. "Can't wait for the next round. You sure do know how to keep a girl hungry for more, Deacon. Is it like this with all the girls? Have you always been so amazing at sex? It was incredible, like I've never had anything feeling this way before."

Damn, if that doesn't make my chest swell even more and make me have a big head. Am I really her first too at experiencing what has just passed between us? Thank God, because I want it to be that way, I want to be the first man that has made her orgasm quite like that. Earth shattering, earth moving and taking her to dizzy heights and beyond. Like she just did to me. I cannot identify what this feeling is that is going on inside my chest, all I know is that I never want to let Daisy go again. I want to hold her like this every day, I want her in my bed forever, until I am old, grey and a gnarly ninety year old man.

"So, you think I'm good in bed do you then, Buttercup?" She gives me a playful punch on my chest.

"Of course. And yes, this is the first time it has felt like this for me. Did you feel it too?" Her voice is a whisper, kind of like she is somewhat nervous to ask. I forget, Daisy is ten years younger than me. Holy crap. Ten years. What have I just done, having sex with her and being Logan's sister too.? The kid with the braces, pig tails, running around with dungarees, who'd have thought that one day she would be in my bed.

Listen, don't get me wrong I have wanted Daisy ever since she began to change when she was in High School. I couldn't help noticing that the young kid, Logan's little sister was growing up, the way she began to fill out her T-shirts, her endlessly long, lean legs, the way her face took on a more grown up look and that smile that could knock a ball right on out of the park. Yeah, I noticed and I was hungry for her then. It seems I have been hungry for Daisy, my Buttercup since she was about sixteen. It makes me feel like a damn, old pervert if I am honest.

"It was different for sure, Buttercup. You made me see white flashing lights and fireworks. You hang the moon, Daisy." She giggles like a teenager and runs her hand over my chest, causing the heat to rise from my groin again. I swear this woman has a magic touch, she definitely has a hold on me. My dick responds to her featherlight touch and I know I am ready to go again. But, I have to remember that Daisy will need a break, she must be sore since she was so tight and I am not built that way.

"Good. I've waited a long old time for you, Marshal Deacon I'll have you know and now I've got you." She sounds like the cat that got the cream. I chuckle and kiss the top of her head and pull her in closer to me.

"And I you too, Daisy."

She props up on one elbow and looks deep into my eyes. She is beautiful, more beautiful than any woman I know. Forget those models in the magazines or those so called hot shot A list actresses, this girl she is real and magnificent. Daisy is the shining star that will lead you through a dark and stormy night.

"Seriously, you're not just saying that? Only, I know you have a lot of experience. More so than me." I lift her chin with my thumb and forefinger.

"Never been more sure of anything in my life, Buttercup. You just rocked my world." I don't tell her that I want her to rock it forever, for the rest of my days. I don't want to scare this beautiful, amazing woman away. I mean, she may just want me to gain experience or to cross me off her list of things she wants to do before she finds The One to settle down with and have kids with. My heart lurches just thinking about her being with a nother man, a man who might put a ring on her finger and betroth her and have kids with her. In fact it grips me so hard I can hardly breathe.

"Hey, you okay?" She asks her eyes widening. "You've got a strange look on your face all of a sudden. Was I being too much too soon?"

"No." I reassure her. "I think it was a bit of indigestion or something." God, now I am becoming a liar. Shit.

"I know you probably think I'm some kind of kid still, but I hope I just proved that I am not." She wiggles her eyebrows at me.

God, this woman will undo me time and time again. I lower her head and allow my tongue to enter her mouth and kiss her with love and longing. I do not want my Buttercup to have any doubts in her mind about how I feel towards her. Is it too soon? Possibly but I want her to know I am not hooking up with her for just a night. If this is her intention then I will live with it. Won't I? Okay, so now I'm lying to myself of course I couldn't. I imagine seeing Daisy on some other guy's arm laughing and joking, smiling up at him the way she smiles at me and it almost causes me to have a seizure.

Her tongue shamelessly plays with mine before she sucks on it, which sends my dick into a total spin. It hardens for her and I am ready to take her again. Without giving her time to think, I turn and flip her over so she is on her back and pin her hands together above her arms, I move her legs apart with my hips and snuggle between her legs. With my free arm I move my hands down to her core and feel her slickness.

"You're so wet for me again, Daisy." I tease her with my head bent over her breasts and suck on her nipples one after the other, teasing them, biting and nipping at them and causing her to moan my name.

"Always wet for you, Deacon even when you're not with me." That makes me even harder and tightens my balls. I like the thought of her wanting me all the time. If it is the last thing I do, I'm goig to make Daisy ruined for all the other men out there. I can't think of her being with another man or not wanting me time and time again. I don't want to be an infatuation that she is satisfied with in a few week's time, I do not want to be the man she used for experience and who she had a crush on and no longer needs. I want to be her everything.

She is consuming me, the way her body wriggles underneath my powerful form. Her legs wrap around my waist as she pushes her pussy up against my stomach trying to get friction on her clit.

"You want me again, Buttercup? You want me to fill your pussy with my huge cock, and make you ache so much you'll never forget whose cock was inside you?" Her eyes widen, she blushes. I'm guessing Daisy has no experience of a dirty, filthy talking man like me. I've got some things to teach her. She nods.

"Yes." Her voice is almost breathless. I nudge her opening with my cock just enough for her to gasp out as I hit her tingling nerves.

"Condom." I rasp. I need to get a damn condom out of my pocket.

"No. I want to feel you." She tells me. I halt everything. Wait, what? "I've been tested and I am on the pill." She tells me. Is she seriously suggesting that I go bareback inside her? Fuck. This is serious, and I don't give that away in fact not going to lie I have always wrapped up before entering any woman. It would be an entirely new experience for me.

"Daisy, are you absolutely sure? We're crossing a line here." Can my heart stand it if she gets bored of me eventually? Will I survive not being with her after tonight if she doesn't want to see me again? She's caught up in the moment, she's all about riding her next orgasm right now, all about the fact that the guy she's had a crush on since forever is above her with his raging cock at the tip of her entrance. I don't think she's thinking clearly. What is a guy to fucking do? Part of me wants to ride with it and give her what she wants, but I am experienced, I am older and I have so much damn respect for this woman laying underneath me. Nor do I want to take a risk in terms of her possibly falling pregnant. For me, I'd be over the moon to have Daisy and my baby in my arms, damn I would be the proudest father in the world, only Daisy is still young, she's still just in her very early twenties and runs her own business, with a whole life in front of her.

"I have to put the condom on, Buttercup. I need to protect you. I am clean too, we have regular checks." She tries to distract me from my own words as she pushes further onto my dick. I inch back slowly, fuck I am conflicted as hell right now. I have to be sensible one of us needs to be, dammit. "The pill isn't a hundred percent fool proof, Daisy. You're not thinking straight."

"Don't tell me what I'm thinking Marshal. I am in control of my own mind." She punches me in the chest. That's a first during sex. Wow, she is feisty who'd have thought it.

"No, I can't Daisy I can't take that risk. I want to, trust me Buttercup I would be honored to slip inside you naked and feel your tight pussy clenching around my bare skin." She groans and bites down on her bottom lip. "But Logan would fucking kill me if I got you pregnant and you're so young Daisy."

"Fuck off with the so young." Her eyes are ablaze.

"You have your life ahead of you, when you have a man uncovered inside you it needs to be *The One*. You hear me?" She bites down harder on her lip, her eyes are imploring me. She goes to say something then stops herself.

"Good girl. When you know who you want to spend the rest of your life with, Buttercup then do it without protection." Shit, fuck and damn. Do I sound like I don't want to be her *One*? It's not how I want to sound.

"I want you more than life itself right now Daisy, I want to be your One, the man you grow old with, the man who holds your hand through sickness, when you bring life to the world, when you cheer a kid on for it's first goal on the soccer team. But you don't know what you want just yet and I can't spoil you for the other men."

"Too late, you already have Deacon." She looks shyly at me, her long dark lashes framing those beautiful blue eyes of hers that I am lost in, drowning in. I lower my head to her forehead, our noses are touching. Our breathing is labored. Dammit I fucking love her.

Chapter 38

D^{*aisy*} He is driving me insane right now, I'm all a quiver wanting him inside me with nothing between us. My body is bone aching for him and I know he feels the same way. He is the One for me, the one and only, always has been and always will be. What does it take to get into his head? Why is he so damn frightened?

Slowly he lowers his head, his lips press softly on mine. My heart is about to burst with the tenderness. My body is sparked and alight for the flame of this man. He is the match and I am the fire, we belong together, I know he feels the same way. This is no ordinary kiss, this is no ordinary feeling, I can feel my heart melting as it races in my chest. I wrap my arms around Deacon's neck, and whisper into his ear.

"You are The One, Deacon for me. I don't want any other man and I am not interested in just a casual hook up. Please." I almost beg him. He kisses me deeper, my hips buck up and feel his thick cock against my stomach. I feel as he takes himself with one hand and gently guides himself to my opening.

He slowly and gently eases his way in as I shift my hips to accommodate him, I raise up slightly and wrap my legs around his waist as he stretches me more to enter. "You feel amazing, Daisy. I'm so sensitive right now without a condom on, you're going to tip me right over the edge. Do not move, Buttercup. Not an inch."

Is he nuts? My body wants to ride his cock, I don't want to stay still it is taking all of my concentration to not move. He moves slowly in and out, with each movement I gasp and groan, he feels divine, my eyes roll to the back of my head and my body feels as if it is transported to an entirely different plane right now. "You feel so good, Deacon. So good." My voice is breathless as he moves deeper inside me, I can feel him right into my core and it's the best feeling I've ever experienced. This man is big yet he is the perfect fit for me.

Is my heart singing? You bet it is as we begin to find our rhythm, one of his hands on my ass lifting me slightly higher. The friction of his groin on my clit is making me wild, the feeling is intense. "Damn it, I am so close," I tell him.

"Me too, Daisy. The feeling of you bare with my cock inside you is breathtaking. This is new for me."

"Me too, Deacon. Me too." I know what line we have just crossed and there is no going back now. We're so close and intimate that I feel as if his body has become part of mine, our hearts are beating at the same time, his breathing as labored as mine. He nuzzles my neck, sucking and biting at the soft skin. I don't care if he marks me, I want the world to know that Deacon and I are together.

"I'm moments away, Daisy. Tell me you are ready." His voice is gruff, low, manly, sexy. His breath tickles my neck.

"I'm ready, *holy* fuck, Deacon. Nowww." My mind goes blank, I see stars, white lights and feel him pounding furiously inside me, moving in and out faster than anything I've ever felt before. His hand is gripping my ass so tight I can feel his fingers digging into the soft flesh, it is a mixture of pain and desire. I buck and buck, getting the friction on my clit until the orgasm washes over me and I scream out his name at the same time as he screams out mine.

The sound of my name coming out of his mouth as he comes undone on top of me, is more than I can explain. It fills my heart. I hold on with my legs and arms around him, not wanting to let him go.

Deacon pulls slowly out of me, I feel like something is missing, that closeness we just felt, the bond, it was so real. He pulls me into his arm, I lay my head on his broad shoulder inhaling his masculinity. "You're a beautiful woman, Daisy. I've never done it bare with a woman before. You are my first."

That fills my heart, me Daisy the girl who has crushed on this man for nearly a decade or so has had the most amazing connection with him. Finally. I bet y'all saying that too because it is FINALLY. I trail my fingers down his stomach. His hard, flat stomach feels delightful to my touch. He shivers.

"Me too, Deacon. You're my first too in so many ways."

"You want a warm cloth, Buttercup?"

"No, I'm liking the feel of you between my legs and on my thighs. We can have a shower together shortly. I guess everyone will know we've headed off to be together." I groan because how am I going to face my brig brother after this? I mean, it is a bit obvious right?

We lay side by side peacefully each lost in our own thoughts. How can two people make something so beautiful is beyond me, it felt as if fireworks had gone off. My toes curl just thinking about it. This man has my heart and I just hope that he is going to give me his.

It's not like Deacon has ever had a long term relationship, I mean he may be scared of them and just because I'm his first solo ride doesn't mean he feels the same way about me. I want to ask him, I need to know yet I don't want to come off like a ridiculous young girl, asking so many questions and laying my heart openly on the line. I guess I will have to see how things go with us, but rest assured, I am not letting Deacon go without a fight.

I want this man in my bed every night, I want to be by his side as I grow old. My heart is only beating for him.

"Let's get in that shower, Daisy. I'll wash your hair if you like." Oo, that sounds like heaven, I can't remember the last time I had my hair washed. Wait, it was when Lottie and I had gone out to Lazy

Duke's bar, I had way too much to drink, Abe had to stop serving me. I don't think we were celebrating just a raucous girl's night out, a few months back. Anyway suffice to say I had too much and was pretty sick. Lottie was staying over and I remember she had to hold my hair when I was over the toilet, but I still managed to get sick in it. She helped me lean over the tub as she washed it all out. Ugh, just the thought of it makes my stomach lurch. Cringeworthy, that is one thing I will never disclose to Deacon. Otherwise, he will think I'm some kind of kid who can't hold a drink or two.

I lift my head for Deacon to move his arm. He grins at me. "Look at the state of you, beautiful but definitely disheveled. I love it, Buttercup. The way you moved against me and came undone, it was the sexiest thing ever."

I blush, he makes me feel as if I am the only woman alive. He extends his arm and I reach for his warm hand. "You want to get down and dirty in the shower, Buttercup?" He has a wicked grin on his face. Do I ever.

Chapter 39

Deacon

Wow what a night. Daisy is a dream, the way her body moved with mine, her insatiable appetite for sex she is a little firecracker. I thought my appetite was voracious but this girl, phew is all I can say. Her in the shower, pressed up against the wall, the water from the shower head running down her body, her budding nipples standing to attention and her legs wrapped around my waist. Damn. I shake my head. I am in so deep and yet it is way too soon isn't it? I mean I know about all this insta kind of shit from the books my sister had read and oh, okay I may have read a couple growing up too. The way Maxine used to blush at the spicy scenes, well let's just say they had me intrigued so hell yeah, I read a few paragraphs here and there. So, I'm a book naughty scene pervert guy, well at least I was as a hormonal teenager.

"Breakfast?" I ask my drowsy beauty who is coming out of her deep sleep. We slept spooned together last night and it felt like heaven having her in my arms. Although I was awake most of the night thinking about whether what I did was the right thing. How can anyone resist Daisy? She isn't a woman to be ignored and the sexual tension that has been building between us over the last year let alone more recently, came to the fore and I simply couldn't resist her anymore and now I know I am well over my head.

"You making it?" She asks, her blonde hair spilling all over the pillows propping her head up. She has the sheet down some and I can see her perfect, pert breasts. My morning wood is in over-drive but I need a rest, Daisy needs a rest, I'm betting she aches a bit this morning.

"Of course, Buttercup. What do you want?"

"Mm, I think some scrambled egg, toast and beans. I'm pretty sure that Sage has everything well stocked in the cabin."

"Your wish is my command, Lady." I bow and wave my arm like I've seen in the movies, it causes her to giggle. Even her giggle is sexy. Everything about this woman is sexy. But laying in the bed right now she looks so young and I can't help thinking what the fuck am I doing? An old man like me, okay not that old in my mid thirties but compared to Daisy ten years younger than me, I'd say that's old.

"I'll be down in a few minutes. Just want to brush my teeth and tie my hair up."

I give her a quick kiss on the head and inhale her minty shampoo from last night. I've never washed a woman's hair before, I've never showered with a woman before and having sex in the shower with Daisy was a first for me. I've always been a man who just likes the basics with a woman, I only ever needed to have the release and the women I've slept with, they were happy with that. Spending a whole night with a woman is a first for me. Already so many firsts with Daisy. It makes me grin.

Downstairs, Logan and Sage are sitting at the island with Eliza her husband, Sadie, Lottie and Ryle. "Good morning." Logan says. Do I feel awkward? You bet I do. He knows I've just slept with his sister, fuck I feel like a kid who has got caught stealing from the corner supermarket, red handed. My cheeks are burning. He raises his eyebrows with that look that says, *don't forget if you hurt her you'll have me to deal with.* And I know that last night, Daisy and I crossed a lot of lines. We've gone from friends to being lovers just like that.

Ryle places a mug in front of me as I take a seat, good, I need a nice strong coffee. "So, we were just saying that a hike would be good today." Sage says. I am grateful for her taking the heat off me even if Logan is still giving me a concerned look.

"Sounds good." I take a drink from my coffee. "I think I'll make some eggs and toast for Daisy and I." I stand up as Sage talks about the hike she has planned.

"You and Daisy joining us?" She asks.

"Sure, sounds good. I've not hiked for a while. Where are we going?"

"I'm thinking we could go to Bear Ridge, take a light lunch at the bar on top then head back down. We've got a dinner planned this evening at the Italian restaurant down in the town here."

"We'll meet you down here at the cabin when you're back from the hike." Eliza says. "My hiking days are over."

"Fair enough." Sage smiles kindly at Eliza. To be honest, I'd like to ravage Daisy some more but I also don't want to rush this, we need to take our time, we need to get to know each other properly.

Daisy enters the kitchen looking adorable in black leggings and a red sweater that hangs off one shoulder, she looks fresh and *young*. God, I feel old just looking at her. With rosy cheeks she goes and gives Sage a kiss on the cheek and hugs her brother. Logan looks surprised.

"Did you have fun last night?" Lottie asks causing Daisy to blush.

Logan coughs. "I don't need the details spare it for your girlie talks, thanks."

"Noted." Lottie shoots back. Daisy comes and pecks me on the cheek with her soft, warm lips. I pour her a coffee from the pot centre of the table.

"What's on the agenda today then?" She asks as she squeezes my thigh when I sit down next to her, and runs her hand up the inside seam of my jeans. Jeez not here at the table, what is she trying to do to me today?

"Hiking." Sage replies. "Up to Bear Mountain, lunch up top then back down. Italian meal tonight. You up for it?"

"You bet I am. I love hiking." I get up, her touch is burning a hole in my jeans, my dick is on fire for her and it's all I can do to stop myself from taking her in my arms and carrying her right back to bed. I need to slow things down between us.

I make our eggs and some toast and we all sit around eating and chatting about the day, Sage tells us she is about done with all the wedding plans and Logan claps. "Finally. I cannot wait to call you my wife." Oh, these two so romantic. His eyes shine with happiness as he looks at her. Daisy gives me a look and I almost choke on my coffee. I mean, we crossed the line but hold on a second, we have a lot to talk about right now and we need to take it a day at a time.

More than anything, I sure as hell need to get my head round this whole age gap thing. When I am nearly fifty she will still be young. It scares the effing hell out of me if I am honest.

"Don't get any ideas just yet, Buttercup. We have to take this whatever it is slowly." I whisper into her ear. She comes closer to me so our lips are almost touching.

"Can you guys please not do that in front of me." Logan blurts out. Daisy chuckles and I go beetroot. She has no filter or limits this girl, none whatsoever. Don't get me wrong, I love that about Daisy, her naturalness, her confidence but I am not used to it and kissing in front of Logan and everyone else, it makes me feel a bit uncomfortable.

Daisy flicks her hair over her shoulder, "sure we can talk, Deacon but ain't anything you can say to me that will change my mind. I already told you how I felt last night." She eats her breakfast like this isn't anything monumental. Only to me it is, it's a huge big deal. Am I ready for a relationship? Am I ready to go both feet into this?

My heart feels ready I know that much. God, I am so nervous and scared. What if I fuck this all up? What if I am not the man she needs in her life? What if I can't be Daisy's everything?

Chapter 40

D^{*aisy*} I love hiking, the way my legs feel strong and the breeze on my face, it's a bit chillier today and the air has that crispness to it that you only get this time of year. Up high it is breathtaking and I am so pleased that Logan and Sage decided for us all to do this today. For a hen and stag weekend, it's the best, who needs to go to a bar or wear those sashes anyway. Lottie and Ryle are behind Deacon and I, those two sure seem to be hitting it off.

I hope my bestie goes easy on Ryle, only she has always stemmed away from any kind of relationship, ever since her daddy left when she was a little girl she has had some major issues with commitment. Ryle seems like a nice guy, and his story about losing his wife is tragic. I can't wait for us all to meet his little girl, she sounds adorable. I wonder if this is just a weekend fling for Lottie and Ryle, it makes me smile. I'm glad they have each other for how long it lasts. I am guessing Ryle won't be going into anything new without a lot of thought, not with a kid to think about.

Deacon is behind me and I can feel his eyes on me even though I am not looking at him. "Are you checking my ass out, Marshal?"

"What do you expect, it's right in front of me and it's like a damn peach, Buttercup. I could bite it."

"You can do that later, I can't wait to curl up in your arms again and feel your hardness against my stomach."

"Daisy, behave. Not out in the open for God's sake. I'm having enough difficulty keeping my dick under control as it is." He chuckles, I love it when he does. It's deep and throaty just like his groaning is when he's about to explode. My that man sure does know how to get a girl all worked up and then some. The way he took me in the shower was out of this world. I've never done it in a shower before, don't get me wrong I am no novice to sex but let's just say the guys I have dated, well it was all over rather quickly. But not with Deacon. He savored me as if I was some fancy dish in a restaurant, he took his time and made me feel as if I was the only woman alive.

"So, you and Molly," I begin.

"Molly?"

"Yeah the woman in Coppertown."

"Oh, that Molly. What about her?"

"You guys were serious?"

"No, Buttercup. She understood me and I understood her. I've not seen her for a while now not since, I caught myself thinking about you all the time."

"Seriously?" I keep my eyes on the ground not wanting to trip and bust up my ankle or sprain it like Sage did not long ago. Oh, boy when she did they had the helicopter out for her and the rescue team. She was spitting mortified and angry. Personally, I think that was the point that brought her and Logan closer together, when he had to make a house call, even though she was still pissed at him.

"Seriously, Buttercup. I've not been able to take my mind off you for quite some time now. Molly and I would only spend a night together a week and then to be honest, we didn't spend the whole night together. It wasn't like that. We both had our needs and that was the relationship. Nothing more, nothing less."

I mull it over, just the thought of Deacon being with another woman makes my chest lurch and knots my stomach right up. I don't want to even think about it, but I do get that a man and a woman have basic primal needs.

"Good to know." I feel his fingers lacing through my own, he stops me in my tracks and forces me to face him, lifting my chin up with his thumb and forefinger.

"Oops sorry." Lottie says as she practically bumps into me. "I'll er, just go round. Come on Ryle, lets leave these two lovebirds to it. We can go catch Logan and Sage up." She pushes Ryle to the other side of Deacon.

I look into Deacon's eyes, there is a tenderness there that I hadn't noticed before, and a hint of amusement. "Are you jealous, Daisy? Of Molly?"

"No, don't be so ridiculous, I was just asking. That's all. Only what I felt last night with you, it was nothing I've felt before and I kind of don't want it to end when we get back to town." He lowers his lips to mine and softly kisses me.

"I don't want it to end either, Buttercup and nobody says it has to. Everyone here on this weekend knows we've sealed our whatever this is. Relationship?" I blush, I like the word relationship tripping off his tongue, it sounds so kinda like we could be going steady. Oh, will you listen to me, I sound like a damn teenager with all that *going steady*. But you get what I mean, right?

"I'd like to see where it goes, Deacon I don't want it to be just sex." I blush. He runs his thumb along my jaw line, it feels sensuous and warm.

"Me too, Buttercup. Me too. I'm scared, I won't lie I mean you might change your mind in a few weeks or a month, but I'm not going to lie, Daisy I really, really like you." I want him to tell me he loves me, but I know for him it's probably way too soon.

I know already that I love Deacon, I've loved him since High School, the way he makes my heart race, sends my butterflies in my stomach all a flutter, there is no doubt in my mind. But I get that Deacon is older, wiser and perhaps a bit more cautious. I guess it's up to me to show him that I am serious about having a proper relationship with him. Sure, I've flitted around with different guys here and there, I've had a few casual relationships but never have I had feelings like I have for Deacon.

When you know, you know, right? Your heart races, he hangs the moon, his words mean so much. He makes my pulse beat and takes my breath away. I love this man more than words can say. I want to have everything with him, I want to have my first last everything with Deacon. There are no two ways about it.

"Deacon I won't be changing my mind, you light up my life, you've made me the happiest woman alive. I've crushed on you since I was in High School, you know that." His eyes dance like I've handed him the moon.

"Have to admit, Buttercup I've kind of had a thing for you since you were in High School. Only I've been so damned blinkered by the whole age gap business that I've let it stand in the way of everything. I don't want to do that anymore." Music to my ears, I am brimming over and my smile must be cracking my face, least ways it feels like that.

"I've never felt like this about anyone before and If I am totally honest, I have always been a bit shy of commitment. In my book I want what my folks have," he tells me making me swoon so much my legs feel like they're going to give way and I'll be a puddle at his feet. "you know to be with a partner for life, someone I can share the small and the big things with, someone who will stand by me, respect me and feels the same way I do."

"I'm your girl, Deacon surely you know that already and as for the whole age gap thing. Honestly, nobody cares. Certainly not me. It's just a number and it only signifies how many years we haven't managed to have together." His lips brush mine sending a shiver up and down my body, warmth creeps through my lower regions up to my stomach and pools. His lips are soft and gentle, his tongue enters into my mouth. Is the mountain moving?

Chapter 41

D *eacon*

The rest of the couple of days up in the cabin passed in a blur, hiking, dinner with the band again and charades out back on the deck with some beers, guitars strumming away, Logan and Sage singing a couple of tracks and Daisy and I snuggled up together, mindful not to be too in her brother's face. Not going to lie, being close with Daisy with her watchful brother, even though I have his blessing being around did make me feel a bit uncomfortable.

Alas, it is a Monday again already and duty calls. We've got a couple of hooligans in from Copper Town who decided over the weekend to graffiti up the wall of the nursery school, one of my guys is with them and their folks now. Needless to say they will only be reprimanded and hopefully they won't do it again. If it wasn't so serious I would have to say I admired their work, they are a group of talented young lads. I shake my head such a waste, it's a shame they are the kind of kids who won't go far in school and miss all the opportunities that are presented to them and to go to an art school.

"Good weekend?" One of my guys asks as he hands me a coffee.

"Very good, we had a great time. Not been up the mountain for some time, good hiking, great weather with sunshine but cool breeze, beer, wine, the band. Sage and Logan chose well to have their stag and hen do jointly."

He nods. "What do you want to do about old man, Jenkins?" He asks me. Indeed what do I want to do with the town's drunk? He's harmless enough but we have to keep pulling him in off the street and with no place much else to go, he spends a night in our cell. We bring him food, coffee, plenty of water and headache pills. What thanks do we get for our troubles? None. Diddly-squat. He always cusses at us and marches right on out to the nearest watering hole, Abe's bar, Lazy Duke. Where we have asked Abe not to sell the old fella any more liquor. Story has it that his wife died when they were a young couple, way before my time and that he took to the bottle. The only saving grace is that they never had kids. Seeing kids brought up with parents that drink is never a pretty sight to see.

"The usual I guess. We'll let him back out on the street but can you make a call to the shelter for me and see if they will take him in and give him a bed for a couple of nights at least?"

"Sir, you know he won't go there or stay, wasting our time."

"We have to give it a try, who knows one of these days he may just decide that a warm place and a proper bed is the best option for him." My guy shrugs but picks up the phone and starts making the call.

"We've got a petty theft at the grocery store, Sir." One of my new officers, fresh out of the academy, Lisa says. I am feeling a headache coming on, since when did Willowbrook have a theft going on at the grocery store? What is the world coming to and all of this on a Monday morning?

"Can you handle it Lisa please, take Clint with you?"

"Sure, no problem, Sir." Paperwork, paperwork and more paperwork is what is coming my way. My phone buzzes on my desk, I take a look and a boyish grin spreads across my face, it's Daisy. We swapped mobile numbers over the weekend and it struck me how strange it was, that after all these years knowing each other and being around one another, we didn't know each other's mobile phone numbers.

"Hi, how are you this morning?" I ask her and place my feet up on the desk.

"All the better for hearing your voice. I miss you."

"Really? It's only been a night, Buttercup."

"What can I say? The morning is okay, I've finished the prom dress I was working on, it looks beautiful on and the bridesmaid dresses for Sage are all finished. Business is quiet today so thinking of taking early lunch over at Bluebell's. You want to join me?"

"Sounds like a plan. Say half an hour, I can get away then?" We hang up once we've made the arrangements and my stomach flutters, whoa do I have butterflies? A grown man like me, well I never. Thirty minutes later I am in my truck not that it's that far to Bluebell's, our station is at the end of Main Street and the diner, café is plop in the middle but I have a house call to make straight after lunch so the truck it is.

The door chimes as I walk in and see Daisy sitting as pretty as a picture at one of the tables in the corner by the far window. Her long, blonde hair is tied in a braid and hangs down her back. Her narrow shoulders taper down to her slender waist and I feel a stirring in my pants. From the back she looks like a kid of about eighteen, but I've worked on the whole age gap thing over the weekend and having spent time with her, I have come to realize that like Daisy says, it is just a number and that millions of people around the world together are in age gap relationships. Apparently, it is only an issue if the couple make it an issue. She told me I need to focus on what makes me happy and she sure does make me happy.

Daisy is like the color on a grey day, the sunshine on your face after a long, hard winter. She turns and smiles, her entire face ligthing up like a picture. She waves as Bab's greets me and asks what my order will be today.

"I'll have a tuna and cheese melt please, Barbara. Has Daisy already ordered?"

"Indeed, funnily enough she is having the same thing."

"Good choice. Thanks, Barbara. And a strong coffee too please."

"I'll bring it over."

"Hey, so good to see you Deacon." Daisy grabs my hand as I sit down, the warmth transcends to my own, our fingers curl around each others. Just being with her makes me feel like a teenage kid again. My mouth is dry and her beauty takes my breath away.

"It's always lovely to see you, Daisy. I thought we were going to you know, see how things went before we you know," shit I am stumbling for the right words here, see, I told you I am acting like a damn teenager. "You know go public."

She throws her head back and laughs. "Oh, Deacon who cares about everyone else. I'm not letting go now we've decided to see where this goes. Why wait? I want you and you want me, we've already had amazing sex so now it's time to you know, just be." She leans over and kisses my cheek. I blush, not being used to any kind of public display of affection.

"Okay, Buttercup. Whatever you say."

"Hey kids, good to see you two finally together. Took you both long enough. Can't wait for the wedding." Barbara chuckles as she places our food down in front of us. I almost choke.

"We're nowhere near the wedding stage yet, Barbara, give us a chance. We've only just begun."

She gives me a wink. "You know how it goes here in Willowbrook Deacon. Once you're with *the* girl, a ring goes on the finger and then there are the wedding bells, oo and some babies."

"Romantic." Daisy breathes, holy smoking cow, these ladies are working a bit too quick. I need to get used to the whole idea of having a girlfriend. It's a first for me. *Girlfriend*, hey I like the sound of it. Barbara pinches my cheek and wanders back to behind the counter.

Daisy is grinning from ear to ear and I swear to God, this woman has already picked out her church music. She is definitely the kind of girl who has dreamt about and planned her wedding from a young age.

We have got some miles to go first but you know what I am thinking, who better than a beautiful, sweet girl like Daisy to spend forever with?

Chapter 42

D*aisy* My oh my, how in this town everybody is always a meddling, I recall just how we all behaved when Sage came back home and we tried endlessly to meddle in her affairs with Logan.

"Hey, don't worry too much about Barbara, I know we have some ways to go. Besides, have you seen how Lottie and Ryle have been all weekend, those two are on *fire*?" I giggle, honestly I have never seen my bestie so taken with a man, she messaged me this morning to let me know that Ryle is taking her on a proper date. Which of course got me to thinking.

"They are going on a *date*." I tell him, he raises his eyebrows then cocks his head, and gives me that panty melting smile.

"Would you like to go on a proper date with me, Buttercup. Only, I think it would be about time don't you think?" Fantastic, he is on the right track, I never thought he'd ask.

"Absolutely, I'd love it. Where will you take me?" I kind of fancy the new Italian restaurant further down on Main Street, I know it's a bit pricey but I like a fancy meal every now and then.

"It will be a surprise. How about I swing round to your place tonight say sevenish, does that give you enough time to lock up the shop and get ready?"

"Yes, plenty of time. I can't wait." I am literally almost bouncing up and down on the chair. He chuckles, his dimple comes to greet me and makes me swoon. Could Deacon possibly be any more handsome than he is right now? His eyes are dancing and lit up, his smile is broad and it looks as if he hasn't shaved for a few days with that alluring bit of scruff on his jawline. How can anyone be this good looking? No wonder all the girls used to be after him in school.

"Wear something warm." He tells me. Wait, what? Warm? I was hoping for a fancy Italian meal.

"Intriguing."

"I think you'll find it very romantic, Buttercup. My lips are sealed just make sure to be wrapped up."

"Okay." I breathe the words, it still hasn't really sunk in how I am finally with Deacon, well you know kind of with Deacon. So far it's been unbridled, hot sex with a lot of dirty words and actions, that are enough to make a girl blush and now we're here having a coffee together and talking about a date. Little me, and Marshal Deacon. A few girls on the other table turn their heads and look at Deacon then turn back to each other and giggle. I know they like the look of him and it makes me buzz knowing that it is me he has chosen.

"You fancy going to a movie mid-week?" He asks. Oo, a second date. This is a good sign and I am might glad that he hasn't brought up the age gap thing, honestly that wearing thin for me at one point. We chatted about it over the weekend away and finally he seemed to relax about it. Having Logan's blessing too means so much to me, I am so relieved to have a brother who is going all caveman on me about who I do or do not see.

"Sure, I'd love that. What will we see? There is a new Reeves movie out."

"I thought you'd like to see the original Casablanca movie, I hear they're showing it again this week but if you prefer a new movie then I am up for that too. He's a brilliant actor, you can't go wrong with one of his movies."

"Casablanca, why Deacon you romantic you. I'd love to see it at the movies, it is one of my favorites. How did you know?"

"I have paid attention Daisy, I also know that you love a good Hallmark movie, that Sandra Bullock and Julia Roberts are your favorite actresses and that you fancied the pants off Brad Pitt." His smile is infectious.

"You *have* been paying attention."

"I also happen to know your favorite author is Tolstoy for classics and that you read an awful lot of smut books."

I blush. "Did you read my books?"

"Not all of them no, but I made a point of reading some of them that I'd seen laying around at your folk's house when you were growing up and I was there for Logan."

My heart flutters, well I never. Deacon reading girlie books, romance books, it's enough to make a girl swoon right off her seat and kiss his feet. "That is sooo romantic, Deacon."

"Told you, Buttercup, I have always liked you. Never thought you'd be interested in me but I had an inkling you did growing up. I honestly thought it was a teenage phase you'd grow out of. Mighty glad it wasn't."

"Me too, I mean that I never grew out of it." Gosh, why am I stumbling over my own words? He does things to me that are out of this world, just looking at him is making me squeeze my thighs together.

His phone vibrates on the table, Deacon gives it a quick glance. "Sorry, Daisy I have to run. There is an incident on Roosevelt Street. I may be tied up for a while but I will most definitely be at yours around seven this evening. So sorry to have to run on you, the nature of the job I'm afraid."

"Don't be sorry, Deacon I can't wait to see you this evening." He grabs his hat, leaves some money on the table to cover the coffees and makes a dash for the door.

"So you two, eh." Barbara comes over. "Didn't want to disturb you two love birds. Have to say, Daisy am I glad to see you two being a lot closer."

"Yeah, me too." My heart is still racing from being so close to him, feeling the heat off his thigh close to mine as we sat together. I cannot wait to have our first proper date tonight. I'm so excited I can hardly contain myself and I know it'll be a quick afternoon.

"I hope it works out just how you want it to, Daisy, I am so happy for you both."

"Thank you, Barbara that means a lot to me. I have a little feeling that it just might." I smile and finish my coffee as she goes off to tend to some folk who have just come in. Honestly, I am so over moon I could literally hug myself. Tonight cannot come fast enough. First though, I need to finish my coffee then head over to the lingerie store and buy myself something fancy and sexy for our first proper date.

Chapter 43

Deacon

My palms are sweaty, jeez I feel like a teenager all over again. My heart is racing and pumping so fast I feel as if I need a goddamn horse tranquilizer to calm it down, and my nerves are shot to pieces. I haven't been on a date since I was around sixteen or seventeen, eighteen at most. After that when I was in college studying, it was just flings here and there with girls, nobody wanted anything from anyone and everything was free and casual. But this date with Daisy, it means the entire world to me. I want it to be as perfect as can be, I want my girl to know how much she means to me, not just as I've already shown her with my body but on a deeper level.

My phone buzzes as I come out of the shower with just a white towel wrapped around my waist. I pick it up from the bed where I slung it after I got in from work and needed to wash the day off me. It's Logan's caller i.d.

"Hey, Bro what's up?" I ask him as I wipe the drips of water off my chest that are trailing down my stomach.

"You want to join us at the Lazy Duke's tonight, just a guy's quiet night out after the full on weekend away?"

"I can't but it sounds like a good idea. What have you done with Sage?"

"Actually, she isn't feeling too good, she said she felt a bit nauseous." I raise my eyebrows not that Logan can see me through the mobile. The first hint of that word is always synonymous with pregnancy in my mind, just the way it works. I give myself a mental slap, those two are careful or maybe they already want to start their family.

"That's rubbish, I hope she will feel better soon and it'll pass. Shouldn't you stay at home with her?"

"She's got Holly her bestie over, talking weddings, invites that kind of thing."

"Oh, right. I thought everything was tied up?" They are after all getting married in only a few weeks time. The whole town has been invited, I will be Logan's best man and Daisy is chief bridesmaid. I'm looking forward to our dancing together, it should be fun and yet another excuse to be able to hold my Buttercup close to me and feel her warm body flush against mine.

"Pretty much, I think it is a run through thing. The rehearsal dinner is next week, you can still make it, right?"

"Listen stop fretting, your wedding is going to go off without a hitch. And yes, of course I am still coming wouldn't miss it for anything. It's just the families right though?"

"Yes. We're keeping it small and simple some drinks afterwards at Lazy Duke's and we've hired Abe's private room out back with the deck for our meal. He's rustling up some special menu with Sage." I chuckle at Logan, usually it's the bride who is clucking away and fretting but he sure does have a case of the old nerves going on. He has waited a long time for this wedding to happen, to have the woman of his dreams in his arms forever.

"I can't twist your arm about tonight then?" He asks me.

"To be honest, I er, I have a date with Daisy. Thought I ought to try dating her so we can get to know each other properly." There is a pause before he says anything.

"Courting hey?" He chuckles. "Good, glad to hear it. Daisy deserve the best, she's special to me. I couldn't think of anyone better to be taking my sister on a date."

"Thanks, Man. I appreciate that. Listen, I gotta go I said I'd pick her up around sevenish and I don't want to be late. This means a lot to me."

"Cool, no problem. Deac. Catch up with you another night. How about Thursday, I've the morning off at the practice on Friday as Sage is covering for me so we could have some beers unless you're on duty?"

"Thursday night is good, I am off on Friday, Carlson is on shift. It's my day off and I'll be doing the Saturday shift."

We chat some more before hanging up. I remove the towel and dry off the rest of the water droplets from my body, slip into clean boxer shorts, a blue flannel and my faded denims, slip my feet into my brown cowboy boots and take one last look in the mirror. I make sure that the cabin is tidy before I grab my keys and head for the truck. I know everything is set up and ready, I got one of the guys to cover for me earlier after I'd gone to see to the incident on the other side. My nervous are all a jingle-jangle I can tell you that much. My mouth is dry as I slip the key in the ignition and head on over to collect Daisy.

Wow, is all I can think when I see her heading out the door in black leggings, cute black Ugg's on her feet and a thick, cream jumper that comes to her hips, thrown over she is wearing an orange puffer jacket and on her head a matching beanie, her long blonde locks flowing from underneath it. She is a vision that makes my pulse beat in my ears and my dick starts to make movement down there. *Down boy not now.*

I hop out of the truck because no lady especially not Daisy needs to open the door on her own, it's my role to open it for her and help her to get in. "You look stunning *and* adorable, Buttercup." Her smile makes my heart flutter. I am loving all these teenage feelings rising to the fore.

"You don't look so bad yourself, Deacon. A proper cowboy look going on there, all you need is the hat." She makes me chuckle. Once she is in I close the door for her and head back round to the driver's side.

"I'm excited to know where you are taking me for our first date. Don't you just love those words, *our first date*." Absolutely I do. I respond by squeezing her delicate, warm hand then bring it to my lips and place a kiss on it.

"This is for you." I hand her a square box wrapped in pink paper with a purple bow wrapped around it.

"Oo, I love this shop I could spend hours in there." She opens the box of chocolates that come from our finest chocolatier in Willowbrook, *Artisanal Cacao Couture*. Dolly the owner has been running it for the past ten or twelve years and her chocolates are the best for miles around, her signature wrapping is pink and purple for the ladies and turquoise with navy ribbon for the guys. She has definitely honed her marketing skills and people from miles come round to buy from her, she's also on the tourist route here in Willowbrook.

"Thank you so much, Deacon." She pops one in her mouth and offers the box to me.

"No, those are all for you, Buttercup." She giggles with delight it sends a direct hit to my dick. Honestly, my lower body has no self control whatsoever where Daisy is concerned. Not that I'm complaining, I think I'd be worried otherwise.

I turn the truck stereo on and put on a soundtrack I created this afternoon at the station just for her. The first track that fills the truck is Tim McGraw's *I Need You*. Daisy sighs as he opens, it makes me feel happy to know that her favorite country singer is coming through the speakers.

"I love his music."

"I know."

She shoots me a look. "Really?"

"I told you, Buttercup, I know almost everything there is to know about you, except what's deep inside your mind but I hope that our journey together will show me more."

"Deacon, you are so romantic, who'd have thought that our town Marshal was a big heart." She leans over and kisses my cheek, her kiss is featherlight and sends a tingle through my body.

"Are we having our first date at your cabin?" She asks as I pull up outside.

"Not per se, no. You're just going to have to wait and see." I hop out the truck once the ignition is off and go round to help my girl down, extending my hand for hers to fit in. She gets down, I use the moment to pull her into my chest and lower my lips to kiss her with longing and passion that leaves us both slightly breathless.

"My oh my, you sure know how to kiss a lady. Must be all those years of practice." She teases me.

"Nope." I pop the P. "It's kissing you, Buttercup that brings it out in me, kissing you is like chocolate melting in your mouth, it's the sun gracing your skin when it peaks out from behind a dark cloud."

If looks could swoon, then that is exactly what my Daisy-Buttercup is doing right now. I take her hand and lead her down the path that takes us down and round the cabin.

She gasps. "Deacon." Her voice is just a breath.

Chapter 44

D^{*aisy*} My eyes well up with happy tears, I've never seen anything quite so romantic. From the back of the cabin, leading up to a round table decked over with what looks like a Damask tablecloth are lights in the ground, leading a pathway right to the table. A waiter stands next to the table with a cloth over his arm and a bottle of champagne in a bucket next to him. "This is, this is stunning." I turn and see Deacon gazing at me like I've just given him the moon.

To the side a string quartet are playing are soft and gentle love song, I can't quite make out what the song is but trust me, it sounds amazing. I've never been to a string quartet before, have always wanted to but never gotten round to it. I wonder if this is yet another something that Deacon just happens to know about me.

He smiles sending butterflies shooting around my stomach, my heart is beating like wildfire and warmth envelops me like a warm blanket on a chilly evening. "Come." He reaches out his arm and then hooks it so I can link arms with him.

Deacon moves the chair back that is draped in cream fabric with a huge bow around the centre. I sit down and admire the candelabra in the centre of the table, the china plates, silver cutlery and ground lights that form a circle around the table. Our waiter begins to pour the champagne once Deacon is seated. I glance up at him and see the warmth and tenderness in his eyes.

"I've never had an outside dining experience, wow Deacon this is amazing for our first date. You are taking my breath away." He smiles broadly.

"Glad you like it, Buttercup. There's more to come." He lays the napkin over his lap, I do the same.

"More? What more could there be than this?"

"You will see. I hope you like asparagus, Daisy we're having sauteed asparagus with butter sauce for starters, olive bread on the side."

"I love asparagus, actually there isn't anything I don't like if I'm honest."

"For main we are having red Mullet with courgette and menton lemon." Now my mouth is seriously watering, and my stomach makes strange noises, I guess it was a while ago since I grabbed something to eat at the diner.

"Sounds delicious. You are spoiling me."

"You deserve it, Daisy. You are important to me and I want the best for you, besides, I can take you to a restaurant any day. I happen to know you've got your eye on the new Italian on Main but I kinda thought something really special for our first date."

"I love it, honestly, Deacon I'm almost speechless." That makes him chuckle, it's deep and throaty, he is one sexy man with his broad shoulders that taper down to his slender waist. All that working out he does to stay fit shows.

"What's for dessert?" I ask him as the waiter brings two dishes towards us and places one in front of me, the other in front of Deacon. I reach for the bread basket and tear some olive bread and dip it into the sauce of the asparagus. "Oh my gosh, this is heavenly. Taste it."

Deacon places a piece in his mouth and murmurs, it's so damn sexy. "It's very good," he swallows. "For dessert we are having sour cherry souffle and vanilla chantilly." Just the sound of it is making my tastebuds fire and crackle.

"Who did you have as chef, or did you order in?"

"Order in, are you kidding me? Not for our first date. I hired Blankavich." I almost drop my cutlery.

"*The* Blankavich as in *Raoul* Blankavich." I am aware my eyes are opening and closing in disbelief. He merely nods like hiring in the top Michelin chef in the State isn't some huge, big deal. The man has won awards, he has restaurants throughout the country *and* has his own culinary school.

"Deacon, seriously? The man is famous."

"Is he?" He cocks his head to the side and raises his champagne glass. "Daisy, you are the light of my life, you shine brighter than the stars at night, you are my color on a dark day. Here's to our first *proper* date."

I raise my glass for the toast. "Thank you so much for all of this, I just don't know what to say. But, Blankavich. I can't get over it. Where is he? Is he in your kitchen cooking?" The thought of someone as famous as chef milling around in Deacon's cabin cooking makes me smile, only the man is famous for his tantrums and temper alongside his fine culinary skills. Deacon chuckles.

"He has gone now but yes he brought what he needed and used my kitchen. We have history." He tells me like he's talking about him and Logan or any other regular guy friend not a chef almost as famous as Gordon Ramsey, a celebrity chef.

"You have history? Tell me more."

"His brother is Dan's best friend."

"Dan as in your sister Maxine's husband?"

"The one and only. We've been at BBQ's together, restaurant openings, they're a pretty tight knit family. And we hit it off and have been in touch for the last five years or so. I did him a favor once by letting his kid sister off on a speeding fine, she was only going a couple mile an hour over and I relented. So, you know he said he owed me a favor." He acts like this is no big deal but to me eating something that chef has cooked is a massive big deal.

The meal is over all too quickly, the quartet continue to play song after song, the music is amplified out here in the open with nothing but stars above us and a quarter moon. "I'd like to have ordered you a full moon tonight, Buttercup but it was a bit out of my reach." Deacon stretches his hand across the table, our fingertips touch and waves of passion flood through my body. I squeeze my legs together. If I hadn't already done the do with this fine, handsome man in front of me, I would most definitely be giving myself up to him tonight.

I've never been wined and dined like this in my entire life, it's exquisite and I never want the moment to end. Just the two of us, the music playing softly and all of this for me. For me, I can't believe it. Deacon looks relaxed and happy. If my heart wasn't singing before, and I didn't see hearts, let me tell you; I am right now.

"Are you finished?" He asks me as I murmur over the last of my dessert. It literally melts in my mouth.

"Yes, thank you so much. This has been wonderful." And of course I don't want our date to end. He gets up and comes round to the chair and pulls it out for me. As I turn I see both his horses behind me, how they got there I have no idea, unless he had someone lead them out but surely I would have heard something.

Around their necks they wear garlands of large, white roses. "Oh, my, Deacon. Look at them, they're beautiful and those roses, honestly. You are making me swoon." He holds his hand to my lower back and pulls me into him, our lips meet, his soft and warm, his tongue probing into my mouth.

"I couldn't bring out Dreamer he's too young to be ridden." He tells me as I pull away.

"Are we going on a ride?"

He nods. "I've got somewhere special to show you, I think you'll like it." Right now I'd like just about anything he shows me. As if the dinner, the quartet, the famous superstar chef wasn't enough, he has more. What possibly could top all of this?

Chapter 45

Daisy
Deacon helps me to get up on Mitzi his Appaloosa horse, she is so docile and bows her head to allow me to stroke her cheek. I nuzzle her nose and she softens into me. Once I am sitting comfortably he goes over to Lady Night, his black Arabian and seats himself, boy doe he look good on a horse with his broad shoulders and strong, muscular thighs gripping the girth. I kind of wish I was between those legs right now. Oh, dear I can't stop thinking about sex with Marshal Deacon. I giggle. He pays no mind and turns Lady Night, Mitzi follows and we begin to amble, all the while hearing the music behind us. It's a soft serenade straight out a Hallmark movie.

Mitzi comes side up to Deacon, he reaches for my hand. "Happy?" He asks me. Is that like a trick question?

"I couldn't be any happier, Deacon. You don't realize how long I have wanted to be your..." I don't say the word instead he finishes my sentence.

"Girlfriend." He gives me a gin. "I like it. Girlfriend. Girlfriend. Makes us sound like a couple of young kids." I squeeze his hand, he isn't wrong there, it sure does. I feel like I'm back in High School on my first date, my heart racing like a speeding train. I wonder where he is taking me. I mean I knew he had a lot of land behind the cabin but this is stretching on for miles.

The quarter moon offers us lighting but the horses seem to know where they are going. "Have you always owned all this land?" I ask him. My hand warm tucked in his, the horses amicably walking side by side, docile, languid, it feels amazing being on Mitzi. I've not been on her for a while, I can't recall when I stopped coming for the horse riding sessions. It was Logan and Deacon who both taught me how to ride back when I was a kid. Logan didn't quite have the patience that Deacon did and to be honest, I definitely preferred having one-to-one sessions with the guy I hero worshipped. I blush just thinking about the things that used to pass through my mind when I was anywhere close to Deacon, not to mention how often my vibrator got used when I was a bit older and my dirty thoughts of all the divine things Deacon would do to me with his hands and his lips. I feel my clit aching and my panties getting wetter.

"I bought the extra land from Carlton's grand-daddy some years back. He didn't want so much land anymore and Carlton only wanted sufficient to have a homestead for the wife and kids. He wasn't interested in having stock or cattle. I bought it and think maybe one day I'll build me a home around this spot right here. The cabin is going to be maybe too small one day. You know for a family and all."

"The views must be magnificent in the day time." Our horses have stopped. Wait did he say for a family and all? He did. Oh, my does he mean a home for him and for me? Am I running away with myself here? It makes me swoon. I can just imagine having a home up here with Deacon, our kids running around, playing and squealing maybe some chickens, a couple of goats. I'm all for the whole Little House On The Prairie scenario. His voice brings me out of my daydream.

"Not as breathtaking as you are, Buttercup. Nothing holds a candle to that beauty of yours." Aw, he makes me blush, it's a good job there is no lighting out here.

"Come on, we're nearly there." The horses trot gently, my ass bumps up and down in tune with Mitzi, my knees pressed against her middle. Riding is like freedom, it's a breath of fresh air on a hot, muggy August day when the air is stifling.

In front of me, I see lights twinkling, I move my head forward and peer though my eyes to make sure that what I am seeing is not my imagination. "Deacon is this, is this the old tree house we used to all come play in when we were kids. Carlton's daddy made it for him?"

He chuckles. "It's the one and only, Buttercup. Of course it's mine now and I have done a lot of work to it."

I exhale, all I can see is the structure outline with fairy lights all around the bottom of the tree leading up the wooden staircase that has been put in, back in the day we simply used a rope ladder. The entire tree house has been decorated with lights that sparkle like magic, music floats out, I can't make out what the track is but it's definitely a country love ballad. I place a hand over my mouth, tears spring to my eyes.

"It's like a fairytale wonderland, a piece of heaven. This is amazing and so beautiful." My voice is but a whisper. Deacon hops off Lady and comes and reaches his arms up for me. I swing my leg over and easily drop into his strong arms.

"You've not seen anything yet, Buttercup." He kisses the tip of my nose as I carries me to the steps that take us up to the front door. On the outside is a large hanging heart made out of wood, with *Deacon 4 Daisy* on it, oh my gosh, my heart is melting. He grins at me.

"This is too much, I love it. Did you make this recently?" He shakes his head.

"No, I have to confess I made it back in school in woodwork. I kinda always hoped that one day you'd be my girl, Daisy." I throw my arms around his neck, this is possibly *the most* romantic thing in the entire world, certainly anything that has happened to me.

He opens the door with his hand mindful not to drop me as my arms hold tight around his neck, inhaling his cologne, it's woodsy and musky, I take a deeper inhale.

"Are you sniffing me, Buttercup."

"You smell so good, it's hard to resist." He chuckles a deep and throaty sound, it shoots straight to my core. As the door opens my eyes pop wide open, heavens it's like something out of a movie. Candles literally cover the entire floor with deep red rose petals. "They're battery operated." He tells me. "Don't want the place to go up in flames."

"Gosh, Deacon it's all so beautiful." He lays me gently on the bed that takes up the space, with it's white fluffy cushions and bedspread on which are rose petals in the shape of a heart. "You're going to ruin the heart." I tell him as I unclasp my hands from around his neck.

"The only heart that really matters, Buttercup is in here," he taps to the very place where his heart organ is. Swooning? Oh, absolutely. "And that will never be ruined. Not with you in my heart now, tomorrow and for always." I lay my head back against the pillows and see a black and white canvas on the wall opposite.

"Is that me?"

"It is. I took it when you were in the meadow picking daisies when you were sixteen." I look happy and peaceful, a daisy chain I was working on in my hand.

"I look...."

"You look serene and beautiful. It was the very moment I realized I had fallen in love with you, Buttercup." My heart fills with such emotion I swear I'm about to cry happy tears. Deacon comes to the bed and lays down beside me, he kisses me with such tenderness it takes my breath away, I can only see his beautiful warm eyes gazing deep into mine.

He pulls away and admires me like I'm the only person existing in the universe, it sends shivers and tingles throughout my entire body. "I want to make love to you, Daisy." I nod, biting my lower lip. I am so ready for this man with my entire being, my head, my heart and my body are all his now.

Chapter 46

D*eacon*
 Damn this woman is beautiful inside and out. Her personality is a ray of sunshine on a cloudy day, her blonde hair flows over the pillows and with the red rose petals surrounding her face, she looks angelic. "Do you need to go home to Bonnie cat or do I have you all night?"

"You have me all night, Marshal and you can do with me as you please." That sends a jolt straight to my dick, not like it needs a jolt. I swear that just thinking about my Buttercup makes my dick perma-hard. It's insane no other woman has ever had this affect on me before.

I lean down and kiss her lips, as much as my body is raring to go and I am aching in my pants, tonight is not about dirty talk and rampant sex. Tonight I want to share my body and soul with her, deeply and profoundly, what I lack in words I want to show her with my body.

Daisy's lips part for my tongue to slide in, my arm tucks under her sufficient enough that I can cradle her head in my large hand. She murmurs as our tongues meet, swirling around, tasting each other. With my other hand I trace down her face, my thumb gently stroking her jawline. She moves to cup into my hand, our eyes never leaving the others. I could get lost in those enormous eyes of hers, now hooded with desire.

My dick strains against my pants but I want to take it slowly. Instead, I ignore the ache and tightness of my balls and trail my finger down to her sternum, moving my lips to leave a trail of kisses down her chin, her neck, her collarbone. "Oh, God please Deacon." She tells me. Slowly I move my hand to the hem of her top and ease my hands up her warm, soft as silk skin. It's enough to undo me, my breath hitches at her touch. Moving her top up I expose her breasts and flat stomach, the sight of her bra that is barely there, causes my dick to stir in my pants, can it possibly grow anymore, I'm already hard as anything for my Buttercup.

"Don't tease me, take me."

"Not just yet, Buttercup. I want to take my time and explore your beautiful body, I want to get to know every inch and crook of your body, every dip, every curve." I place kisses on her stomach, she giggles.

"That tickles, but oh, I love it." Her voice is sweet and girlish. I unhook her bra then sit up to help her take her top off over her head and remove the bra and cast it aside to the floor. Her nipples are perfect buds of pink, pointing straight at me like headlights in a snow storm. Lowering my head and I take one in my mouth and nip at it, she squeaks, I nip again then flick it with my tongue, easing one hand down to her core, between her legs where I feel how warm and wet she already is for me.

"You're so easy, Daisy." I chuckle.

"Only for you, Deac." That makes me swell, I swear my chest puffs out. Damn, this beautiful angel is all mine. She moves her hips, I push my hand further against her pussy to give her some leverage and friction as I lower my lips to the top of her waistband.

"Take them off, please, Deacon. I don't want to wait, I am aching for you." Her voice is breathless, her breathing is more rapid and I can see the blush on her chest, neck and cheeks. Daisy is divine and so damn sexy how I'm managing to restrain myself is beyond me. All I want to do is rip the rest of her clothes off and bury my face between her sweet thighs and feel her wrap her legs around my neck.

Kneeling I place my hands on the waistband of her pants and guide them down her hips, down her legs and help take them off her feet. I place them on the floor and take a look at her body splayed out needy and wanting me. Her barely there thong is the only garment remaining and I can see she has soaked it already. I use my knuckle and rub between her legs right on her clit, she bucks and gasps. "Fuck." She hisses out.

"You are so wet, Buttercup." She nods and bites her lower lip as I lower myself to lay flat on my stomach and bury my head between her legs, moving her thong to one side with my fingers. My tongue touches her softness, she isn't just warm damn, her body is on fire, she is alight for me.

My dick is groaning in my pants, as I suck at her lips, run my tongue up and down her slit, enjoying how sweet she tastes, like pure honey from the jar. Easily I slide a finger inside her, Daisy moves her hips, I slide in another and wait until she has adjusted herself to be comfortable. Her legs come up around the back of my head, as she moves slightly further and begins to rub her pussy against my face. It is like going to heaven, floating on a cloud. I swear she is my sweetest addiction as I lap and suck, moving my fingers in and out whilst she begs for more. I use another finger and slide it into her wetness and reach under her ass to help lift her to get a better position and enjoy getting herself off all over my damn face. Her movements increase, the pressure against my mouth and my nose is noticeable as she uses her fists to hold onto the sheets, her head moving from side to side, I glance up and watch as her chest rises and falls. I know just from feeling inside her as everything grips my fingers tightly that she is about to orgasm all over my face.

"Oh. My. God. Oh. My. God. Fuck, Deacon." She screams out then screams out my name again. I am telling you, it's a good job I have so much land an no neighbors. Her body tenses then releases as her thighs move away from my face, she brings her legs back down.

Slowly, and very gently I move my fingers out of her pussy and suck her juice off them. Her eyes are wide.

"Wow, that was amazing, so intense." Her voice is full of emotion. I move my body to lay beside her and pull her into me. She's soft and warm, her one arm goes across my chest, I hook an arm under her and cradle her head into my shoulder.

"Deacon that was beautiful." Her breathing returns gradually to normal.

"I love you, Buttercup. I want to spend the rest of my days with you." She trails her fingers down my chest and settles on my stomach. My dick stirs. I place a hand on my crotch.

"Good, because I want to be with you forever, Marshal Deacon. You have spoilt me for all the other guys out there. You have since I was a teenager and now I've got you and I feel like pinching myself."

"I like the sound of that, Buttercup. You ready for the next round?" Is it too soon, maybe she needs more time to relax?

"You bet I am, besides, I want to feel your cock in my mouth, I want to swallow all the cum you've got to give me."

Fuck, this woman is going to be the undoing of me that's for sure.

Chapter 47

D^{aisy} The evening in the tree house was more than perfection, the way Deacon made love to me and made me feel like I was the only woman in the universe, still leaves me swooning. We kept telling each other how much we loved one another and played the game of secrets, you know the one. You tell me yours and I will tell you mine. It turns out that Deacon has very few secrets although he did have a massive crush on Shania Twain and loves 90s music, adorable, right? I don't have any secrets, growing up pretty much together, Deacon already knows just about everything there is to know about me. I did, however, divulge that I write in my journal most evenings and that I love to read the journal from my grandma. He thought that was a special thing to have and to do.

We held hands and laid and talked for what seemed hours, we explored each other's bodies, savoring each precious moment like it would be our last ones and when I fell asleep the best thing ever, was waking right up beside him the following morning, his body spooned against mine, his protective, strong arm folded over me and holding onto my stomach. Bliss, such bliss. My idea of heaven.

It's been a few days since we were at the tree house and today is the day of our fall fundraising event for the kids. I've got all my crafts ready and Sadie is on the stall next to me, her hair today has gone from her shocking pink to a muted kind of purple color, you know like those tiny violet sweets you can get from the old fashioned candy store. It suits her and on her lips she is wearing the pretties shade of pink lipstick, I need to remember to ask her where she got it because I sure do fancy me some.

"All set?" My mother asks me as she swings by laden down with some divine looking cakes.

"Yes, all set, I'm so excited for the grand opening, our very own mayor Hank Rindell is opening up and his wife, the adorable Betsie is cutting the ribbon, it's tradition and the whole townsfolk look forward to it. Deacon is not, however, looking forward to being dunked time and time again by the kids, and I know for sure that Logan will be throwing the balls to help the kids too, so Deacon is going to look like a drowned animal by the end of the day. But hell, he doesn't mind too much, we all know today is about the kids and every cent we make goes into the coffers for the baseball ground, the kit they wear, the stadium, the kids and those who can't really afford to play. Logan, who I think I've mentioned before set all of this up some years ago and my folks and I are really proud of him.

"These bags look beautiful, when did you have time to make all of this stuff?" Mom asks as she sets the cakes down on my stall and has a turquoise, beaded bag in her hands, it has a long strap and would easily fit a mobile, set of keys and a couple of other small items.

"Just around doing the bigger stuff, Mom and sometimes in the evenings. I also had a bit of stock left over that didn't sell over the Christmas holidays and brought those out too." Sadie hands me a nice steaming hot chocolate with plenty of whipped cream on top. "Thanks, Sadie."

"Sure, no problem. I love that bag your mom has in her hands, I'd like first dibs on that please."

"Absolutely. My first sale of the day and I have my eye on your knitted scar and hat set, the one with the white fur pompom on top."

She grins. "It's got your name on it, Daisy. It'll look adorable on, let me take it off display."

There is a slight crackling and buzzing you know that sound when someone is trying to get the sound system to work. I am guessing our major has arrived to Main Street with Bessie. "Good morning good folk of Willowbrook and welcome to tour fifth annual fundraiser for the Baseball ground, started as most of you will all know by our very own Doctor Logan. Please let's give Logan a huge clap of hands and welcome him to the stage."

My heart swells for my brother. Deacon comes round the corner and stands beside me, running an arm around my waist and plants a gentle kiss to my cheek. He smells woodsy and slightly of cinnamon, mm I could inhale him all day long. "I brought you your favorite blueberry muffin from Bluebell's."

"Thank you, you're such a sweetheart." I give him a kiss and wait for Logan to go up on the stage that has been erected for today. We have all had a hand in decorating it. The iron pagoda has come out and is draped with fall vines and pumpkins sit at the foot of the stage with a pumpkin each side of the steps leading to the main area. Logan strides up the four steps and gives everyone crowded around a wave.

"Good morning everyone, firstly thank you all so much for coming out to support us today, it means so much to us that you come and support us year after year. I can't believe we are already into our fifth year and looking forward to many more years. All your efforts and hard work into making this event happen on an annual basis means so much to all of us and I thank you all from the bottom of my heart. Now let's get this event opened and on the road." He gives everyone another wave as they clap, whistle and cheer. I swear I've gone all emotional with some tears prickling at my eyes. Deacon hands me a handkerchief, how sweet, I mean who carries these anymore these days? I take it and dab my eye like something out of an 1800's scene.

"I'll catch up with you two lovebirds later," my mom says as she picks up her cakes and heads a few stall down where my dad is waiting for her now that he has set the table up, placed the orange tablecloth over the trestle table and a brown small one on top. It looks so fall-ish.

We went all out this year for Main Street since the mayor gave us a little bit extra funding, the whole street is decorated with lanterns hanging from the trees, lampshades are decorated with fall bunting and foliage. It's so pretty like living on a Hallmark set. I sigh with contentment, I live in the best place in the entire country, I swear I will never leave Willowbrook.

Yeah, I did have designs on heading to Paris to study fashion and close my shop up and spend a year or two over there, but you know here is where my heart is right with Deacon, with my family and my friends. Why would I want to go anywhere else? Besides, I can always go there on a holiday with Deacon some day. That'd be funny though, to see Deacon outside of Willowbrook, I'm not sure he's ever left the State. I grin and chuckle.

"What are you giggling at like a High schooler?" He asks me.

"Oh, nothing. Nothing at all. But I have made a decision."

"You have? Care to share it, Buttercup?"

"I have decided that I'm not going to Paris after all to study and be away for a year or two. I'm so happy here Deacon that I don't need Paris. Everything I want right now is here beside me. Everyone, you, my folks, Lottie, Sage, Logan." I hug myself.

"Are you sure, Daisy? It's a big decision and a three-hundred-and-sixty degree turnaround. You had your heart set on Paris."

"That was before I realized how much in love with you I am, Deacon and you are with me, that was when I thought I needed the adventure the change of scenery but now I have all the scenery I want every time I look into your eyes."

He grins from ear to ear, lowers his head down and kisses me so tenderly that it literally takes my breath away.

"I don't want to stop you," he says when we finish, and I try to catch my breath. "Your dreams are important, Buttercup don't let anyone ever stand in the way of them. Not me, not Logan, not Lottie nobody. You need to do what is absolutely right for you. We're strong, Buttercup, even if you decided to go to Paris, I'd be waiting right here for you with a warm bed and Bonnie who by the way I'd take care of."

"You'd take care of Bonnie?" Now I am melting in front of him.

"Of course, I love that little Satan cat of yours." He makes me giggle, okay so Bonnie can be a bit satanish with Deacon but not often and only when she gets kicked out of the bedroom when he wants to be amorous with me. It's kinda funny and adorable.

"You are my dream, Deacon I knew it from the time I was fifteen, hell I knew it before then but I hadn't figured it out until I was a bit older. Nothing more to be said, I want to be by your side every day. Besides, we can fly there on a holiday or something sometime."

"If you say so, Buttercup. You really do hang the moon, Daisy. I promise never to let you down, I promise to always protect you and Bonnie, I promise to be the man you want and need in your life." Okay so right now I am that puddle at the bottom of his size ten boots.

Chapter 48

D *eacon*

Thanksgiving is already upon us and boy has the time gone quick. Daisy and I have been seeing each other almost every night and to be honest she spends more time at mine than she does at hers now. Which suits me just fine. Bonnie has become a permanent fixture over at my cabin and it also means that Daisy gets to spend more time with Dreamer, who is growing and will be a fine horse for her in no time at all.

Sage and Logan will be getting married in just over a week, I shake my head and chuckle, Logan got his girl. I'm stoked for him. It takes me back to when we were all at school and he had this crush on a girl with long legs, long hair and a smile to make Julia Roberts jealous. You got it, Sage and now that ring is firmly fixed on her finger and the cabin has had some adjustments, because Sage insisted they extended to accommodate two additional rooms. For what you may ask, let me tell you the woman is talking babies and Daisy is beyond excited for her brother and Sage to have those little ones. It's giving her all sorts of ideas and now she's not going to Paris anymore, she keeps looking all doey eyed at all the baby stuff that Sage shows her. I tell you, it makes me chuckle some, because I know what I have planned even though I am as nervous as a cat on a hot tin roof.

"Sir, needed down on Fraikin Street. Someone has apparently broken into the Jones' house." I scratch my head and reach for my hat.

"The Jones' house you say?"

"Yes, Sir," Clint says as I look at him.

"We never have a problem in town who would want to break into that sweet elderly couple's house. I am betting it's Mr Jones who has forgotten his darn key again, you know that man has memory problems. In fact, Logan was telling me the other day that he saw Mr Jones."

"That as it may be, Sir but Mrs Jones sounds like she's a woman in labor hollering and screaming down the phone that someone is trying to get into her house."

"Okay, okay. Well get someone on it, Mackie is out on patrol right now, he can get there quicker than we can. I'll go along as back up and you keep an eye on things here. No need for us all to show up. I have a hunch it's old man Jones trying to break into his own home." At least I hope that's what it is.

My phone rings I can see it is Daisy. "Hey lover boy, how is your day going?"

"Well there is some kind of ruckus down at the Jones' house so I'm about to leave to go check it out. How is your day?" I grab my keys and start to make my way out of the station.

"It's going well, listen I was thinking should I stay at mine tonight only I have been over at yours for weeks now ever since you spun that beautiful romantic night on me and only been home a handful of times."

"About that, Buttercup, why don't we talk about this later when I see you. I want you to make yourself perfectly at home at the cabin," I'm at my truck now and get myself seated and belted and start up the engine, placing my phone in the cradle so I can continue with the conversation. "You know I want you to stay over tonight. I have a suggestion for you but I can't talk right now beautiful."

"Sure, no problem. In that case I'll bring some cake over from Bluebell's and can cook us a nice stir fry. What time should I expect you?"

"Say five ish, I get off early today, Clint is on shift tonight. And Buttercup, wear that lace purple number you've got you know how hard it makes me for you." She gasps like she's never heard my dirty mouth run with me before, I can just imagine her in her shop with a customer close by and blushing beetroot.

"Marshal Deacon, I'll have you know not to speak to me like that on a public line." Public my ass, the girl has a customer, knew it.

"Gotta fly, Buttercup." I've already pulled out of the station car park, down Main Street and turned at the bottom to the street where the Jones' live. Mackie's car is parked outside and he is standing with Mr Jones.

I hop out of the truck. "Everything alright here?"

"Hi, Sir. Yes, Mr Jones had forgotten his key and has been trying to get into their house. Mrs Jones won't open the door, she said that all he had to do was knock on the door or ring the bell. Mrs Jones is accusing Mr Jones of scaring her half to death and now won't let him in." I take my hat off and run my hand through my short hair. The problems in Willowbrook can give you a headache that's for sure, but thankfully this is a minor issue.

"Let me go speak with her." I make my way up the front steps to the wrap around porch of the two up, two down clapboard property painted in yellow. "Mrs Jones, it's Marshal Deacon." I wait cap in hand.

"Yes, Marshal."

"We need to let Mr Jones in, he seems to have forgotten his key."

"He scared me half to death." Gingerly Mrs Jones does open the door and I am greeted by the tiny, frail old lady who is in her late seventies dressed in her green housecoat looking perplexed.

"Thank you, Mrs Jones. Now you know that Mr Jones has been to Dr Logan and needs help don't you?" she nods at me. "Okay then, so if this happens again you need to let Mr Jones in. You don't want to cause him anymore distress now then do you?" she shakes her head.

"Mackie please bring Mr Jones over so he can come on inside and I'll call Dr Logan have him make a housecall." Mackie brings Mr Jones towards the house, Mrs Jones opens the door some more then comes to the porch and gives her husband a big hug.

"There, there darling it'll be okay." She gives him a kiss on the cheek.

"Thank you, sweetheart, I didn't mean to frighten you."

It pulls on my darn heartstrings it does at that, and I imagine how lucky I will be if Daisy and I can make forty years together when I'll be an old man like Mr Jones.

We leave them to it and I place the call into Logan and ask him to come by and visit the Jones' after work and start putting things in place for the couple and have some home assistance and a day nurse at the very least.

A few hours later and I've been to the basketball ground where some kids were having a fight, seen to a cat up a tree and a small girl bawling her eyes out because she thought her feline friend would be trapped for eternity up in the tree. It's now home time and I am tired but excited to see my Buttercup.

"Hey, rough day?" She asks as I step inside the cabin, Bonnie glares at me, like what am I doing in *her* home. I raise my eyebrows at her, she hisses and moves away and goes to rub her head on Daisy's shins. Yeah, the little madam.

"So-so, just another day in Willowbrook with the residents. The food smells good I am starving. How was your day, Buttercup?" She proceeds to tell me about a new order for bridesmaid dresses she has come in and a bit of town gossip.

"There's a new girl in town," she stirs the food in the pan as I stir the rice next to her. I am loving this domesticity, our closeness and the way she looks as pretty as a picture with her hair in pig tails, dungarees and a red jumper underneath. Her face is natural, Daisy doesn't need any of that cosmetic stuff, she's a natural beauty.

"I haven't seen a new girl in town, I'd have noticed not a lot gets by me, Buttercup."

"I think her name is Montana or Cheyenne, either way rumor has it she's been to Abe's bar and has been causing a bit of trouble with the locals."

I raise my eyebrows, "trouble?"

"There was a bar fight the other night according to Lottie, when she came in and took offence to one of the local kids trying to touch her ass," that makes me chuckle.

"I'm not surprised, how'd you like it if some guy touched you up?"

"Fair point," she moves the pan off the hob and takes it to the stone with granite top island and sets it down and reaches in a cupboard for two plates. I drain the rice.

"Apparently, Abe was not best pleased he asked her to leave."

"He did what?"

"Asked her to leave, he said he didn't need any trouble in his bar."

"Did she leave?"

"Nope. Lottie said the girl put her hands on her hips and told Abe he'd have to physically pick her up and throw her out, she said she had every right to come on in and have a drink at a public bar. Apparently she's got tatts up and down her arms and is some kind of barrel racer or something. According to Lottie she's a stunner and she saw the way that Abe looked at her."

"You girls and your gossip. I'm pretty sure if she's a barrel racer she'll only be passing through." Daisy serves up our food and we go sit on the knotted pine dining table in the open space that separates my kitchen area from the lounge area with it's sofa, easy chair and fireplace which Bonnie is now sitting in front of.

"I sure love being here." Daisy says once we're finished and at the sink doing the dishes together.

"And I love having you here, Daisy." I wrap my arms around her and press my body into hers, my stiffening dick pressing up against her butt. She giggles like a school girl, it's adorable and sexy.

"I have been thinking," nerves get to me, what if she says no.

"Don't do that, it'll hurt your brain, Deac."

"Very funny, Buttercup." I clear my throat. Is it too soon? What if she still wants her independence? Hell, I've got nothing to lose and everything to gain.

"How do you feel about moving in with me?"

Chapter 49

D*aisy*
The last ten days has been a whirlwind of everything I could wish for. Of course you guessed it, I said yes to moving in with Deacon. For a few seconds back then I thought he was going to pop the question to me, but you know this is a step in the right direction and honestly, he seems a bit nervous of late so I am thinking that Marshal Deacon has got something on his mind and if it's wedding bells, then I am more than ready.

My brother's wedding is tomorrow and everyone is beyond excited especially our mother. She's like a fussing hen the way she keeps checking everything is ready, Sage has got the patience of a saint. Lord knows how she will be when it's my wedding one day.

Deacon and I have spent nights being cozy on the sofa watching movies, mostly Hallmark movies, I think I've converted him, *finally*. I love the way that we sit together snuggled up with Bonnie now used to the idea that the cabin is our home. She roams around outside to her heart's content, she's stopped giving Deacon the evil eye when he has his arms around me or cuddles me in bed. In fact she has taken to sleeping down at his feet at night, after she's given him a chin bump with her tiny black head at night before settling down. It's adorable.

"Hey, Buttercup are you ready yet?" Am I. He's taking me on a surprise. Another surprise, the man is full of them. The other day he took me to a new restaurant in Copper Town, a smart fancy, French restaurant that has just opened, we had the entire restaurant to ourselves. Is he leading up to something do you think? It kind of feels like it.

"Won't be a minute." I slip into my riding boots, since he said we were going out on the horses, his horses since Dreamer is still too young to be ridden but oh my, he's becoming so beautiful. Every time I go to the stable he comes to the door and leans his head over my shoulder and comes in for a proper big hug. I love Dreamer so fiercely and to think that Deacon bought him for me, makes it even more special and that he rescued the little thing for me.

Deacon's sister, Maxine has got all the permissions through for Deacon to open up for a riding school for the underprivileged children *and* for children with disabilities. He's taken on two volunteers who are trained to work with the children and two full-time staff. Next week he and Maxine are heading to a different horse auction to select a few more horses, he says they'll buy four more horses at this juncture, and see how it goes. If the demand increases then they will get a few more. It's not like he doesn't have the space. The land he acquired at the end of his land stands in at a few thousand acres.

The fall sun streams through the bedroom window casting a gorgeous glow across the oak flooring, and the large bed with crumpled sheets from our love making this morning. I ought to make the bed but Deacon is hollering up at me again. Bonnie is lying on the bed on her back, her paws in the air. I snap a quick picture of her and post it to my Instagram account with the hashtag #caturday since it's a Saturday.

I grab my cream cardigan from the balloon backed chair in front of the antique dressing table, which Deacon told me had belonged to grandma and give Bonnie a kiss before heading down the wooden stairs.

"Okay, ready." He looks at me, a smile spreads across his face. Have I told you how handsome this man is? He's a dream come true with his broad shoulders, the way he tapers down nicely to narrow hips and those muscular thighs of his encased today in a pair of tight black jeans. He wears cowboy boots and I swear I'm lusting after him, even though we were up until the early hours exploring one another's bodies. I could never tire of this man. I am the happiest woman alive right now, well okay, maybe except Sage who is going to be my brother's wife tomorrow.

"You look radiant, Buttercup."

"I'm not surprised, you gave me some serious multiple orgasms last night, Deacon." He reaches out his hand, I take it and he leads me out the front door. I hook my arm through his as we walk towards the stable.

"So, what's the surprise?"

"I can't tell you that, it wouldn't be a surprise."

"Mm. Not even a clue."

"Nope, not even a clue, little Miss Impatient." I squeeze his arm. He smells woodsy this morning and of fresh shower. The horses raise their heads as we come into their domain, Dreamer whinnies. I go over and wrap my arms around his neck and kiss his forehead, He nuzzles in, it's like a slice of heaven, this love that surrounds me, not just from Deacon but Bonnie and Dreamer too. Honestly, I feel like I'm in some kind of princess dream.

"Are you taking me back to the tree house?" I lead Mitzi out of the stable and start to get her ready, Deacon hands me the saddle then changes his mind and puts it on her for me and makes sure it is fastened and secure.

"Not to the tree house, but you're close."

He saddles Lady Night and then helps me get up onto Mitzi. We ease the horses out and Deacon steers us towards the trail which leads to the end of his stretch of the boundary. As we ride we talk about Logan and Sage's wedding, how I'm getting on with my business and that my new seamstress starts in two weeks time. I've gotten busier and it's time to have someone in to help me, that and I like being at home when Deacon comes in to have dinner ready for him. It's like something from Little House on the Prairie and I absolutely love it. It's an honor to take care of a man like Deacon.

The views are amazing from up here as we slowly go up the trail, you can see the mountains in the distance and all of Willowbrook below us. "It's breathtaking." I tell Deacon as he pulls Lady Night to a stop.

"You think?"

"Yes, it takes my breath away. Just look at the mountains today with the sun bouncing off them, the colors are magnificent."

"Which way is your favorite view?" He asks me sitting on his saddle, one hand resting on Lady's neck the other on his thigh. He looks good enough to seduce right now.

"Oh, definitely out to the mountains and Willowbrook below for sure, but the forest behind us sure is pretty too."

"You reckon a mountain view from the kitchen window would be the best?" He asks.

"Gosh, absolutely." I reply without thinking. Wait, what? A kitchen? Huh?

He starts to chuckle. "What do you mean a kitchen view?" I ask him not following anything.

"Buttercup," he pulls Lady Night closer to Mitzi and takes my hand and kisses the top of it. "I'm building you a house."

"A what? You're doing what? We have the cabin."

He chuckles some more, a twinkle in his eyes, the skin around them creasing some, making me swoon at his feet. If I weren't sitting right on top of Mitzi, I'd be a puddle on the ground.

"We'll need somewhere to fill with all those babies, Buttercup."

"Babies?"

"Babies, I'm thinking maybe five or six, hell we could have ten. I'm building you a five thousand square foot house, Buttercup and we can fill every room with babies." My mouth drops to the ground, I am lost for words.

"Buttercup, I love you from the bottom of my heart. Ever since I can remember I have loved you. You are the reason I want to be a better man, you are the reason I take every breath. You fill up my life, my senses and everything that makes me, me. Buttercup, would you do me the honor of being my wife, to put up with me as I grow old and grumpy, to have my children, to sit out front on the porch with and watch the sunrise and the sun fall at night?"

Oh my gosh, the words, the way he's looking at me right now the ring box he's taken out from his pocket, black velvet. His hand leaves mine as he opens it and shows me the most beautiful princess cut diamond. "You are my princess, Buttercup." I'm choked, the happy tears start to fall.

"Yes, absolutely, yes." He reaches over and slides the ring onto my finger and boy does it glitter. "It's stunning and it fits."

"I had Lottie help me with the ring size, she said you were both the same size."

I am speechless and breathless. Deacon brings me closer, our lips meet and I swear to God my heart is soaring and bursting.

"I can't wait to tell everyone, wait I don't want to take Sage's day away from her though, tomorrow." I say once we pull apart.

"Don't worry, she and Logan know I was asking you today, I asked your father for your hand a few weeks ago." He winks, so old fashioned, right asking my dad for my hand in marriage but then Deacon is a gentleman through and through.

"Let's head back, I want to show you the plans for your new house and I am guessing everyone will want to see your ring tonight. I arranged for everyone to meet for drinks at Lazy Duke's."

"Thank you, Deacon, I'd love that and to show it off."

"Buttercup, for you anything, the world, the moon, the stars, whatever you want you've got it. I will do everything in my power to make you the happiest woman alive."

Chapter 50

Daisy

"Oh My God, it's stunning, damn Girl you are going to get married. It's unreal and to the man of your dreams. Someone pass me the tissues." Lottie screams out when she sees the ring on my finger and Deacon sitting next to me in Lazy Duke's with his arm draped behind my back, along the top of the chair. Sage laughs at her exuberance, Lottie is known for being totally and utterly over the top. But I love her anyways.

"I want to be chief bridesmaid," she declares fanning herself. Ryle sits next to her and smiles then rolls his eyes, yep in a short space of time he sure has got the measure of my beautiful bestie and her dramatic ways.

"Of course you'll be chief bridesmaid, and Sage will be my second. Mom is over the moon and can't contain herself. We stopped by before coming to meet you all," I tell her. Lottie leans over and gives me a huge hug, I can spot little tears at the corner of her eyes.

"Look at us, all grown up and now you're going off to be married and Sage here, our ex-babysitter is getting married tomorrow. I can't believe it."

"Me neither, hell where did all that time go, from when we'd sit on the school bench in recess and chat about books, the boys and our favorite teachers?"

"I have no idea but oh my gosh, I'm so overjoyed for you. And you," she points at Deacon, "it's about time, what on earth took you so long? This girl has been waiting since she was at least fifteen.

Honestly, some days I could have stuck a rocket up your ass, talk about slow at going forward, Marshal Deacon." To which he grins and places a kiss on my cheek. Logan isn't with us tonight, according to Sage it's because it's bad luck to see the bride the night before the wedding, even though they've been under the same roof for months now.

Still, he likes his traditions and so does, Sage and of course my mother kept banging on about how it's tradition and he should honor that. Deacon and Ryle decide to head up to the bar and grab us some drinks. "I'll only have one glass of white, please. I want a clear head for my wedding day," Sage tells them. Deacon nods. Ryle claps Deacon on the back, no doubt they're going to have some man talk and stuff.

"When do you plan on getting married?" Lottie asks. Sage grins.

"Give her a chance, he's only just proposed today."

"Well, I know already she'll want a spring wedding, it's her favorite season."

"I'm not sure, I definitely don't want to get married in the summer, it's way too hot and the thought of being in a long wedding gown in the height of it all just doesn't appeal to me. So, probably spring or maybe fall next year. That way we've got a year to plan and by then Sage here may be expecting a little baby."

Sage raises her eyebrows. "I think Logan and I want to wait a while before that happens. You know he's expanding the practice, right? We need to take on additional staff you know he wants a couple more doctors in and an extra nurse to help Sadie. Eliza isn't getting any younger and wants to drop her hours, that means we need an extra pair of hands for the front desk and everything she does for us. Honestly, babies aren't on the agenda just yet."

"You can do both, besides, if Logan is getting extra doctors in, don't you think it's because he wants to make sure you can have as many babies as possible and he'll be covered at the practice?"

Sage cocks her head. "Ah, so he's being devious is he, intending to knock me up as soon as possible?" she chuckles, "I like that idea, could you imagine little Logan's running around?" She looks wistful with a beautiful smile on her face.

"God help us if they turn out like Logan," I tease her. "Just joking, I can't wait to be an aunty and Deacon will make the best uncle."

Speaking of Deacon, he and Ryle turn up with two trays of drinks and a couple of beers each for themselves. "Here's to the bride to be." Deacon says. We raise our glasses to Sage.

"And to the soon to be Mrs Deacon." She comes back with. We all clink glasses and turn our heads when we hear an almighty roar coming from Abe behind the bar.

"OUT. NOW." We all raise our eyebrows and turn to the door to see *the* most stunning woman I personally have ever seen. She's got a full, thick mane of long blonde, unruly hair, tan skin, ink up and down her arms to where her T-shirt sleeves end. A leather jacket is slung over one shoulder, she stands with her hands on her hips.

"Aw, Man don't start that bullshit with me again."

"I asked you not to come here again after you caused my locals to fight with each other." Abe says as he glowers at her, his cheeks slightly flushed. I cock my head because since when does Abe ever blush? And he's licking his bottom lip. Hold on a second what is going on with Abe?

"It ain't my fault them backass locals of yours wanna fight over a pretty little thing like me now then is it?" She moves closer to the bar, all eyes on this woman who has got *the* longest, jean clad legs I've ever seen, narrow hips, a tiny waist and a modest chest. But it's the wild hair I'm loving that spills down her back, it's all blonde waves and looks like a waterfall. Her eyes, I can't quite make out because her back is now to me as she takes a seat at the bar. We're all still gawping at her.

"Now, I'll have a bottle of Bud and a tequila shot, thanks Bear." She tells Abe whose jaw drops to the bar.

"My name ain't Bear. Don't call me that." He growls at her.

"Will you stop glowering at me and just get me my drinks already."

"Oh, hell, looks like Abe's got some trouble on his hands." Deacon says and pulls me in for a kiss, his lips are soft and warm.

"Seems to me he's got a bit of fire come on in from outside and I reckon she's about to rock his world." Sage offers. You know, she might just be right. I for one can't wait to see how this pans out.

We go back to chatting about the wedding tomorrow, Lottie takes another few looks at my ring and places her hand on her heart. "You are so lucky, Daisy. I'm really happy for you. I can't wait for your wedding."

Deacon grins, he looks like the proudest man alive. "Me neither." We stay for an hour then make our way home, tomorrow is going to be a long, but beautiful day. My brother is finally getting married to the woman he loves. We leave Abe still glowering at the new girl in town, and I can't help notice that even though he has other customers to serve, he can't stop checking her out.

Chapter 51

D^{aisy} Everyone is seated as the chairs line up on two sides of the isle that lead to the platform Logan and his band built. An arch of flowers surrounds it from one end to the other and it is as pretty as a picture, all with poinsettias, white and blush roses and foliage. It's fitting for a winter wedding. Logan had one of his fir trees by the stage decorated with baubles of white and silver, with the snow fall there is a dusting on the branches, it is breathtaking, I can't take my eyes off it.

My peach bridesmaid dress hangs to the floor, it's an A-line and makes me feel like something out of the Victorian era with it's square neckline and velvet matching ribbon that ties under my breasts and then there is Deacon. Oh my, he cuts a dashing figure in his charcoal grey dress pants, a striped waistcoat, a dark charcoal tail coat to match his pants and a starched white shirt. He wears his cowboy hat in typical off duty, Deacon style and I can see that Logan has his on too. These two they think they're damn cowboys, it's adorable. And it makes my heart lift, I recall the two of them in their baseball sweats and outfits as kids, the way they'd bum around in torn jeans in their teens, chewing gum, combing their hair and trying to be cool. Here they are standing as fine men, in all their finery awaiting the beautiful bride.

I'm grateful for the faux fur, cream stowel around my shoulders as the air is fresh this morning, the sun is out and there are drifting clouds in the sky. It couldn't be a more perfect day for these two to get married. I cannot wait to see Sage in her ivory dress with lace bodice and long sleeves, tiny buttons up the back from the base of her spine and a gentle floating skirt with a trailing piece. She has opted for no veil saying that at her age she really doesn't need a veil and besides it's a bit too old fashioned for her. I kid you not, the woman is only in her thirties, that's hardly old, right?

Sadie looks adorable dressed just like me, her hair has been toned down for the wedding and is a gorgeous chestnut color, I'm telling you with her stunning green eyes with amber flecks in them, she looks amazing.

I see my mom dabbing her eyes with a hankie, dressed in a powder, pale blue skirt suit and matching shoes. They're an old pair she had that we dyed together and they have come out beautiful, exactly the shade of her outfit. Dad has his arm around mom and wears the same outfit being father of the groom, as Logan and Deacon. On the opposite seats sits Sage's mother, elegant and beautiful in an ivory lace skirt over satin fabric that swishes as she walks, on her top half she wears a high necked cream, lace blouse that is identical in lace as Sage's bodice. All my hard work can be seen and I am going to admit, I feel mighty proud of myself right now. I even made the wool camel colored coat she wears over the top.

Fallon stands beside Sadie, gorgeous as ever with her cascading hair falling around her shoulders and a single blush pink rose tucked behind her ear. The photographers snap away and the music begins, all heads are turned towards the back of the cabin where we see Sage appear her arm linked in her father's hand. The bouquet of white lilies hangs down setting off the dress perfectly, she's elegant, beautiful and the epitome of femininity. I feel the lump in my throat, oh God not now. *Do not cry, Daisy, do not cry you'll ruin your make up that took a while.* I wipe a tear away, how can I not cry? She's beautiful like an angel gliding down the aisle with Eliza in front throwing out blush rose petals. I glance at Deacon who gives me a wink, that one that makes my knees go weak.

Sage's father looks so proud to have his daughter on his arm, and leans in to whisper something in her ear. Sage grins and nods her head. The special moment between father and daughter as he walks her down the aisle to the man who will look after her, support her and be with her for eternity. I put a hand to my heart. Deacon smiles and blows me a kiss. Sadie has tears in her eyes and Fallon wipes hers away.

Logan puffs out his chest but he isn't fooling me either, I can see tears welling in his eyes. She is a vision.

Her father lets go of her arm, Sage looks like she's going to cry too, this is such a pivotal moment it's charged with emotion. He kisses her cheek and says something to her. Sage gives him a hug careful not to crush her bouquet. Logan steps up, they look deep into each other's eyes. Oh, I swear this is too much. I'll be a puddle of emotional tears in no time. He kisses her softly on the lips.

The preacher coughs, "er sorry no kissing until after the ceremony." Logan shoots him a look.

The ceremony starts then Logan begins his vows.

My darling Sage,

From the moment I met you, my heart recognized you as its home. In your eyes, I see my future, in your smile, I find my joy, and in your heart, I discover a love deeper than I ever dreamed possible. Today, as we stand here, I am overwhelmed with gratitude for the incredible journey that has led us to this moment.

I vow to be your steadfast partner in all of life's adventures. To support you in your dreams and to celebrate with you in your successes. I promise to listen to you with compassion and understanding, to speak to you with kindness and honesty, and to cherish every moment we share together.

You are my best friend, my confidante, and my one true love. I promise to stand by your side through the highs and lows, to hold your hand when times are tough, and to dance with you when life is beautiful. I will be your rock when you need strength, your cheerleader when you need encouragement, and your safe haven when you need peace.

As we embark on this new chapter together, I vow to nurture our love, to respect our differences, and to cultivate a life filled with laughter, adventure, and endless affection. I will love you with all that I am and all that I will become. Today, I give you my heart completely, for now and forever.

There isn't a dry eye anywhere close by, even Sage has tears rolling down her face. Oh my, I fan my face, Fallon and Sadie hold hands and Sadie grabs mine. "So beautiful, right?" I say. They nod.

We listen as Sage says her vows, her mother is almost blubbering as she blows her nose and finally, the preacher claims them both as man and wife. Logan hands his hat that he was holding in his hands in front of him, to Deacon and places an arm around Sage's waist, the other hand resting on the back of her head as he leans her slightly back and kisses her. The photographers are having a field day. They come up for air and we all clap and cheer. This has got to be the most romantic wedding I've ever been to and I've attended a few, the setting, their horses by the end of the aisle waiting to take them down the track to where Logan and Sage have a large marquee waiting to entertain us all.

Logan and Sage hold hands and lead us down the aisle, followed by my father linking arms with Sage's mother, my mother linking with Sage's daddy then Deacon linking arms with me.

"So, Buttercup. It's going to be us next, just a few months and I'll be the proudest man alive."

He kisses me as warmth floods through my body, I melt to his touch. Hell, I know we're holding up the procession but nobody cares. Deacon's eyes twinkle, his chest puffs out. "I can't wait to make you my wife, Daisy. We are going to have the wildest adventures, the cutest babies, and I swear to God, I will never let you down."

My heart is soaring on angel's wings right now, I know aside from Sage at this very moment, that I am the luckiest woman alive.

THE END

Thank you from the author

Thank you so much for reading Daisy and Deacon's story. These two have a special place in my heart. I love the exploration of friends to lovers and the risks to a sound and trusting friendship for two people unsure if it could work out for them.

Whilst writing Daisy and Deacon's story I learnt so much about deep and bonding friendships, close families like my own and the harnessing of warmth and strenght from those cloest to us. Above all to trust instinct and allow it to guide and lead.

A hearfelt thanks to my beta readers who give me invaluable insight, correct me when I have made a plot error somewhere, and put me straight when I seem to go off on a tangent, which is quite often when my characters do not conform. A major headache for most authors.

Thank you to you the reader for spending your time with my book and for trusting me as your chosen romance author for the morning, afternoon or evening. It is a special feeling to know that someone out there is cosying on up with a book of mine, loving it just as much I do some of my favorite authors.

If you enjoyed reading this story maybe read Healing Hearts if you haven't already which is book1 of the series. Coming in 2025 will be Love At Lazy Duke's the third in the series.

Love to you always,

Xoxo

Connect with me on social media
HTTPS://WWW.FACEBOOK.com/KerryKennedyAuthor[1]
https://www.instagram.com/kerrykennedyauthor/
https://www.tiktok.com/@kerrykennedy_author

---

1. https://www.facebook.com/KerryKennedyAuthor

https://www.pinterest.co.uk/kerryjocket/
https://www.youtube.com/@kerrykennedy_author
For my Webnovels you can find me on
   *Wattpad   https://www.wattpad.com/user/
KerryKennedyAuthor*
Inkitt https://www.inkitt.com/kerrykennedyauthor
Goodnovel
Heynovel
1001Novel
Eratu
HiNovel

Don't miss out!

Visit the website below and you can sign up to receive emails whenever Kerry Kennedy publishes a new book. There's no charge and no obligation.

https://books2read.com/r/B-A-SGNY-LAOYC

BOOKS2READ

Connecting independent readers to independent writers.

Did you love *You Hang The Moon*? Then you should read *Healing Hearts*[2] by Kerry Kennedy!

Dr. Sage Bennett thought she had it all - a thriving medical practice, a comfortable life in the bustling city, and a promising future with her charming boyfriend of ten years. But when her perfect world comes crashing down after a devastating breakup, she decides to return to her small hometown of Willowbrook for a fresh start. Little did she know that her journey home would lead to unexpected second chances, both in love and in life. Willowbrook, a picturesque town nestled in the rolling hills, is where Sage grew up and where she first fell in love with medicine. She takes a position at the town's modest clinic, working alongside her childhood friend, Dr. Logan Turner. As Sage adjusts to the slower pace of life and reconnects

---

2. https://books2read.com/u/49ak2d

3. https://books2read.com/u/49ak2d

with the tight-knit community, she starts to realize that perhaps the happiness she's been searching for isn't found in a bustling city but right where her heart has always belonged. Logan, too, has his own share of regrets and heartbreaks. As they work together, their friendship rekindles, and they find solace in sharing their stories of lost loves and missed opportunities. As they support each other through life's challenges, their bond deepens, and they begin to wonder if there's room in their hearts for a second chance at love. But just as Sage and Logan begin to explore the possibility of a new romance, Sage's ex-fiancé arrives in Willowbrook, determined to win her back. Sage is torn between her old love and her new feelings for Logan. She must make a choice that will not only impact her heart but also the future of her medical career in Willowbrook. "Healing Hearts: A Second Chance in Small Town" is a heartwarming contemporary romance that explores the themes of forgiveness, healing, and the power of second chances. Set against the backdrop of a charming small town, this story reminds us that sometimes, the path to true happiness leads us right back to where it all began.

Read more at https://linktr.ee/kerry_kennedy_author.

Also by Kerry Kennedy

Willowbrook
Healing Hearts
You Hang The Moon

Standalone
Santa Fe Billionaire
Hidden Desires

Watch for more at https://linktr.ee/kerry_kennedy_author.

About the Author

Kerry is a multi genre author currently living in Spain and hailing from the UK. Five years ago she and her partner made a life decision to move to warmer climates and to be close to the mountains they climb.

An avid writer and reader, you will usually find her with a book in her hand.

Her pleasurable activities include rock climbing, hiking in the Prades mountains, biking along the trails of Catalonia with stunning mountain backdrops and of course drinking too much coffee.

She lives with her partner, four cats and her chihuahua.

Read more at https://linktr.ee/kerry_kennedy_author.

Milton Keynes UK
Ingram Content Group UK Ltd.
UKHW040834300924
449047UK00001B/96